William Arthur

The Life of Gideon Ouseley

William Arthur

The Life of Gideon Ouseley

ISBN/EAN: 9783337333263

Printed in Europe, USA, Canada, Australia, Japan

Cover: Foto ©Raphael Reischuk / pixelio.de

More available books at **www.hansebooks.com**

THE

LIFE OF GIDEON OUSELEY.

BY

WILLIAM ARTHUR.

LONDON:
PUBLISHED FOR THE AUTHOR AT THE
WESLEYAN CONFERENCE OFFICE,
2 CASTLE STREET, CITY ROAD,
AND SOLD AT 66 PATERNOSTER ROW.
1876.

TO

SIR FRANCIS LYCETT,

MY OLD, TRIED, AND DEAR FRIEND,

This Volume

IS INSCRIBED.

PREFACE.

—◆—

At the time of Mr Ouseley's death, his papers were in the hands of his nephew, the late Alderman Bonsall, of Dublin. He was to prepare and arrange them for the late Rev. Thomas Jackson, who had undertaken to write a Biography, after he should have completed his Life of Charles Wesley. But his designation to the office of Theological Tutor at Richmond compelled him to write to Mr Bonsall, reluctantly withdrawing from the task. The latter then declined to give up the papers to any other person.

In this state of things, the Irish Methodist Conference requested the late Rev. William Reilly to prepare a Biography. His Memorial of Mr Ouseley will ever remain a faithful and affectionate record of his venerated colleague; but, though all which the materials then at command enabled him to produce, it was necessarily defective in the information, which was to be had only from Mr Ouseley's own documents.

Twenty years have now elapsed since Dr Robinson Scott extracted from me a promise that I should attempt to prepare a Biography, if Mr Bonsall placed the papers at my disposal. This he at once consented to do, but said it would still require a considerable time to arrange them. Year after year passed on ; and at the time of his death he had not completed his task. It proved that he had not only written out at full all that he had himself taken down from the lips of his uncle, but also recast the matter, framing a more complete narrative. The latter often supplies links of connection, and items of explanation, without which the original notes would have been hardly intelligible. He had, moreover, undertaken to copy out letters, even printed ones, from magazines, missionary notices, and newspapers; and it might have still taken him years to complete all that his love and veneration for Mr Ouseley would have led him to do, before handing over his materials.

At the death of Mr Bonsall, the papers fell into the hands of Mr R. Moynan, who, with his excellent wife—a grand-niece of Ouseley, and a daughter of the Rev. Arthur Noble, one of Mr Ouseley's most respected colleagues—speedily, and with the greatest cordiality, placed them in the hands of the Rev. John Hay. To him the work of preparing them for me was a labour of love, and with loving diligence was it performed. He arranged, classified, and indexed the entire mass of materials. He culled out all the bits of strictly original matter belonging to Mr Ouseley himself. There were altogether twenty-eight manuscript-books, besides numbers of lesser documents, copies of writings, and so on.

It is now more than eighteen months since the papers came into my hands. The task of dealing with so much manuscript has been for me one of great physical difficulty. Even in reading printed books I am obliged, not only to use spectacles, but a large hand-glass, such as people employ in looking at photographs. Consequently, I have often been ready to despond. Had I been willing to make two portly volumes, it could have been comparatively soon done. Letters, journals, and extracts from writings would have easily filled up the space. But I felt that it would be a disservice to the cause of God to bury Gideon Ouseley in a big book, and that if I attempted the work at all, I must master my material and try to give the life and soul of it in as small a compass as possible. This I have attempted, and am now thankful that, however ill, the work is done.

One of the most valuable portions of the book will be found to consist in contributions from different gentlemen, who knew Mr Ouseley and describe him

in action.   These are, one by one, acknowledged
as they are inserted, and I here beg personally to
tender my thanks to every one of those who have
rendered me this important help.   To Mr Hay, whose
labours have been altogether special, I can only repeat my brotherly and affectionate acknowledgments.
The Rev. Oliver M'Cutcheon took the pains of making
a journey to Dunmore, and collected local information
with the greatest possible accuracy.

Many readers will blame me for not correcting
loose sentences, and local idioms ; and probably they
will be right in doing so.   But I felt as if any such
editing would take away from the reality of the
book.   We have here the talk of a man who tried to
convey great truths into the hearts of the people by
the very tones, terms, and phrases which they would
have themselves employed.   What he wrote would
often be written late at night, in a poor room, by
the light of a small tallow candle.   So I have left
the "shalls" and the "wills," the "woulds" and
the "shoulds," with all their kith and kin, just where
I found them.   They who cannot approve, must forgive me.

If I have said something of physical difficulty in
preparing this book, I must acknowledge that,
mentally and religiously, the task has been a very
delightful one.   From the first time that Mr Hay

went over the papers with me to the present moment
I never had a doubt that, if God spared me to complete the work, He would make it a blessing. Many
of its pages will be found full of defects, but every
page will go out with prayers, that it may be made
a means of raising up other Gideon Ouseleys. In
these prayers I believe that I shall be joined—and
here affectionately ask that I may be joined—by
those who will take an interest in the work, from love
to the memory of Mr Ouseley, and from the higher
motive of love to the work of God.

Let me take the liberty of adding one word, out of
pure self-interest. I am not open to applications to
write biographies, and wish to be spared the pains of
declining. Already I am pledged to more work,
either by promise or by commencements made, than
I have any reasonable prospect of living to complete.
Besides, working for a biography is working on
manuscripts; and many times during my labour on
the Ouseley papers have I been reminded that it
would be wrong ever to enter into any fresh engagement of the sort.

WM. ARTHUR.

December 1875.

CONTENTS.

LIFE OF GIDEON OUSELEY.

CHAPTER I.

HIS BIRTHPLACE AND FAMILY.

DUNMORE, the name of the place where Gideon
Ouseley was born, means the Great Fort. Perhaps,
when Connor, King of Munster, took the "fortress of
Dunmore" in 1133, and burned it, the stronghold
may have been of some importance. It has left a
sturdy ruin, seated in a pleasant vale, in the north-
east of the county of Galway, about ten miles from
Tuam, on the way to Castlereagh in Roscommon, and
not far from the borders of Mayo.

The town, however, never grew to any considerable size. At present, though still enjoying the name
of a town in Connaught, it has rather less than six
hundred inhabitants. It was never so much as heard
of a couple of years ago. In 1873 a farmer saw
a black mass on the surface of the fields, which
seemed approaching, as if the ground had changed
colour, and was moving. It proved that the bog,
which lay some two miles above the town, had
broken bounds, and was slipping down the course of
the stream which runs through the place. It swept

A

away a few farmhouses, submerged some hundreds of acres of land, and threatened the little town. So, for once, all the journals had news, and the illustrated ones pictures, from Dunmore.

Besides the church, chapel, and market-house, the only building which could be named, even by a guide-book, is the cavalry barrack, which must not be omitted here, on account of its connection with our history. It was originally a hunting-lodge of Lord Ross—an extinct title of the Gore family not to be confounded with that of Rosse, which the scientific tastes of the Parsons family have associated with the stars.

Some hundred years ago, Dunmore was a place of more consequence than it has been of late. Several families of gentry, each enjoying incomes of a few hundreds a year, lived immediately around it. The most prominent among these would appear to have been that of the Ouseleys. Their stock, originally from Shropshire, had settled at Corteen Hall, in Northamptonshire. Losses sustained in the Royalist cause during the Civil War compelled them to part with their seat to Sir Samuel Jones. Two brothers, Richard and Jasper, on leaving Corteen Hall, settled, the first in Wexford, the second in Limerick. A son of Jasper bearing the same name removed to Dunmore, and lived, according to Sir Bernard Burke, at the Castle, which probably does not mean the old ruin, but a house close by. His eldest son was William, and his fourth Gideon. The eldest sons of these two brothers were respectively Ralph and John. Each of these cousins had two remarkable sons.

The first pair, the sons of Ralph, became Sir Gore and Sir William. Gore was an orientalist and diplomatist. He distinguished himself as our pleni- potentiary at the court of Persia, and left the Ouseley name enriched with a baronetcy.* William also became a diplomatist, and won a knighthood and considerable reputation in Oriental literature.

Of the second pair, the sons of John, Ralph, after distinguishing himself under Lake and Wellington, became a major-general in the army of Portugal, and, besides an English knighthood, bore four foreign orders, not to speak of eight medals. He was ten years junior to his brother Gideon, who was never presented at court, and never wore a star.

Either of the two sons of John Ouseley might have been chosen, in respect of natural character, for a typical Connaught-man. This was so much the case, that for the sake both of the patriots and the ethnologists, we ought to be able to prove that, at least on the mother's side, they were descended from some ancient chieftain of the province. But we remember the canon laid down by Moore—

> " By ' Mac ' and ' O '
> You'll always know
> True Irishmen, they say;
> For if they lack
> Both ' O ' and ' Mac,'
> No Irishmen are they."

---

* Sir Bernard Burke states that he was also plenipotentiary at St Petersburg, but that is incorrect. He returned from Persia through Russia; and as he had negotiated a treaty between the two countries, he was received with extraordinary distinction, and at least one city was illuminated in his honour. In the capital the empress-mother in person stood sponsor for his infant daughter. See " Memoir " by the Rev. James Reynolds, prefixed to his work on the " Persian Poets " in the publications of the Oriental Translation Fund.

Now, so far as the pedigree of our Ouseleys is given by Sir Bernard Burke, or in the family papers before us, or in Mr Reynolds's Life of Sir Gore, it does not afford a single " O " or " Mac " to encourage imagination. There is one intermarriage with an O'Dowd, a name which might have made the fortune of an essay on the persistency of types ; but the blood of the O'Dowd took the wrong direction, and never reached our branch of the family. In it the names are stubbornly Saxon. Morleys and Wakes, Willises, Broughtons, and Johnstons, are not stock to grow Kelts from. The wife of John Ouseley was Anne Surridge, daughter of Francis Surridge of Fairy Hill, in the county of Galway, and nearly related to the Seymours of that county. The Keltic characteristics which stamped her two sons had come by the subtle channels of communion and example.

Gideon, the eldest son, was born on February 24, 1762. In that year John Wesley penetrated for the second time to the city of Galway, and little knew what a successor in his labours was then cradled in a remote corner of the county.

CHAPTER II.

GIDEON grew up under the conflicting influence of two parents, both of whom appear to have had a well-defined character. The father read, and so did the mother; but they seriously disagreed in their belief. To John Ouseley the measure of the worth of religion was the lives of its ministers, and, as he knew these, they were of little worth indeed. Closely connected with the Protestant clergy, and well acquainted with the Roman Catholic, he had a poor opinion of both. The former were more honest, the latter more diligent, but neither bore any trace of spiritual life or moral elevation. How far he was read in deistical works we do not know, but a deist he had become, and would not even go to church. He thought that it would be hypocrisy in him to do so, and further thought that there was enough of that in the world already. Nevertheless he meant to make Gideon a parson, for that was a good profession. How he reconciled this intention with the honesty which would not put on as much appearance of religion as consists in going to church, it is not for us to explain.

Mrs Ouseley, on the contrary, maintained that the lives of the clergy affected themselves, and not the truths they taught. She diligently attended church, and took her children with her. That is, she attended except on those Sundays when there was " no church to-day " — at that time no rare occurrence in Connaught, or any of the remote parts of Ireland. The Rector of Dunmore had other parishes, in which it sometimes took him a good while to collect the tithes, and during such terms of absence the church would be shut up. The same would also take place when he went to spend a few weeks in Dublin, or elsewhere. Whatever religious help Mrs Ouseley could get for herself and her children in a church thus served, she diligently sought, and, besides, made the best use of the means at her command at home.

In her view, the training of Gideon for a clergyman had higher aims than that of giving him a profession. She had some feeling of the honour of the calling, and of his possible usefulness in it if properly qualified. Her grandson, Mr Bonsall, says that in both her family and that of the Ouseleys there had been some who bore a part in the work of the Reformation, and the spirit of such an ancestry had not quite died out. In the house they had valuable works both of Churchmen and Puritans, and she turned them to good account.

Mr Ouseley did not try to teach his Deism to Gideon, while his mother was careful that the father's opinions should not infect the children. As a means of training for her boy, who was to be the teacher of others, she habitually made him read to her out of

the Bible, and also out of Tillotson's " Sermons,"
Young's " Night Thoughts," and his " Last Day,"
with other similar books.   The boy imbibed much
religious thought and sentiment from constant reading of this kind.   Like others, he confusedly judged
of the power of religion in general by the lives of
those who taught it.   Yet a sense of something
deeper sometimes arose, with thoughts of infinite
and awful things, and movements of the heart in
prayer.

His tutor was a priest, called by Mr Bonsall
" one of the old school," which means one educated
on the Continent.   Those who remember Connaught
forty or fifty years ago, are able to contrast a few of
that class of priests, then still surviving, with the
pupils of Maynooth.   They were at that time men
with white heads, long blue coats, shining Hessian
boots, and manners both dignified and winning, if
somewhat self - conscious.   Father Tom Keane of
Kilmeena was a fine specimen of the class, whom
a few old men will still remember; one also whose
hospitality in his remote cottage had some of the
charm exerted over Rousseau by that of the original
of the " Vicaire Savoyard."

In the days of Gideon's boyhood, " the old school "
was the only school, and his tutor was the man of
his age, not a relic of a generation that had died off.
He is said to have been " a perfect Latinist and
mathematician."   At all events, his pupil was diligent.   Up early and up late, he worked so hard
that fears were entertained for his health.   The worst
of it was, that when the time came for him to enter
Trinity College, though unusually well furnished with

Latin and mathematics, he had not sufficient Greek to
pass, because the priest could not teach him. Of course
this was a disappointment to his father, who began
to arrange for sending him to Dublin to learn his
entrance Greek, as good schools were not at hand.

Just at this time an accomplished scholar from
Dublin, Dr Robinson, was brought down by Mr
Ralph Ouseley as tutor to his sons Gore and
William.* It is said that he gave them the first
start in those Oriental studies which carried them
to honour. It was arranged between the two
cousins that Gideon should join Gore and William
under Dr Robinson. The qualifications of that
gentleman must have been high, for Sir Gore, on
hearing of his father's death, records in touching
terms his sense of the debt he owed him for that
education which had been the key to open his way.
The same provision which elicited this testimony
kept Gideon, for the present, from breathing the
cis-Shannon air.

It is hard to say what the effect of early entering
on city life would have been upon him; but his
character, as finally formed, was such as only a
remote province could nurse. The open-hearted
ways of folk who seldom see a stranger, and never
but as an object of interest, had full time to mould
the habits even of his manhood, before he ever felt
the air of a big place—that air which numbs your
consciousness of the presence of the stranger, as well

---

* Ralph Ouseley is called Captain in our papers, and in notices of
Sir Gore in biographical dictionaries. But Sir Gore always addressed
him as Esquire. Probably he was a lieutenant in some local corps, in
which case he would be called Captain in the neighbourhood.

as your sense of the importance of the individual.
So to his latest day he never lost a keen sense of
the value of one.

The same causes laid the basis of that quick
sympathy between him and the common people
which was the greatest among the natural elements
of his power. Living in uninterrupted familiarity
with bog and cabin, with mountain-road and secluded
lake ; with frieze coats, red petticoats, shoeless feet,
and beggars' wallets; with the Irish tongue, or
English spoken with a glorious brogue ; with two
or three little fields for a farm, and for a table the
potato-basket set on an iron pot ; with the wake and
the " berrin," the weddings and the " stations," the
village market, the rollicking fair, the hurling
matches, the " Patrons," and the rows which made
up the sum of peasant life, he was prepared to stand
close home upon the hearts of people for whom he
was to live. He had got into their bosoms before
one differently trained could have seized the tips of
their fingers.

The postponement of his going to college was
thought to be only temporary, but it proved to be
a putting of it off for life. A valuable farm in Roscommon fell to his father, who removed to that
county with his family. Whether he now thought
that he had better prospects for his son than the
Church would offer, we do not know, but it is certain
that he wished him to take to land instead of tithes.

How long the Ouseleys had settled at Green Lawn
before Gideon met with Harriet Wills of Wills Grove
we cannot tell. What she was as a girl is not clearly
stated by any one who has supplied us with materials,

but as a woman, she became such as those friends of her
husband who set him highest thought nobly worthy
even of him.   She had the advantage of Gideon.
He had never been to Dublin, and she had been
educated there.   Moreover, there was a religious
secret, almost forgotten by herself, in her past short
history.   When her father's health had failed, he
had taken her with him to Bath, where she spent a
couple of years.   One evening, passing a place of
worship with her governess, she was struck with the
lights and singing, and entered and stood for a while.
The words of the hymn impressed her as she had
never been impressed before.   Thoughts of God and
eternity rose up within her, she knew not how.   She
afterwards several times begged the governess to
take her back to the same place, unknown to her
father, and the feelings were renewed.   She never
knew what place of worship it was, or to what
denomination it belonged.   On returning to the
thoughtless life of Wills Grove, the sense of things
unseen which had been awakened at Bath faded
away; but when happy days dawned for her soul,
the memory of it came back, as of a morning-star
before the morn.

The young people were both under age, but their
attachment was pleasing to the parents on either
side, and Mr Wills gave his daughter the house and
lands of Woodhill, situated near his own.   It requires
little imagination to see Gideon's brother Ralph, then
a boy of eleven years old, first in the fun of the
wedding, and beginning to show that affection for
his new sister which, when a battered veteran, with
his own domestic ties pitifully broken, he poured out

in letters from London and Lisbon, as if he had still been a big boy in Roscommon. Nearly fifty years after her bridal-day he says, " My mind is in such a state that all things are disagreeable to me. Except in regard to you, I have never changed."

Doubtless the wedding would look more like the introduction to such a life as Ralph led, than to the one which, in the silent future, lay before Gideon and his Harriet. It is not so probable that the ceremony would be performed at church, as at the house of the bride's father. And as we are speaking of ninety years ago, it is pretty certain that the guests generally did not arrive in carriages, or even on jaunting-cars, but on dashing horses, the ladies on pillions behind the gentlemen. Moreover, when the drinking, dancing, and cards came on, probably the parsons were first and foremost. If no fray occurred, and no fall from horseback on the scamper home over bridle-paths, it would be, as the gentlemen would have said, " more by good luck than good guiding." He would be a proud man who could boast the next day that he brought home his sister, himself, and twelve tumblers of punch without any mishap. This quantity may seem absurd, but we can testify that, though it was always mentioned as implying a feat, it was not impossible on an occasion. Half-a-dozen tumblers was a handsome allowance, but great men gloried in leaving such performances behind.

CHAPTER III.

WHATEVER may have been the festivities of the wedding, the bridegroom, though not yet twenty-one, now found himself his own master, with the cares of study dismissed, and those of want or serious business not pressing. Hitherto his character had been steady, and, considering his age and surroundings, moral, even grave. Now, however, he was set among wild hunters, gamblers, revellers ; and his affection for his young wife, though strong, was not strong enough to keep him from following their lead. What the Connaught gentry of that day were has been told by more than one. It seemed like a society organised so as to show youths how they could best throw away a birthright of fine qualities. Emulation ran chiefly in absurd hospitality, in drinking and sports ; public spirit culminated in a hunt or horse-race ; duelling was recognised as the highest form of brilliancy ; and, on the whole, the calling of a real gentleman was to do nothing and spend much. The honour of ladies was tenderly prized, but the purity of gentlemen was another matter.

Maxwell's story of the man who would not do for Galway was written about half a century later than

the time of which we speak. Any one who reads it
will not wonder that property thereabouts should have
exhibited the disposition to make to itself wings, in
abnormal force, and will be able partially to understand how so many in Ireland have had to gaze, as
strangers, with hungry eyes on acres that belonged
to their forefathers.

Gideon's powerful frame and dreadnought courage
made him naturally leader in wild sports. His
agility is said to have defied all attempts at competi-
tion. His mental gifts and furniture would be considerably beyond the average of the squires and
squireens who were his comrades. His ready wit
and free flow of words, with the drollery of his
fancies and his eye, would be an additional element
of power. The fatal superiority in saying nothings
and doing follies, which had lured many a man of
noble capabilities to self-waste, led him on and on.
" The companion of fools " was the bitter record
which throughout the whole of his after-life his
judgment kept evermore writing in regard to those
squandered years.

How much poor Gideon lost by horse-racing and
other kinds of gambling, how much went in " the
drink," and how much in other forms of dissipation,
it is not in our power to say. However, it is plain
enough that after a while he had got himself into the
ordinary condition of men who run such a race, even
when they have more to start with than he had.
Already he was embarrassed and ashamed of himself,
and was plunging deeper and deeper into whirlpools,
trying to forget the shame, when his father-in-law
died.

The heir-at-law of Mr Wills disputed the title of Mr Ouseley to the house and lands of Woodhill, alleging some invalidity in the deed by which they had been granted to his wife. So on the back of his self-made difficulties came a new and cruel one. His nephew, Mr Bonsall, could never exactly determine what particular reason led him to the course he then took, which was the very strange one of leaving the property without a struggle. Until his last day he kept the disputed deed, of the validity of which he had not a shadow of a doubt, and his legal advisers said that there was no reason whatever to cast a doubt upon it. The possible impulses under which he took this unaccountable course are suggested by Mr Bonsall as inexperience, unconquerable shame at his embarrassments, and hasty pride. The last and the first are probably the true reasons. Men whose heads are frequently heated with " more than is good for them," if given to pride, are liable to grotesque fits of that passion. We know of a case in which a grant considerably larger than that of Woodhill was. thrown up in one such fit. The habit of gambling, also, has not a little to do with rash sacrifices of this kind. Those who often wilfully run risk from mere caprice are not unlikely rashly to do what cannot be undone.

In after-life Mr Ouseley clearly saw that this strange movement of his had proved to be the turning-point in his history, and in that of the devoted wife whom he carried away from her home. Whatever may have been the impulse under which he acted, when he afterwards looked back upon life, he adored the hidden hand that led him away from

Woodhill. Had he continued to live there, he felt that he would also have been one of the most heedless and godless of the circle in which he was involved.

Injured himself, and having injured his wife, he left the scene of his joys and follies, and again returned to Dunmore.

It would appear that by this time his father also was once more resident there. On land belonging to him Gideon settled. But what he had suffered had not brought wisdom. In Dunmore he found the same kind of companions as those who had been his curse at Woodhill. Things he had read and heard came up at times in an array of awful thoughts. Especially when alone in the fields, he remembered the great Creator, and felt, as he says, " a desire to serve that Being who, by the word of His power, had made the world." But lower desires of the flesh bore these nobler ones down, and he ran with fools in their folly, day after day, and night after night. He was what the world calls gay—what his renewed self abhorred as grovelling; and sometimes he endeavoured to quench conscience by making himself an infidel, but in this he does not appear to have had complete success. He used to say to his friends, that whatever was true, Popery was false; and from a letter written very late in life, it would seem that at this early time, in addition to all he saw with his own eyes, the reading of one of the fearful anathemas of the Church of Rome had inspired him with a horror of the cruelty embodied in the system, which made him, even then, try to persuade companions that it was wrong.

A severe scarcity of food occurred, and a com-

mittee of relief was organised at Dunmore. Of this
Gideon was a member. One day, after having
discharged his duties, he was walking down the
street, and approached some of his friends who were
engaged in a frolic, or a fray, as it might be considered. Returning from a day of field-sport, they
had gone into the village inn to have " some refreshment." The refreshment was of a kind much sung
for its social virtue. If it is really a cement of
friendship, it nevertheless sometimes stirs up
strife. Thomas Hart started away from his companions in a heat, with his fowling-piece, loaded with
shot, under his arm. One followed to bring him
back, and a scuffle ensued, in which the piece went
off, and Gideon Ouseley, who was coming up, fell
on the street, with the entire charge lodged in the
right side of his neck and face.

They took up the bleeding man, and believing
him to be mortally wounded, bore him home to his
poor Harriet. She had often waited for him through
aching hours of night; assailed, it may be, by
thoughts against which her woman's heart would
fain have barred all the doors of imagination. Perhaps while he was away she had sometimes wished that
there were children in the house to help to keep him
there. And perhaps, sometimes, when he did reach
the door, she was glad there were no children to see.
No doubt that in subsequent years the remembrance
of these dark days helped her not a little to that
sweet patience with which she always waited when
he was long and far away, and to the joy with which
she gave him up to shame and danger for the
blessed business he had then to do.

She had no need to care how many eyes looked upon his present return home. It was only sorrowful ; for the blood that was flowing was not due either to his folly or his sin. It proved that his life was not in danger ; but when the shot struck the face, a single grain entered the right eye, and drove the day out of it for ever.

Now the strong man was a prisoner. Leisure and solitude were imposed upon him. Death had knocked at his door, and he felt that God alone had saved him. The brain became cool, and gradually clear. The one female figure constantly near was that of his admirable wife. Time, not now "killed" by the gabble of fools, but living and moving, stretched its long wings, full of eyes, and, slowly floating past under the broad vault of eternity, searched him through and through.

We have already said that his readings with his mother had not been quite lost. The truths of Scripture, and the images of "Night Thoughts," had often troubled his dissipations. But now they came in companies, and lifted up their voice. The passages upon death and eternity were much before his mind. He could not read; but Harriet was at his side, and she read to him. These readings bore no unimportant part in the mental processes which went to form Gideon Ouseley. Several statements, written and oral, which we have respecting them, agree perfectly in substantials, but show a discrepancy on one point of detail. As, when, years before, he read for his mother, so now the writings of Young held the leading place. Among these all concur in giving prominence to the "Centaur not Fabulous;" but only

Mr Bonsall names it as among the works read to his mother, which statement we take to be improbable. There can be no question that it had a chief part in making the impressions which rendered the time, of which we are now speaking, memorable. The testimony of the Rev. John Nelson is distinct, that this was the book to which Mr Ouseley always referred as the one that made the deepest impression upon his mind, and also that he spoke of it as having been introduced to him by Mrs Ouseley. Mr Nelson, however, adds that she had misconceived its drift. By another informant this mistake on her part as to the drift of a work is referred to the " Infidel Reclaimed." The particular object which Mrs Ouseley had in view is taken to be the same in both statements, and for that object the " Centaur not Fabulous " was the book.

Doubtless the " Infidel Reclaimed " was read, and with still more attention the " Last Day." At that time the terrors of this poem had, if not an attraction for the mind of Mr Ouseley, a certain affinity with its state. To quote the book that touched him most, he now had time to converse with the two greatest strangers—God and his own heart—and " neither of them at peace with him." The setting forth of eternal things in the poem recalled feelings, which often had arisen in earlier years, but had always died away. The blasts of the last trumpet awoke the echo of many a sentence of self-condemnation. Passages referring to the follies of licence and excess came upon his ear in the soft, warm accents of a Connaught lady, with which, doubtless, would often blend the undefinable but tell-tale note of a wife yearning for the reformation of her husband.

The fact that returning health might bring on its golden wings new sins for him, and new sorrows for her, was not to be kept out of sight. And so the subtle language of tone would now and then tell how she was hoping and praying that the big and often clouded lines (veiled, however, with translucent cloud) would somehow make her Gideon good.

It was not with them now as it was when, after having travelled together till both had reached the age of seventy-seven, she once more sat by his sick-bed reading, while the hour for the last farewell drew on. *Then*, the book was not Young, but the Bible; and the favourite passages were not those describing a wicked life, a miserable death, and a doleful eternity, but those of which the retrospect was redeeming love, and the prospect glory, honour, and immortality. In the first case, they feared what the little space of time given by recovery might produce; in the second, they did not fear what eternity, introduced by death, would bring forth.

But the prose of Young struck deeper than his poetry. The conceit under which the sharp lessons of the "Centaur not Fabulous" are couched, was suited to engage the imagination of Mr Ouseley. He could vividly see the picture of a monster in which "the brute runs away with the man . . . galloping with more than human haste after temptations." Many of the passages touched sore places. The death of Altamont was one to which, if we do not mistake, he often referred as having made a very deep impression. In reading the passage where the man of pleasure is put to the question as to whether he

ever did ask himself to what species he belonged—
an immortal or only a rational creature, or a mere
animal — we find the kind of thoughts which
seemed to be native to his own mind.   But here
they are dressed in velvet, instead of his Connaught
frieze. The conclusion of that passage might have
been introduced by his own clinching *ergo*—" He is
an immortal without the sense of his immortality.
He is a rational dethroning reason, and an animal
transgressing appetite."   Perhaps the affinity with
his own modes of thought was still more striking in
the following grotesque definitions of the man of
pleasure :—

" He is an immortal that has two marks of a man
about him—upright stature, and the power of play-
ing the fool, which a monkey has not.

" He is an immortal being that triumphs in this
singular, deplorable, and yet thoughtless hope that
he shall be as happy as a monkey when they are both
dead, though he despairs of being so while yet alive.

" He is an immortal being that would lose none of
its most darling delights if he were a brute in the
mire, but would lose them all entirely if he were an
angel in heaven."

In the illness to which we are now referring, Young
was performing for the future Gideon Ouseley, the
double service which he had already rendered to
many labourers in the field on which the latter was to
enter.   He was filling the imagination with vivid
and active conceptions of life and death, sin and
justice, heaven and hell, and storing the memory
with terms, phrases, and illustrations by which to
convey those conceptions to others, not to speak of

passages. for quotation. The appeals of Mr Ouseley in future life bore testimony of his debts to the bard of Welwyn, from whose wing he often feathered his arrows, as did many another good bowman in the Methodist advance. This eventual use of the readings from Young was, for the time being, distant from the thoughts of both husband and wife. So far as Mrs Ouseley was concerned, we have no reason to believe that her views went beyond such a reformation as would give her a good husband, though perhaps this was connected with some vague feeling after God, " if haply they might find Him." Her husband's language to Mr Bonsall shows that his own ideas of amendment were limited to a similar range. He speaks of them as founded on " temporal and bodily " considerations, rather than on any correct conception of God's holiness and justice. Probably he just intended to be such a man as Harriet would be proud of, and to follow such a course as would secure his character and prospects, and bring no peril to his health. He had plenty of will, and when he took a matter in hand, was noted for being able to set it through. This, of course, he was now going to do in the great affair of turning over a new leaf. Doubtless, however, he would offer some prayers, formal or informal, to fortify his judicious resolutions.

Wise with the many reflections of his retirement, and strong in the purpose to be good, he once more set foot on the highway of life. He had not travelled far, when the dismissed follies began to come about him again; not, indeed, at first with any claim to be masters as of old, but seeking only

for occasional employment, and that ever so little,
as inferior servants.

To yield now would be worse than his first errors
at Woodhill, and even than his deeper plunges after
returning to Dunmore.   Now he would have to
tread upon deliberate resolutions and mature judgments.   He had coolly determined to make a good
man of Gideon Ouseley, and surely he was not to be
foiled.   Had he not force of will, and command over
himself?   Yes, perfect, when the thing to be done
was bad or indifferent.   But now?   The thing to be
done was to cease to do evil, and to learn to do well,
and had he not strength of mind for that?   Here
was the true trial of the strong man.   Alas! failure
after failure, leading on to fall after fall, till it
became a prisoner's conflict between fetters he could
not cast and longings he would not quench.

"The evil that I would not, that I do," began to
be his bitter feeling; and then came the still more
mysterious experience, "The good that I would, I
do not."   Vaguely, but with distressing effect,
disagreeable truths begin to make themselves felt
rather than seen.   First, that his "good heart"
was far from being good after all; and secondly,
that he was not his own master, but really a slave.
In happy days of subsequent liberty, after his Lord
had made him free, when referring to the bewildering
conflict of this time, he would say, "It is not I, but
sin that dwelleth in me"—the dark master who
held the castle forced him to do work that he abhorred.

His old comrades thought he was now all regained
to them.   No doubt his poor wife thought he was

all lost, and lost for life. But neither could see what divine checks the new course of sinning had to contend against within the bosom of the sinner himself. If the dark spirit cast him down and made him wallow, the Spirit of Light was standing above and speaking soft words, but words of power. He often afterwards said that his own feeling was best put into the language of another—"O wretched man that I am! who shall deliver me from the body of this death?" We seldom realise how much God may be working in the heart of those who seem to be loosed from all restraint. At this particular point of his history Mr Ouseley had concluded that his case was incurable—that he must go on sinning, and be lost to all eternity. He knew that he had sincerely meant and sought to establish his own righteousness, and the only result was deeper guilt and worse depravity. What cure could such a disorder admit of?

CHAPTER IV.

HIS CONVERSION.

WHEN a detachment of the Fourth Royal Irish Dragoon Guards marched into the cavalry barracks of Dunmore, it did not strike any one in the town that the event was to have any connection with the future religious life of Gideon Ouseley. But it had not long been there before the little place was ringing with the news of strange doings at the head inn. This was kept by Mrs Kennedy, a Roman Catholic, who had a large room, called in the place " the public room," which she let to showmen, conjurors, and such other worthies as were candidates for an audience in Dunmore. Some of the new soldiers, headed by Quartermaster Robinet, came to inquire about the room, and engaged it for frequent use to hold meetings. That dragoons should resort to a public-house was nothing new, and as to what kind of meetings theirs would be, few people would think it worth while to guess.

But when the new soldiers assembled, there was something strange about their proceedings. Voices and singing were heard, and there was no drink. What could they be doing? The people of the inn listened, and others gathered; and it came to be credibly reported in the town that the troopers met to pray, and that they sang hymns and read the Bible, and did something like preaching. The quartermaster seemed to be a kind of parson for them, but he had no prayer-book. This was enough to excite a place more exposed to events than Dunmore. What could they be?

The clergy of both " Church and Chapel " combined to lead the laugh against the praying soldiers; but some of the people, perhaps, thought that the parsons themselves had better be more given to prayer. Some affirmed that the quartermaster and his band were Methodists, and the bulk of the people asked what was that, to whom the wiser replied that it was a new religion. But the great question was, What could lead men to act so? and each very wise man in the place had his own view as to that deep secret. Had they met for any kind of folly and wickedness, the town's-folk would not have found it necessary to seek below the surface for motives. But meetings for worship! It was, however, remarked that, whatever else the men might be, they were *steady*.

The soldiers seemed open enough, and asked everybody to come and see. Presently one and another of the poorer classes did come, and the plain words of the quartermaster told upon both heart and life. But the oddity of a man in that military array, such as the cavalry uniform then was, standing up and preaching, and that without any book to preach from, passed everything, and still the wonder grew.

Mr Ouseley, of course, heard the talk, shared in the wonder, and adopted some wise man's notion that they had an underhand design, to cover which

all this show was adopted. Still he wanted to know
what their design could be, and no two agreed on that
point. But he was so sure that there was something
of the kind, that he would not venture into their
meetings. After a time, however, he resolved to do
so, feeling perfectly confident that he would detect
" some design, some trick."

It was in April 1791, that the powerful man of
twenty-nine years of age, with one eye blind, and
the other full of shrewdness and roguery, came in
and faced the quartermaster, determined to find
him out. With the one keen eye he watched every
movement, and with both ears hearkened to the
exhortation and to the prayers of Robinet, and of
some of his men. When all was over, what had he
found out? He was compelled to confess, nothing—
not even a new religion; for, using all the theological lore which he had laid up in his various
reading, he found he had not heard anything but
what seemed to be in agreement with the Bible, and
with the prayers of the Church.

However, what he had not detected at first sight,
he felt sure he would on further search. So he came
to the meetings again and again. But still the same
failure to discover any design, any trick; and somehow a new light seemed to glide inward to the hidden
places of his own breast. He began to have different
views of himself. His sins put on the appearance of
more than follies and mistakes, and gradually were
placed in the odious light of offences against a very
good and holy God. Before, he took it for granted
that he could not be cured, and so must sin on.
Now, while on the one hand sin began to look more

exceeding sinful, and eternal danger to be close at hand, on the other hand the possibility of a real cure ever and anon crossed the darkness, as with a gleam from heaven.

Gradually he felt that he had done injustice to the quartermaster, and that, whatever he might be, he really had no design or trick covered under his appearances, but, on the contrary, was a true man. Soon esteem and confidence replaced his old suspicions. He invited Mr Robinet to his house. Their conversation led him to the Bible, and eventually gave a personal interest and reality to things which hitherto, though very awful, had been rather vague and distant. He felt more and more that sin was hateful, and yet that there was a way of repentance.

Encouraged by the appearances in the place, the quartermaster had appealed to the Methodist preachers to visit Dunmore. We have different statements as to who was the first who came, the balance of opinion appearing to be in favour of Mr Thomas Davis, from the Athlone Circuit. Among these early visitors, David Gordon, of the Parsonstown Circuit, is particularly mentioned. Mr Ouseley, rather strong in his own theological attainments, was careful in judging of the doctrine of the preachers, and his first impressions of them were simply that he had not any fault to find with what they said, rather approved of it, but he received no particular religious influence from it. However, at a second, or subsequent, visit of David Gordon, in the month of May 1791, the preacher selected as his text, "Thou art Peter, and upon this rock I will build my church, and the gates of hell shall not prevail

against it." We should have expected that this
would be the text for a highly controversial sermon.
It would seem, on the contrary, that Gordon's was
entirely practical. And then, for the first time, one
of those living impressions, which are never afterwards forgotten, appears to have been made upon
Mr Ouseley. He says that the earnestness of the
preacher, and his remarks upon the text, affected
him so deeply, that, both while hearing him and
afterwards, thoughts of eternity crowded upon his
mind. He adds, "I then more fully resolved upon
reformation, and changed from evil practices, and
withdrew from the society of my ungodly asso-
ciates."

By this time he appears to have come to the all-
important point of habitual and deep study of the
Holy Scriptures. There he sought to know the will of
God; and then the passages in the "Night Thoughts,"
the "Infidel Reclaimed," and the "Centaur not
Fabulous," which had often affected him before, and
been buried under the rubbish of his life, rose up again
and held awful converse with him in the dark. One
day, when at home and alone, he was overwhelmed
with thoughts of eternity. He says, "The question
came to my mind, Is there an eternity?—is there
a hereafter beyond the grave? My mind replied,
There is. The next question was, What will you do?
Then instantly all my sins sprang up to my mind's
view like a hostile army. I then reasoned with myself, If all this remains, and comes against me
in the day of judgment, I shall be ruined most
certainly." Then encouraging passages of Scripture
began to be suggested to his mind. "But I felt

as if I was too vile a sinner to warrant hope that there was mercy for me. Yet I remembered that there was mercy for even the chiefest of sinners, and I thought of the invitation, in Isaiah i. 18, to reason with Him. The thought of my heart was, If God will forgive you all the past, will you serve Him, not as many do, but as He will have Himself served—that is, according to His own Word, and not heeding what men may say or do? I replied, All this is reasonable; but I never could serve Him in that manner. It was then suggested to me, God is almighty, and He is merciful; and if you labour to promote this result as you have done in other things, failure is impossible. To this I said, I believe so; but I must count the cost. I am a young man, and may live, say forty years, and to be under restraint all that time, as if buried alive, would be dreadful. I am not willing to undertake to be tied down to obey that book (the Bible) for the remainder of my life. Then I considered the possibility that I might die before the morning; and even should I survive for forty years, and then be cast into hell for all eternity! This decided the matter. I had such a view of eternity, of being cast into everlasting misery, never—never—never to be released! I fell upon my knees, and cried, O God, I will submit! The moment I consented, and cried, I submit, I submit, cost me what it will, the scripture came to my mind, 'When the wicked man turneth away from his wickedness that he hath done, and doeth that which is lawful and right, he shall save his soul alive.' This is good, said I; it is great encouragement. Another scripture followed, 'Blessed are

those servants whom the Lord, when He cometh, shall
find watching' (Luke xii. 37). So then I said to
myself, If I begin to watch now, and obey the Lord,
and do no more evil, but obey Him according to this
book, He will count me a blessed man, and He
will never go back. The next thought that occurred
to me was, But what will you do with your past
sins? I replied to that question, Even if I cried
my eyes out, I could not make my sins less than
they are; but when God agrees to regard me as a
blessed man if I watch, what need I vex myself?

" Now, said I, what shall I begin to do? I do
not know, unless somebody teach me. Then three
classes of Christian teachers passed in review before
me. The first the Roman Catholic priests, and the
voice inquired, Will they do? No, no; they are a
set of mercenaries. Secondly, the Church clergy;
they are not schemers like the others, but then they
are as little good as myself. They won't do; they
are as careless as I am. Thirdly, the Methodist
preachers; they look very smooth, but they may have
some evil among them, and I had better not have
anything to do with them. They won't do. What
shall I do.? I have but one soul; and if that is gone,
all is gone! Then the voice sounded, Read the
Scriptures, and do what they bid you. I was going
to say, I will, when another thought arose, How
do you know that the Scriptures are true? I do not
know, said I, but of all things they appear the most
probable. God knows I know no better; and I
determined to read and obey. But I found myself
so stupid and forgetful, that I could not obey as I
expected."

It would now seem as if Christian had fairly turned his back upon the City of Destruction, and with his burden upon his shoulders, was bent on getting far away from it. Mr Ouseley was at last consciously fleeing from the wrath to come, and felt that at any cost it was best to press forward. He knew little but that he could not be saved in his sins, and wondered that, when he had resolved to give them up, and watch for the future, all did not go well. He read the Bible to gain more knowledge, and prayed to get more strength. Still the result was outward vacillation, and inward darkness and misery.

"Then I thought of going to the Lord's Table in a way I never had done before, hoping that the terror of damnation due to eating and drinking unworthily would arouse me. A dispute I had had with a gentleman a few days before occurred to my mind; because the Scriptures say, 'If thou bringest thy gift to the altar,' &c. I found I could not go, because of this disagreement. But *he* was in fault. But I said, This is no palliation; and I took my hat, and went immediately to the gentleman's house, and said to him, We have had a dispute: I am going to the Lord's Table, and I cannot go with that upon my mind. So we shook hands, and were reconciled. I went to the Lord's Table, and it was some relief to me from the dreadful stupidity I felt.

"Soon after I had come home from church, a drunken beggar came to the door. The thought struck me, Give him nothing. Another thought came, Never turn thy face away from any poor man, and the face of the Lord will never be turned away from you. I have promised I shall obey God, and now I will. So I went to order something to be given to the poor man, and the scripture occurred to me, 'The Lord loveth a cheerful giver.' I said, I am not the man. But I went forward, and did as I purposed. All the day after I was in heaviness; and on going to bed, I said on my knees, Lord, I am not a cheerful giver, and I cannot help it.

"All this time I knew not the way of salvation by faith in Christ." In fact, to him, as to most men before conversion, the authority of God had appeared hitherto in the same aspect as public justice does to a criminal—that, namely, of the greatest danger and the most dreadful enemy. It does not strike a thief that public justice is the most earnest friend of the whole community, and that, the case arising, it would prove the best friend even to him, and would make the difference for him between being mutilated by wild revenge and being moderately punished by a responsible tribunal. The two alternatives of innocence or punishment—the only ones which strict law can recognise—naturally fill almost the entire field of view in an unenlightened conscience. True, there is then some glimmer of a doctrine of pardon, but it is a pardon viewed only as a very slight modification of the law of innocence—a mere passing over of sin, as something that may be treated slightly. When the law enters; and is put by the finger of God into the mind and heart of a man, all these trifling views of sin go out, and it becomes to every thought and feeling exceeding sinful.

Then the conception of a free pardon upon repentance granted on no heavier condition than simply pleading the death of Christ as our substitute, and relying on that alone, is difficult to admit. The unforgiving nature of man teaches him that some reparation ought to be made by him who has done the wrong; and, moreover, his pride is hurt by terms which, in a case of such heavy offending, take away all pretext of offering the least consideration for being reinstated in favour. The very greatness of the mercy implies the completeness of his own guilt and inability; and the very simplicity of the way whereby that mercy may be made his own, brings it so near, that a man ready to perish feels as if the news were too good to be accepted, at least for the present.

This free, plain, ready method of justification it was which Mr Ouseley was slow to learn. He says, "Thank God, I did learn it before it was too late. I was seeking salvation by the works of the law; and because my efforts were futile, I murmured against God. I condemned Him, and not myself. I asked, 'Why did God make me as I am; and why expose me to eternal ruin for what was His fault, and not mine?' I was like one enclosed in a net, and was becoming more and more entangled by my efforts to extricate myself."

Now came one more noticeable turn in the out-ward path along which the inner life was advancing. Some time in the month of May 1791, on a week evening, after the ordinary meeting, the preacher invited " any seriously-disposed person " to remain for the meeting of the Society. Mr Ouseley had determined not to have anything to do with their Society; but he was now so anxious for every ray of

light, that he thought he would try even what this
might bring.   Mr Reilly has quoted his words, and
they are plainly genuine, as he must have often heard
them from his lips : " I will wait and see what they
are about; but if I find any juggling, any Freemason's
tricks among them, I will have nothing to do with
them."   It is strange that one so shrewd did not ask
himself if it was likely that those who had anything
among them which they feared being "found out,"
would give so wide an invitation as to "any one
seriously disposed," so that, in fact, any person might
come in and play the spy.   Not seeing this, he once
more set the sharp eye to watch for signs of some
black art.

What did it find ?   People in such privacy as consists, not in secrecy, but in being of one mind, giving
themselves up with feelings of family cordiality to
communion on the things of God.   It was Brother
this, and Sister that.   The hymns sung were such as
speak of mercy as a pearl in possession ; of peace as
felt and flowing ; of God as a Father near at hand and
strangely loving ; of Christ as perfect Priest, Sacrifice, Mediator, Righteousness, and Redemption ; and
of heaven as a happy, happy home, only on the other
side of a thin cloud.   The prayers were very like
those offered up in public, and yet, upon closer attention, seemed rather more as men would pray when
no one was within hearing.   Instead of secrets to be
kept, each one openly spoke of God's good dealings
and loving-kindness.

This was something different from making the
discovery of some jugglery.   The work of God in
the soul of man was now brought closer home to

his thoughts than it ever had been before. The generalities of a sermon were here dismissed. It was now man for man and woman for woman. The language was not They and Them; but it was I, and You, and We. We have no particulars of what was said by the respective persons then present; but we know very well how the conversation would run, and thousands would be able to set it down in substance just as well as we.

The words of each particular person would vary, and yet, somehow, all would support the testimony of the others. The great theme was the pardoning love of God, and simply believing in Christ crucified was constantly alluded to as the means by which it came to be felt and known. This brother had long looked to his own efforts and self-healing, but only grew worse and worse; but, when in despair and ready to perish, he cast all on Christ alone; salvation came with joy, while power over sin sealed the change. He would be encouraged to "run with patience the race set before him." Another simple soul would say that he wanted to tell to all around "what a dear Saviour I have found."

Another had fallen again and again, but had been renewed and restored by the inexhaustible patience of redeeming love. He would be warned to "watch and pray, lest he should fall into temptation." Another had formerly walked in the light, but he had been unwatchful, and now felt as if closed round with mist and cloud. He would get a cheering word —he must not despond. "Sorrow might endure for a night, but joy would come in the morning." Another was full of hope, feeding upon foreseen glory; and he would receive the exhortation to be "faithful unto death." Yet another felt the struggle against the world, the flesh, and the devil very hard, and sometimes thought he should be overcome; but he was determined to do his best. He would be affectionately reminded that " not by might, not by power, but by my Spirit, saith the Lord ; " and that, if he trusted in his own strength, he should fail, but if he laid hold on that of the Lord, he should be strong with "the Spirit's might in the inner man." And so the conversation, ever changing yet ever similar, would run on, almost every word teaching the stranger, while no one intended to teach. It is possible there may have been present some of those whose marked individuality no general type will ever cover, who often by a single phrase, a quotation, or a metaphor, convey to the bewildered captive of sin a light which volumes of formal discoursing would fail to bring.

As we said before, we do not know the details of what was then spoken; but " it was the very thing for him," and especially "the experiences he had heard." What he had found was very far from being the discovery of a new religion; yet it was the discovery of a Church in a new aspect as to Gideon Ouseley. Here was a Church in a house, not a Church with her tongue always tied, except when vicariously opened on Sunday in the pulpit; but a Church seated at home like a joyful mother of children, with her sons and daughters holding free fellowship in family communion. Of course, he had read of Christians "exhorting one another," and "praying one for another," and " admonishing one another in psalms

and hymns and spiritual songs,"—and more to the
same effect; but he had never known of anything of
the kind in practice, except as the clergyman might
do all this, or at least as much of it as needed to be
done. He had read of one calling " all that feared
the Lord to come to him, and he would tell them
what He had done for his soul; " but he did not know
that anything of the sort was ever thought of nowadays.
He had also read of Christians " confessing their
faults one to another," and had seen in the sacred
writings many instances of such confession as might
be properly made before any of the brethren, as in
the Psalms and Epistles; but all he had ever practically known of confession was that cataloguing and
detailing of particular transgressions which is fit
only for the secret ear of one initiated as a scrutineer
of sin. Here, however, was plenty of confessing—
fervent and touching. One was " unwatchful,"
another " hard and ungrateful," another " the chief
of sinners," another had " grieved the Spirit;" yet it
was such confessing as needed no secrecy or priest-
craft, but only called forth the prayer of one for the
other, as of those who felt their common need, and
sought the common help.

He here found that Gideon Ouseley was not the
first who had determined to make a good man of
himself, and miserably learned that " the leopard cannot change his spots;"—that he was not the first that
had said he never could be cured, and might as well
sin on; nor the first who had gone to the Lord's Table,
and done much to set his house in order, and yet
found no rest to his soul. Then, as to this new way
of faith—they called it " resting on Christ," commit-

ting all to Christ, laying down the weapons of rebellion, renouncing all merit but that of Jesus, beholding the Lamb as slain for them, looking only to the blood of Christ, and so on. And yet, again, as to the love, and joy, and peace they spake of! Was it not wonderful to hear men talk as if the things said in the Bible were real, and as if people actually did feel and know them in Dunmore?

It is not clear in our narrative whether it was. Quartermaster Robinet who invited him to the class-meeting, or John Hurly; but just now mention occurs of the latter. He was one whom Gideon did lovingly remember—"an earnest, zealous preacher, and his ministry was much blessed to me." It is evident that in his discourses the law had no small place; and hitherto this seems to have been the only part of scriptural truth which made much impression upon Mr Ouseley. Now his views of sin were gradually becoming more defined, both as to its being grievous in the sight of God, and being the natural fruit of his own evil heart. But of John Hurly he says, "He did not leave me to the horrors of the law. He unfolded the plan of salvation. He preached the glad tidings. He assured me of the willingness of God to pardon my sins though faith in Christ, to blot my name out of the book of death, and write it in the book of life."

This, and especially the testimonies to which he had listened at the class-meeting, brought the idea of pardon nearer home. Now the blotting out of sin was no longer an undefined something to be obtained or not as the case might be, but in any case not to be felt. It had become in his view a real reconciliation with God, having its effect in the mind of the prodigal, as well as in that of the forgiving Father, involving the healing of the breach and the establishment of peace on both sides. He saw in the Holy Scriptures that they whom God forgave were abundantly forgiven—tasted His love, and were made happy. He felt sure that others had actually found the pearl he now eagerly sought after; but was not his own case an extreme one—that of a sinner beyond the pale of ordinary clemency?

Thus agitated, and yet led onwards, Mr Ouseley was now nearing the foot of the cross. His views of God's plain way of mercy were still far from being clear, but he had a dawning knowledge that salvation was of grace alone, through the merit of Christ alone, and received by faith alone. The bitterness of his sin and its burden became more and more intolerable. He would cry, " O God ! my wicked nature ! Fain would I be made a new creature, but I can no more do this for myself than I can touch the stars or create a world." He had now both the satisfaction and the pain of one who was in search, not merely of some hid treasure of a sort unknown, but of one goodly pearl—the satisfaction of having a definite object to seek, and the pain of seeking and not finding. " Oh that I knew where I might find Him, that I might come even to His seat !" was his cry, as again and again he sought the witness of God's Spirit with his spirit that he had been accepted as His child. " I would order my cause before Him, and fill my mouth with arguments." And he did so, urging the great good argument, " God be merciful to me." Yet no answer. " Behold, I go forward, but He is not there; and backward, but I cannot perceive Him; on the left hand where He doth work, but I cannot behold Him. He hideth Himself on the right hand that I cannot see Him." But He that had said to him, " Seek my face," was not to hide it long.

John Hurly had evidently succeeded in teaching him that mercy was at the door, and that redemption was to be looked upon as nigh at hand; and one Sunday morning, about the middle of May 1791, when in his own house seeking his Saviour as he long had sought Him, he was enabled to behold the Lamb of God slain for him, and felt that the load and darkness were taken away, and that the long-sought peace had been bestowed at last. At the meeting of the class, Hurly asked him, " Are you getting power over your sins?" " Yes; but the axe must not boast against him that heweth therewith." Probably there was a new tone and look with these words, for Hurly replied, " Do you believe that the Lord has pardoned you?" " Yes; 'my soul doth magnify the Lord, and my spirit doth rejoice in God my Saviour.'" The blessed Spirit had put a new song in his mouth, which all along the wind-beaten path he travelled to the grave was sung and sung anew.

Mr Reilly has made emphatic mention of the way in which he often had heard Mr Ouseley in later life tell of " that Sunday morning." And thousands heard him allude to it, in accents they could never forget, when weighted with years and labour, after hard experience of life and clear tokens of coming decay had sufficed to dispel illusory recollections, and even to damp the joy of such as were real, if it had not been unquenchable. To the last, when he referred to the great deliverance then granted to him, just as when speaking of it at Dunmore at the first, "his soul did magnify the Lord, and his spirit rejoiced in God his Saviour." Always with thrilling voice, and often with flowing tears, he gave praises for the mercy then bestowed, whereby life had been rendered thrice happy. Even to the present time, though he has been already thirty-five years in his grave, many of his children in Christ survive whose memories will yet echo the tone in which he spoke of "that Sunday morning."

Forty-six years subsequently, a youth lately from Edinburgh was seated in the chapel in Mount-melick, curious to hear the old missionary of whom so much was said, and not at all supposing that the "great change" in his own case was to be linked on to one which had been wrought upon Ouseley in Dunmore so many years before. The hearer is now my friend the Rev. John Hay, without whose loving labour on the Ouseley papers I could never have undertaken to prepare this Memoir. He says, "I wish I could reproduce his testimony as I heard it on the morning of the 24th December 1837; but Montgomery's illustration seems as applicable to it as it was to the impassioned and eloquent Summerfield. The solemnity and loving earnestness of his manner, the melting tone of his voice, the beaming look of grateful joy, the flowing tears, the impassioned character of his appeals, cannot be produced on paper. He spoke with a childlike simplicity and an overflow of heart which impressed me with the guilelessness and gratefulness of the preacher. It seemed as if the change were with him the great

event of his life, a continual wonder unto himself.
On the Sunday morning he had gone into his room,
with the resolution to remain there until he had
found peace to his anxious and alarmed soul. He
locked the door, and threw himself upon the floor,
and there groaned and cried for mercy. In the
exercise, to his amazement, a growing sense of hardness of heart came upon him, and with it the
wondering thought, 'Am I ever to be saved?' and
then the appeal, 'Ah, Lord God! is there no mercy for
me?' and still the growing sense of hardness. At
length, in the midst of his renewed and resolute
appeal, the thought of entire and instant submission
rose up within him,—'Lord, I submit—I submit!'
and with that came up the thought of Jesus the
Saviour—the Saviour for him! 'I saw Jesus—
Jesus the Saviour of sinners—Jesus the Saviour for
me. I saw Him as the gift of the love of God to me.
Jesus loved me, and gave Himself for me; and the
hardness of my heart all passed away. It melted at
the sight of that love of God to me, and I knew—
yes, I knew—that God had forgiven me all my sins;
and my soul was filled with gladness, and I wept for
joy. Oh,

 ' " Where shall my wondering soul begin?"

And ye all may be as I am. Yes, ye all may have
your sins forgiven, and your hard hearts softened,
and made blessedly happy in the love of God. God
loves you all, Jesus died for you all—ay! for the
very worst of you. Come, O my guilty brethren,
come! Won't you come, John? Won't you come,
Mary?' And thus he proceeded, till all the congregation seemed affected, many of them to tears."

Now the news ran that Gideon Ouseley had joined the Methodists, and no doubt he was going mad. In the mind of the young believer himself, fears soon began to enter, troubling his new-found rest. "I quickly fell into doubts and fears, thinking I had deceived myself; but the Lord soon relieved me again." We are not quite sure whether the relief thus spoken of is the same as that manifestation of the Comforter which, in his own interlocutory way, he thus describes : "In a few days, while standing in the street, God poured His Spirit upon me, so that I felt wonderful happiness, and indeed cried out, 'What is this?' not understanding the thing properly. Then I began to fear that I was guilty of presumption in supposing that the Almighty should have a regard to a thing so insignificant as I was. 'True,' said I, 'it is presumption.' Again, however, I reflected that I now possessed what before I had not. 'Did any man give it to you?' 'No,' said I. 'Did any angel give it to you?' 'No,' said I. 'And yet you say that God did not give it to you?' 'Oh, oh,' said I, 'God did give it to me.' I became so happy then that I cannot describe my feelings."

The Methodists had kept directing him at every point to the Bible; and now he became so hungry and thirsty for what he found there, that he wanted to know the whole of it at once. He was very far indeed from being patient with his own stupidity, there was so much of the Bible that he did not know, and so much of what he did know that he could not understand. With regard to these latter parts, ofttimes in following years he proved what angel-work was reserved for him, when, bent over the places not yet understood, he searched diligently for new gems in their depths of ever-brightening light.

He mentions that, some time in the month of August—that is, after a period of some three months, during which he had been sometimes happy and sometimes harassed with doubts and fear—he felt greatly perplexed, and asked himself what he must now do. The reply was, "Fast." But he was not quite ready for this. "What good will that do me?" And so he had a conflict with himself for some time, but eventually commenced the practice of fasting, and very often recurred to it in subsequent life.

He now became convinced that, beyond all the mercy already granted to him, he needed " a clean heart ; " but he thought that it was "too much for me to expect." Here the same conflict between law and grace, which had to be fought out in seeking justification, had to be fought over again, in seeking entire sanctification. On grounds of law, we can expect only what our obedience entitles us to ; and at first sight this principle seems specially applicable to sanctification. Indeed, so much is this the case, that many who carefully teach that justification is by grace through faith, practically, if not theoretically, take it for granted that sanctification is only by works. In so doing, they confound sanctification as a cleansing act of the Holy Spirit with sanctification as the manifestation by the human soul of its own state as cleansed. Life, as the secret force in a germ, differencing the egg of an insect from a mote of clay, is confounded with the development of life in growth, motion, and habit. Human eye sees not the force, nor does human ear hear it, nor can the heart correctly conceive what it is. Not we, but God can put it there; and if we want the mote changed into an egg, all human skill fails us. But if any one says, God has changed this mote into an egg—we shall see. Life will tell its own tale. The mote that He has made to live will grow and move, and put forth beauties and powers that dead mote never could put forth.

It is obvious that his doubt turned on his personal unworthiness, not on the question whether cleansing was promised or not in the Word of God. He found the promises clear, strong, exceeding great and precious. It was plain that God did not appoint His children to uncleanness, but to holiness; and that the precious blood of Christ was of efficacy to cleanse us from all sin, as much as from any.

But grace so great and full seemed to stand in infinite contrast with his past life and present deserts. "What I may expect," is judged not by what the Lord hath said, but by what I am. Yet, when the first principles of salvation by grace, and of faithful promise-keeping, are understood, this soon appears unreasonable, and the standard of hope rises to the level of the Word.

About the middle of August 1791, one Sunday after returning from church, "not having broken my fast till then," his wife was reading to him a narrative of the conversion of two clergymen, John Janeway and his father. While listening to this, he was marvellously affected; more especially when Mrs Ouseley read a prayer of John Janeway for his father, and how the latter said, "Oh, son! now it is come, it is come, it is come! the Spirit of God has witnessed with my spirit that I am His child. I can now look up to God as my dear Father, and to Christ as my Redeemer. I can now say, This is my Friend, and this is my Beloved. My heart is full, it is brimful, it can hold no more. I know now what that sentence means, ' The peace of God that passeth understanding.' " It was forty-six years after that memorable reading when Mr Ouseley, in 1837, telling Mr Bonsall, said, "This passage was so applicable to my state, so encouraging, that ' as I sat listening,' a mighty power from heaven fell upon me,"—and here the old man paused, wept, and broke out in thanksgiving to God. It was some time before he could resume his tale, during which he praised the holy name of his Redeemer that the fulness of the blessing which was given in 1791 had never been withdrawn. When able to resume, he said, " The manifestation was such as I never anticipated or thought of; but it is written, ' Eye hath not seen nor ear heard, neither have entered into the heart of man, the things which God hath prepared for them that love Him ; but God hath revealed them unto *me* by His Spirit.' " The words of several scriptures were brought home to him with wonderful force. " Though ye have lien among the pots, yet shall ye be as doves, whose wings are as silver, and their feathers as yellow gold." " The light of the moon shall be as the light of the sun, and the light of the sun as the light of seven days." " Then the Lord shall bind up the breach of His people, and heal the stroke of their wound."

" Like the father of John Janeway," he says, " I was unable, I am still unable, to express what glorious discoveries God made of Himself to me. Astonished and bathed in tears, I fell on my knees, and cried, ' My God, my God! I never thought that such happiness was to be attained in this world.' The reply was, ' See that scripture, The kingdom of God is at hand.' I said, ' O my God! I thought " at hand " meant that I should go to heaven when I die.' The voice replied, ' You are mistaken.' I got up from my knees greatly rejoicing, and then went to the prayer-meeting, and began to tell, with tears and joy, what God had done for my soul. From this time forth, wherever I went I spoke of the ' things of God,' " telling of a kingdom, not in the golden clouds of a distant world, but within you—a kingdom of righteousness, peace, and joy in the Holy Ghost.

The Lord had long been training a harvest-man, and now He was thrusting him forth into the harvest. When He seeks labourers, He·goes not to the places we should have thought of, nor does He cast in the moulds we should call most becoming; and He gives only one certificate, which, though generally admitted by the wise of the next generation, as a rule, is satisfactory only to the simple in the present one: " By their fruits ye shall know them."

CHAPTER V.

THE candle was now lighted, and could not be hidden under either bed or bushel. First, it had to show light to those " who were in the house." The change which had passed upon Gideon was naturally matter of remark among all his friends. His father took it as one phase of his development, which, like the rest, must run its course. His wife was pleased with it so long as it remained within bounds; but the intensity of his religious feelings, and the absorption of mind which followed, alarmed her. All admitted the wonderful moral improvement, and, so far as that was concerned, were delighted; but his zeal was very objectionable, and still more so his Methodism. Could he not have gathered the strawberries without bending his back to that plant growing so low ?

Still, so long as he confined himself to private exertions among his friends, the opposition did not rise to any head; and before that took place, she who stood nearest to him was gradually entering into sympathy with his views. On the one hand, she gently tried to persuade him that he was allowing religion to absorb his mind too much, and that both reason and health might suffer. On the other hand, he sought by all means to bring her to the knowledge of that blessed Saviour who had made the earth a new world for him. Whatever Mrs Ouseley might privately think, she was too amiable not to accommodate herself to her husband's ways. Gradually, his prayers, the frequent conversations she heard between him and his new friends, and the books that were continually in his hand, told upon her own mind. She too, feeling that she was a sinner even as others, sought mercy as he had done. In about a twelvemonth after his own conversion, she became a partaker of like precious faith, happy in the Saviour who had made him happy. Thenceforth husband and wife were as one soul. It would be very hard to conceive union more sympathetic and practical. If he was the one to brave the storms, she bore the cold; and many observers felt, what both Mr Huston and Mr Reilly have put into words, that it was hard to know which to admire most, the husband in his labour or the wife in her solitude, so well did both fulfil the peculiar parts to which they were called by the common Master.

It would seem as if the solicitude of Mrs Ouseley concerning the health and reason of her husband was not the idle fear often indulged by those who wish to check promise of decided Christian devotedness in the bud. At first, Mr Ouseley no doubt showed extravagances, which in one remarkable case came to a crisis, and so wrought their own cure.

Like all young converts, when meaning to follow the Lord fully, he says, "I was very strict over myself, and judged and condemned myself with severity for forgetfulness and mistakes, though, as far

D

as I know, few of them were intentional.   I pined for
unbroken fellowship with God, to be saved from every
doubt and fear.   As I afterwards discovered, I wanted
to be saved from trials and temptations.   When
tempted, I accused myself of unfaithfulness ; and on
some occasions properly so, for my faith was dull, and I
tampered with evil suggestions, instead of resisting."

In this state of mind occurred what might well
alarm Mrs Ouseley, and what, indeed, to make it perfectly credible, requires his own words, which we have
before us.   It is a proof of his tenacity of resolution,
and also of his bodily strength, such as required the
subsequent course of a long life fully to corroborate.
He says, " Shortly after the late gracious manifestation I had received, darkness came upon me, and I
thought of St Paul's fasting, I resolved to try to
fast three days.   I did so, and found no pain on
account of the fast, and continued three days more
doing so, and did not eat a morsel or even drink a
drop of water during those six days, till I received
the sacrament in the church on Sunday, and all
through the time I felt sweetness as if I had been
drinking honey.   After that I had a great fit of sickness, and thought I should have died.   When in the
greatest agony, my happiness subsided for a little
while.   Then a thought struck me, ' Whither shall I
go when I die ? ' not having the witness then.   But
that scripture occurred to me, ' Him that cometh to
me, I will in no wise cast out.'   Another voice seemed
to say, ' Do not touch that promise : did you come to
Him ; did you come off from every sin ? '   I replied,
' Lord, Thou knowest that, from such a time (about
thirteen weeks before), I did quit every known sin,

and submitted to my Redeemer.' Then the promise came home fully, and I became exquisitely happy. I thought I should die, and got up and settled my affairs, without telling the reason to my wife. After that, my health began to recover rapidly, and I was soon restored."

Here we have a will strong enough to beat down the most imperious of our appetites; and yet we remember, that when this man fought his desires in his own strength, he could not overcome them. What a proof is this of the power of sin to lead the strongest will captive! His continuous fasting was not the wild enthusiasm of a weakling, but the dogged will-force of a very resolute man, whose former want of self-command is easily accounted for by those who believe in the fall and depravity of human nature. Those who deny that doctrine, when they take to explaining such a fact, resort to odd means, as untrue to the philosophy they profess to serve as to the religion they wish to shun.

It was not for long that speaking of the things of God merely to his friends and acquaintances would suffice. He soon began to feel a loud inward call to go out into the highways and hedges, and summon the people to repentance. Even his private efforts brought ridicule. "I was laughed at, and looked upon as an enthusiast, and ridiculed for giving myself to such a people. But I maintained that their doctrine was only what I had learned as a Churchman from my youth up, except that they directed my mind to the inward experience of it through the Holy Ghost; and therefore the reproaches moved me not. Through grace I persevered.

Those who most derided me were, in general, the sober professors of religion."

But the call to go forth publicly resounded louder and louder within. What could he do? He felt that he neither knew how to begin a sermon nor how to "carry it on." But this did not decide the conflict. He would say, as Mr Hay tells, "The voice said, 'Gideon, go and preach the gospel!'" But he so felt his ignorance and unworthiness that he pleaded, "Lord, I am a poor ignorant creature. How can I go? Ah, Lord God! behold, I cannot speak, for I am a child." Then it would rush into his mind, "Do you not know the disease?" "Oh yes, Lord, I do." "And do you not know the cure?" "Oh yes, glory be to Thy name! I do." "Go then and tell them these two things, the disease and the cure; never mind the rest; the rest is only talk." "So," he would conclude, "with the knowledge of only these two things I went forth; and here I am, these forty years (or more, as it might be) telling of the disease and the cure." This seems to me to agree almost exactly with what fell from his lips the only time I ever heard him preach, when I was yet a boy. While his mind was divided by alternate urging and reluctance on this subject, he says, "I was afraid Satan would deceive me, and I often went into the churchyard to reflect on the state of the dead. One day I was standing over the grave of a man named Murphy, who had been buried the day before; and I asked myself, 'Am I to lie among the dead?' I felt a recoil from it, and said, 'Ah, what means this?' The scripture came to me, 'This is my beloved Son, in whom I am well pleased;

hear ye Him:' but if ye will not hear Him, I never will be pleased. I then became determined, and said, ' I will make no more excuses, should it even cost my life, should they dash out my brains.' I saw that I must speak to the people in the streets; and I promised God that, as my way opened, I would devote myself wholly to His service."

The parish burying‑ground lay within view of his own residence. While his heart was full of these feelings, the funeral of a neighbour entered it. The wild " Keena " rose from the women and rung in his ears; and no doubt the whole bearing of the crowd showed that the mourning was, as he says, formal and ceremonial. The hour had come. Forth he went, entered the sacred enclosure, and began to address the crowd.

" The rude forefathers of the hamlet " is a familiar word; but it would be hard to find a ruder church‑yard than that of Dunmore. And it is vain to look, at present, for any trace of the particular gravestone, among the many weather‑worn ones wherewith it is crowded, on which or by which the robust man stood, and round which his peasant‑hearers clustered.

We have no record of that first sermon or of how it was received. They all knew him, and what he had been. He had nothing to tell them but the two points, the disease and the cure. These he told as well as he was able; and all we certainly know is, that on that day began a course of labour which has borne much fruit. It would appear that he soon took other similar opportunities of preaching. " I had to go forth sometimes to churchyards when the Roman Catholics were burying their dead, and told those attending, generally in the Irish tongue, the sinful state that they were in,—that no effort of man, nor any 'service' could relieve them; that God only, for the sake of Christ, could or would give His Holy Spirit, whereby alone they could be saved. The priest told them not to heed me, that I had lost my senses; but they frequently replied to him, 'If you would hear him, sir, you would find there is good sense in every word he says.'"

Hitherto any opposition he had met with from his friends had been mild. Their relief at witnessing the moral change wrought in him blunted their feelings of antipathy to his decided godliness; but now it was becoming too bad. By this time we find a curate added to the personalities of Dunmore. He was specially indignant. Mr Ouseley plainly says respecting him that he was "neither sober nor moral." Nevertheless, he had his æsthetics of religion as well as other people, and greatly resented the unseemly proceedings of Gideon. "It is bad enough that he has himself embraced these new opinions, but to propagate them, and make others as bad as himself, is intolerable." Hitherto the curate had been proud of his large-mindedness; he "allowed every man to go to heaven in his own way;" but Gideon's way would never do. He actually taught the people that Christ was to save them, not in their sins, but from their sins, and that the Holy Spirit was not merely a solemn name in the Creed, but a living agent, operating on the hearts of ordinary people.

So one Sunday morning the curate came out with a great sermon against the Methodists, whose doctrines were "rank nonsense," and their motives bad.

" They taught," says Mr Bonsall's representation of Mr Ouseley's words, " that man is fallen, utterly gone from righteousness ; and that while he cannot recover himself from sin, or do any work, or even think a thought, to be approved or accepted of God, there is nevertheless a way of recovery, through the agency of the Holy Ghost, whereby repentance towards God and faith in our Lord Jesus Christ may result. All this, he denounced with severity and anger."

When the preacher closed, Gideon stood up in his pew, and affectionately but firmly urged that the doctrines denounced were exactly those of the Bible, and, indeed, those of the Liturgy, which the clergyman had just read, citing the words as witness. Greatly excited, the curate cried, " Do you know what you are doing, sir ?" " I do, sir," replied Gideon ; "I am striving to persuade you that you should not preach false doctrine, and to guard those that heard you from its effects." Little wonder that the curate replied, " Only that you are John Ouseley's son, I would do as the law empowers me—fine and confine you, sir."

One can imagine the stir made in a place like Dunmore by this event. If it had its bad side, it had its use. " Many," says Mr Ouseley, " heard in a few words truths they never had heard before, and were induced both to hear and to converse on sub-jects which they had shunned. The rector came and called upon Gideon, accompanied by his own father, and both " reprobated his conduct in the severest terms." The rector said, " But for regard for your family" (his wife was Gideon's cousin), " and that I believe you to be crazed or the dupe of fanatics, I would proceed against you in the Bishop's court."

His father told him that he disgraced him, and
insisted that he should give up preaching, or he
would disown him.   He gently replied, that to give
offence was no design of his, but at any risk he
would obey God rather than man.   Even on the
point, which he would have been the last to defend
when more experienced, he then insisted that, however painful to his feelings, his sense of duty to God
and the people would oblige him to correct misre-
presentations either in church or out of it.   Years
afterwards, he learned that his father would have
thought worse of him had he not acted up to his
views of duty.   Still, for the present, the east wind
blew keenly.   Mr Richard Ouseley of Prospect,* who
would seem to have been the most important of the
Ouseleys at this time, strongly joined in the petty
persecution.

One day his father came to his house, and asked,
" Where is Gideon ? "   When Mrs Ouseley told him
that he was away somewhere preaching, " He looked
at me," she said, and replied, ' I pity you, my child;
indeed I do.   That fellow will ruin himself and bring
you to beggary.'   I replied, ' Sir, why are you so
violent against your son ?   When he has spent nights
in sin, and when you have seen him scarce able to
walk home, you administered no reproof, and you
evinced no displeasure; but now that he has broken
off from practices that were sinful, and that must
have brought ruin upon him, and when he is striving
to serve God, you speak against him and oppose him.'
He hung his head, but made no reply."

* Probably Mr Ralph Ouseley, the father of Sir William and Sir
Gore, had then removed to Limerick, where he ended his days.

But if his father rated him, he would not let others speak ill of him, and behind his back would say, " Gideon is right, and we are wrong." Mr Richard Ouseley also, before his death, expressed the same feeling, and showed great sorrow for the course he had taken with regard to Gideon, and his last days were lighted with cheering Christian hope.

Gradually Gideon extended the sphere of his efforts, pushing out to neighbouring places, and even into neighbouring counties, preaching in the graveyards and the streets, wherever he could find hearers. He sweetly used the Irish tongue, which won a way to the ear of the multitude as nothing else could do ; and yet they often opposed, and actively persecuted him; but, as if a supernatural shield was always over him, he escaped any serious hurt. His own house became a home of the disciples. A class of a dozen members was formed in it. Probably when the soldiers of the regiment through whose instrumentality he was himself led to join the Methodist Society removed, the class had been changed from the public-house to his home. Of the dozen members meeting there, about one-half were of his own relations, who had formerly been opposed to his new ways. Mrs Ouseley became a nursing mother to the little flock. When he was away on distant excursions, she was both praying for him, and endeavouring to supply his place by Christian attentions to those who came to his house, and efforts to edify them.

Some five years passed in Dunmore in this kind of labour, irregular only in the fact that it depended entirely upon his own impulse and will. Of those

efforts we have no formal record, but traces of them
still exist, which show that they must have been prodi-
gious.   Families in widely-distant neighbourhoods,
which traced their conversion to his instrumentality in
those days, are still to be found, and some of his sons
in the gospel, who afterwards laboured in the same
fields, rejoiced to trace back their conversion to these
his earliest efforts.   Among such, the name of Rev.
William Cornwall was particularly well known, and
is to be held in remembrance ; for it was he
who, in years long subsequent, became the happy
instrument in the hands of God of the conversion
of Mr Ouseley's aged father; and it was with no
ordinary feelings that the former regarded this
precious fruit given to his spiritual child.   Writing to his brother Ralph, only about a year
before his own death, he thus reminded him of his
father's case : " This did my dear father find, even
in his last illness, that his guilt, oppression, and
terror were removed.   While looking between despon-
dency and feeble hope to Christ, who saith, ' Look
unto me, all the ends of the earth, and be ye saved.
. . . Him that cometh unto me I will in no wise
cast out,' he testified this to our sister Anne, then
attending on him, as she told me."   This same
spiritual son of his, Mr Cornwall, was also the instrument in the conversion of the excellent lady at
Ballinahinch Castle, the wife of the celebrated author
of " Martin's Act against Cruelty to Animals." *

    The " Patrons " of the country, of which we shall
hear more in the sequel, were one of the gathering-

* An interesting notice of this is found in an article in the " Sunday
at Home " on the Martins of Connemara.

places to which he resorted; and he did not forget
either the "Stations" or the wakes. The latter
formed one of the most striking features of the community in the midst of which he lived. However
poor might be the family at the "dead house," and
however ruinous the loss which they had sustained
by the bereavement, they were bound to furnish pipes,
tobacco, and snuff for as many as would come, generally as many as the house would hold, and who
spent the entire night in revelry. If whisky was
not also provided, the people were mean; and if
plentifully supplied, they were excellent. In apple-
season, the guests generally furnished themselves
with that fruit, at the cost of any orchard that might
be within reach. All the fellows in the neighbourhood who were wits, or thought themselves such,
looked on the wake as a stage for the development
of their talent. Whoever could invent the most
boisterous sport was the greatest man. It was a
theatre for the antics of which the grotesque side of
the Irish character is capable, and for training the
young to think that such foolery had a kind of sacred
sanction. The anguish of the death-wail mingled,
at least repeatedly alternated, with indecorous songs
and jokes, and many a wild oath found its place
between. Folly and Vice were formally presented in
the chamber of Death, and installed there as if fit for
any presence. This mixture of the deepest sorrows
of humanity with the grossest levity was enough to
undermine all depth of character, and form a people
governed only by impulse, taking up any feeling for
the moment, and trifling with them all.

Into scenes of this kind Mr Ouseley would make

his way, and kindly greeting the people, would, with
solemnity and pathos, entreat them to prepare to
meet their God.   Before the interment took place,
the scene at a wake was often varied by the presence
of a priest, who said mass, and collected " offerings "
for the soul of the departed.   Carleton sketches a
scene where the altar is a little table, and the first
offering is laid on a plate placed on the altar;
whereupon the priest carries the plate round, and
the name of each contributor is proclaimed with the
amount he has laid down.   He makes the priest
appeal to a Protestant gentleman, who expresses a
doubt whether his guinea did not bear a heretical
mark, but the priest replies that, in that case, the
only thing to be done is to restore it to the true
Church, and then it will be within the pale, assuring
him, moreover, that he will find it before him when
he goes to St Peter.   In certain neighbourhoods, if
not generally, this process of raising money for the
good of the departed was called " canting " (that is,
auctioning) " the soul."

Mr Reilly has related an instance of the appearance of Mr Ouseley in the midst of such a scene.
Two or three other versions of the tale are before
me; and I remember having heard it from the late
Rev. John Holmes, nearly forty years ago, during
the lifetime of Mr Ouseley, and all the forms of it are
substantially identical.   As the priest was reading
mass, and the multitude were on their knees, a
stranger suddenly rode up.   Dismounting, he knelt
in the midst of the congregation with manifest solemnity.   As the priest went on reading in a tongue of
which the people knew not a word, the stranger

caught up passage after passage, selecting, though unknown to his hearers, those portions which conveyed
directly scriptural truth or solemn warnings. He
suddenly turned the words from Latin into Irish,
and repeated aloud after the priest. Then, with deep
feeling, he cried at the end of each passage, " Listen
to that ! " The priest seems to have been overwhelmed
and awed, and the people 'completely melted. When
the mass was ended, and all rose up, Mr Ouseley, with
a face beaming with affection, urged upon the people
the necessity of having their peace made with God,
telling them they must become reconciled to Him,
and that it was possible so to do by real repentance
and true faith in the Lord Jesus Christ.

As he was taking his departure, the crowd cried to
the priest, " Father ——, who is that ? Who is he
at all ? "

" I do not know," said the priest : " he is not a man
at all ; sure, he is an angel. No man could do what
he has done."

Mr Ouseley was forthwith mounted and gone.

Long afterwards he met with a peasant, and accosting him, had a conversation, which we give in the
words of Mr Reilly :—

" My dear man, would you not like to be reconciled
to God, to have His peace in your heart, and stand
clear before the great Judge when He will come in
the clouds of heaven to judge the world ? "

" Oh, glory be to His holy and blessed name, sir,
I have this peace in my heart ; and the Lord be
praised that I ever saw your face."

" You have ! what do you know about this peace ?
when did you see me ? "

" Don't you remember the day, sir, that you were at the 'berrin' (burial), when the priest was saying mass ? "

" I do very well.   What about that day ? "

" Oh, gentleman, you told us then how to get that peace, and I went, blessed be His holy name, to Jesus Christ my Saviour, and got it in my heart, and have had it here ever since."

Another fact connected with this period is related by Mr Reilly, which I do not remember to have seen elsewhere.   A Roman Catholic gentleman, a neighbour of Mr Ouseley's, on calling found him engaged in some mathematical work, and made some remarks in praise of the science.   " Yes," he replied, " there is Euclid " (pointing to the book) ; " if you abide by him, he will bear you out ; but if, in any one instance, you depart from the principles laid down by him, you forfeit all claim to his support, and you will inevitably go astray."

" That is very true," rejoined his neighbour.

" Very well, sir," continued Mr Ouseley, " take up the New Testament, read it ; and if you abide in the truth revealed in it, you will be infallibly right, Christ the Lord, the great author of that book, will stand by you.   If, however, you forsake it, you deny Christ ; and if you are priest, or bishop, or pope, Christ will disown you."

One day when travelling, a strange gentleman rode up to him.   Mr Ouseley very soon introduced his one great theme, how Christ, the blessed Lord, had come down from heaven to give salvation to His creatures, rich or poor.   The gentleman expressed doubts as to the truth of Christianity; and then began one of those typical series of questions, which he used with effect throughout life, commencing with generalities, which his interlocutors readily conceded, and going on, until he was prepared to clinch a nail which they did not know he had been driving.

" Don't you think, sir, that Jesus Christ was at least a good man ? "

" Why, ye-e-s, I do."

" Do you not think He was a good Teacher ? "

" Indeed, I must acknowledge that I think He was."

" Another step, sir. Is it not your opinion that He was really the best Teacher that ever the world saw ? "

The gentleman said with some hesitation, " Well, in candour, I must admit that it was my opinion that He was. But then"——

" But then ! What then, sir ? Can you blame me for learning from the best Teacher that ever the world saw?"

The gentleman seemed more surprised and pleased, says Mr Reilly, than confounded ; and it is hoped that the conversation resulted in convincing a sceptic at least of the truth of Christianity.

Many years later, Mr Ouseley, in describing how one of his spiritual children was awakened and brought to the knowledge of the truth, had to refer to an anecdote he told when preaching. This anecdote belonged to the time of which we are now speaking ; and yet, as long afterwards as 1823, the relation of it to a crowd in the street was made the instrument of a remarkable conversion. He met a poor man on the road, whom he would probably

know at first sight to be a pilgrim.   He found he
was coming from the Reek, as the majestic cone of
Croaghpatrick is called, which stands on the south
of Clew Bay.   The mountain is very holy; indeed,
it ought to be, if it is not—the very one from which
St Patrick gave all the venomous reptiles their final
orders to depart from the Green Isle, and to bury
themselves in the depths of the sea.   A text in the
classics of Connaught, which perhaps represents less
the faith of the writer than his knowledge of the
faith cherished by many around him, says—

> " 'Twas on the top of that high hill
>   Saint Patrick preached his sermon."

When Mr Ouseley met the pilgrim, he asked him
where he had been.

" To the Reek," was the reply,—the distance
being fourscore miles.

" What were you doing there, poor man ? "

" Looking for God, sir."

" On what part of the hill did you expect to find
Him ? "

The poor fellow replied, with tears in his eyes, " I
did not think of that, sir."

Mr Ouseley then put the question, " Where is
God ? " to which the reply naturally was, " Everywhere ; " and now came out the point.

" When the sun is up, where in Ireland is the
daylight ? "

Of course the poor pilgrim replied, " Sure, sir, it
is everywhere."

" So, then, it is about your own cabin as much
as in any place.   Would it not, then, be a strange

thing for you to go fourscore miles, and bruise your poor feet so, looking for the daylight?"

The man paused. "Oh, the Lord help us, sir! and sure I never saw the folly of it before. I will never take another pilgrimage."

This was the kind of training which Mr Ouseley underwent for the duties of the ministry. The theory of the Methodists is that no training for the work of God is like training in it; and that, however valuable study in preparation for the ministry may be, actual service is absolutely indispensable; and when that is voluntarily rendered, in such a way as to give full proof of call and qualification, it offers a certificate with which no other can be admitted into comparison.

During this period, Mr Ouseley never seems to have had a thought of being "called out" by the Methodist Conference, as he was past the ordinary years, and a married man. He none the less burned with an inward fire—a fire in his bones, impelling him to spend all his time in seeking, like his Master, in order to save that which was lost.

He very deeply felt, however, that it was hard for him to subject his wife to all the consequences of such constant devotion to public work as his own heart yearned for, involving almost constant absence from her, and neglect of home interests. Although I have no written authority, I have verbally heard, from more than one, that in some journeys he visited the markets for linen yarn, and purchased for trade. This seems not improbable, as the linen trade, though chiefly carried on in Ulster, is not wholly confined to it. He wished to leave Dunmore,

E

for what reasons we have no clear information. His devoted wife, seeing his perplexity, said to him, " I will go with you, my dear, and you can go from town to town and preach." These words seem to have formed a sort of crisis in his life, as if he had felt them to be a kind of paper of manumission; and to her he always felt unfeignedly grateful for so entering into the spirit of his calling. They prepared to leave Dunmore.

CHAPTER VI.

WE have not light enough to enable us to form even a conjecture as to why he settled in the little town of Ballymote, in the county of Sligo, after removing from Dunmore. This took place in 1797. He took lodgings, however, in the house of Mr Farquhar, and forthwith commenced a course of evangelistic labour such as he had long pursued. He pushed it so far, that, according to the testimony of Mr Jackson Hawksby of that town, given to the Rev. Graham Campbell, he was soon put into the Black Hole of the barracks in Sligo for disturbing the peace by preaching. No trace of this imprisonment is to be found in his own papers, but that proves nothing; for many of his sufferings and dangers, even long after his character had become public, were never put upon record. Mr Bonsall truly says, that often the first his relatives would hear of some peril and escape would be when notices of it occurred in public papers.

I distinctly remember a statement made respecting the town of Ballymote by a highly respectable Presbyterian clergyman. He had come from the north of Ireland to undertake for a while duties in a congregation not very far from the town, at a period, I should think, about twenty years subsequent to the time that Mr Ouseley sojourned there. On the first Sunday morning, his mind was naturally pre-occupied with the Sabbath-keeping ideas of his native country. He looked out of the window, and saw a gentleman in a dogcart, with a shooting-belt across his chest and a fowling-piece beside him, driving down the street accompanied by dogs. Turning in horror to Mrs Lougheed, the wife of the excellent Methodist doctor, at whose house he stayed, he asked—

" Who is that ? "

She looked out and said, " It is the Rev. Mr ——, our rector."

" And where is he going ? "

" To church, to perform the service."

" To church ! "

" Yes. He will put a surplice over his shooting-jacket, and when he is done, he will go on to his sport."

By the time the rector had done duty, and reached the outside of the town, the congregation of the " Chapel " was dispersing. He pulled up, and the parish priest came out and mounted beside him. His name I forget, but I very distinctly remember that of the Presbyterian minister, who lived some considerable distance in the country, and was to join the party. However, when rector and priest reached his door, the Rev. Mr —— was too tipsy to go along with them.

About a twelvemonth after hearing this story, I had an opportunity of asking Mrs Lougheed if she remembered the facts. She very well remembered Dr B—— (the Presbyterian clergyman who told me), and how he was shocked at something on the first Sunday morning he was with them; and as to the details of his statement, they offered no difficulties to her, but she did not profess particularly to remember them. She had stories of her own to tell. It ought to be added, to the credit of the Presbyterian Church, that the one of those three worthies pertaining to it was brought under discipline. He long survived his degradation, making a penny by marrying runaway couples.

One such fact as this illustrates the state of religion and morals then prevalent in Ireland better than could be done by a string of general assertions. If things were in that state twenty years after Mr Ouseley began his toil, what had they been twenty years before. It is no wonder that, in the remote regions of Ireland, scattered Protestant families rapidly merged into the mass of superstition around them, and that in some districts they were lost wholesale; and their descendants now form the bitterest enemies of Protestantism and of England.

Mr Ouseley seems to have had no idea of anything short of constant itinerancy. Not only in every one of the five counties of Connaught, but in several towns of Leinster, and a few of Ulster, he made his appearance on horseback, the people wondering who he was, where he came from, what had sent him, and altogether feeling as if a voice from the unknown had reached them, and brought strange things to their ears. In fair or market, at burial or patron, he took his stand, and cried aloud. He also succeeded in gaining access to the jails, visiting both the debtors and criminals.

The mutterings of the storm which burst in 1798 were already disturbing every part of the country. Lawless bands, called Whiteboys, Rightboys, Defenders, and other such, were being formed everywhere, in preparation for the combined outbreak. The intellect and craft were generally supplied by the priests; and of those whom they deluded, some would every now and then be found in prisons, frequently under sentence of death. Mr Bonsall tells us, that in the town of Roscommon, Mr Ouseley visited a convict sentenced to death. While he preached Christ to him, the man at first heard with sullen and stupid disregard, but after some time, looking up at him with a feeling of astonishment, inquired, " Are you an angel or a man; or who or what are you?" Mr Ouseley prayed with him, and when taking his leave, the man importuned him to visit him again, and also to visit a fellow-convict in the same prison, like himself, sentenced to death, for some crime connected with what was then called the " Threshers." The first of these two men was savingly converted to God. He expressed a strong desire to have Mr Ouseley with him at the time of execution; but this he was not able to comply with, as he was bound by promise to visit others, who were also appointed to death, lying in the jail of Carrick-on-Shannon. He advised the man that, when he came to the place of execution, he should not attempt to speechify, but should keep his mind occupied in prayer, looking unto God. His conduct was according to this advice, except that he counselled his wife and children to attend to their eternal interests; otherwise he spake not, except to God in prayer, and with a grateful heart testifying that it was God who had sent Mr Ouseley to him.

The other man, whom this one had requested Mr Ouseley to visit, feeling sure that as soon as he heard he would embrace the truth, raged like a fiend and refused to hear. Even at the place of execution, he prayed for vengeance upon all who were concerned in his detection and death.

Now, for the first time, Mr Ouseley begins to appear as seen by the eyes of other men. Hitherto we have only had jottings of his own recollections, as taken down by his nephew—very broken, and always saying as little about himself as possible. In 1836, before Mr Ouseley's death, the Rev. Matthew Langtree published an autobiography full of material illustrating the condition of religion in Ireland, and the early work of the Methodist preachers. Speaking of Boyle, a town in Roscommon, which he visited when he was junior preacher on the Sligo Circuit, he says :—

" It was here I first saw my friend and brother Mr Gideon Ouseley, that eminent Irish missionary. He was not then in our itinerant ministry, though exceedingly zealous in his public and private, ordinary and extraordinary labours, calling sinners to repentance, particularly the Irish. The night before he came, I had a most impressive dream respecting a man I had never known, with solemn aspect, and a defect in one of his eyes. He appeared to be present when I was about to preach. Satan endeavoured to exert an uncommon influence to prevent my first prayer. This stranger, I apprehended, came forward and overthrew him, and immediately an

astonishing work of God commenced. When I saw
Mr Ouseley the next day, I was quite surprised;
his face was familiar; he was the man I had seen
in my dream. A remarkable influence attended his
ministry that evening; and I shall scarcely forget
his conversation and pleadings with God the same
night when we retired to our bedchamber."

We find that in the next year, 1798, the memorable year of the last great Rebellion, he took up his
residence in Sligo, and there opened a girls' school.
One says it was a large school; but no one explains
how he kept it together and at the same time pursued his work. Perhaps, during this interval, he
was not so much occupied in itinerant labours as at
other times; yet we have hints of his being here
and there, falling in with parties of rebels by night,
having the shoes taken off his horse's feet to make
pikes' heads, and so on, as if he had nothing else to
do but scour the country preaching everywhere. He
always spoke as if at this time he had known but
very little as to the doctrines of Christianity. His
early impatience to understand everything in the
Bible had not worn out, but the spirit which urged
him to seek that which was lost led him to address
Protestants and Roman Catholics indiscriminately.
He no more thought of passing by the latter than
the former; and when he came to urge them to seek
the Lord, he found that so much of what they believed
had " nothing whatever to do with the Bible," that
it was absolutely necessary, if he would converse with
them intelligently, to study the Missal, the Catechism
of the Council of Trent, the Canons of the same
Council, the Christian Doctrine, and so on. He also

painfully felt that, as a rule, Protestants did not take
the trouble to comprehend the system of the Church
of Rome, or to fit themselves to reach the understanding of the Roman Catholics. Moreover, he had
a very strong impression that, in what Protestants
chose to call "argument with Roman Catholics,"
they generally preferred imperiously denouncing
errors, with "the ascendancy strut," rather than
meekly selecting and acknowledging any common
truth and turning it to account.

The gracious spirit that was preparing him for his
future labour, led him early to adopt an opposite
course. Perhaps the very first time I ever heard
his name, but if not, certainly the very first definite
recollection I have as associated with it, was hearing
a gentleman, who had been educated for the priesthood, but had left the Church of Rome, contrasting
Mr Ouseley with other Protestant preachers, and
saying what an effect he had seen him produce in a
crowd, when, in their own tongue, and with a heart
overflowing with love, he entreated them to turn from
their sins, "for the sake of the Son of the Virgin."

He would often begin by talking about the Virgin
and St Peter. "The Virgin," he would say, "had
the best religion in the world." This was enough to
fix attention and conciliate feeling. Then he would
say how Peter too had the true religion, and what
Peter's religion was. He would go on to tell how
both Mary and Peter had learned it all from the one
perfect Teacher, and how they owed everything that
they had to simply obeying and listening to Him.
He would also show that they taught us to render to
Jesus just the same absolute obedience and implicit

trust. Thus, in the name of Peter and of Mary, he preached the glory of Jesus alone.

Mr Bonsall quotes, as one of his sayings, that in regard to the Roman Catholics as well as others, the order of Christ had been reversed. He said, " Behold, I make you fishers of men." " Now," said Mr Ouseley, "fishermen seek after the fish ; but we find those who are called fishers of men waiting for the fish to seek after them." Mr Bonsall, in noting the fact that his uncle's usual plan was carefully to seize upon common grounds of truth in dealing with Roman Catholics, makes the remark, that with priests or men of education he acted differently, at once impugning their system, and exhibiting its antagonism to the truth revealed in Scripture. This is probably to some extent correct, but it will prove, as we go on, that with them also he was very careful so to allege and to reason out of the Scriptures, that he rather made personal friends of his opponents than otherwise.

During his residence in Sligo the Rebellion came to a crisis. North and South were in a flame. The chronic tidings of broils and murders were now exchanged for news of battles here and there. Wherever the Roman Catholics gained a temporary advantage, horrid butcheries were perpetrated on the Protestants. Yet, in the midst of all this, he would hear that the Methodist preachers were enabled to hold on their course, traversing the most disturbed districts, and, though sometimes seized and doomed to death, in the end escaping, as if an invisible cover turned danger from their heads. Suddenly a French force landed in the neighbouring county of Mayo, at

Killala, and marched through wild mountain passes straight upon Castlebar, where a considerable division of the English army was drawn up to meet them. It broke and disgracefully ran, the shame of the day being redeemed only by the bravery of some Highlanders, and that of a small detachment of the Leicestershire Regiment, commanded by Gideon's younger brother, Ralph, then only a lieutenant.*

* In the " Gentleman's Magazine," volume lxix. page 18, under date of September 1800, we have the following letter : " Mr Urban,—I have seen your genealogical account of the Ouseley family, many of whom, it appears, have served in the army. May I then beg permission to furnish you with a memoir of an officer of that name,

" ' Whose tiger brow,
Though charged with death, smiled mercy on distress.'

"In August 1798, when the French under Humbert invaded Ireland, Lieutenant Ouseley commanded a detachment of the Leicester Fencibles in the action at Castlebar, which his example inspired with such firmness and intrepidity, that while the army right and left—a few Highlanders excepted—shamefully gave way, not a man of his evinced the slightest disposition of timidity. However, after a bloody resistance, a superior force broke his little phalanx, most of whom were instantly killed or made prisoners. Thus situated, he rushed into the midst of the enemy, crying out to the remainder of his party (Prince of Wales's), ' To the bayonet, boys ; to the bayonet ! ' and at the same time laying about him with such rapidity and success, that he cut his way quite through the enemy's ranks. But in getting over a fence he was made prisoner. Then, after a few minutes' respiration, he disengaged himself by a *coup de désespoir*, and came off, though covered over with sweat and blood, with very little injury—*Lupus fuit canibus et cæsim cursimque evasit*—holding in one hand a bayonet, and in the other a reeking scymitar, with which to my knowledge he inflicted many a deadly wound.

"This soldier (to whom I am still unknown), though the enemy was close on his rear, afforded me all the assistance he could. On approaching where I sat bleeding on the ground (whence I could distinctly hear or see most of the transaction), he raised me up; and while he was in the friendly act of helping me over the wall (being unable to render myself the least assistance), the enemy forced him from his kindly office, three of whom however he laid by me wounded mortally.

Sligo was not captured by the rebels. The French marched upon it; but one regiment, the Limerick Militia, boldly advancing to Coloouey, faced them with determination, so that their General, thinking this small body must be the van of a large force, changed his line of march.

In the meantime, Mr Ouseley was traversing this part of the country, and was often stopped by the rebel bands. He fearlessly told them his gospel message, and never failed to point out their own errors. He knew, as well as any man did, when he was in danger, and he had no liking for it; but whenever it was a question of avoiding it or leaving his blessed work undone, he never thought twice; when he found himself in the midst of danger, he believed that the best way out of it was by outspoken candour.

There is a story of Ralph about this time, which I have often heard repeated, and of which a version is before me from the Rev. Graham Campbell. Mr Ouseley's own papers do not make any mention of it; but that must be taken to be of no weight whatever; for, excepting in letters which passed between themselves, I find hardly an allusion to his brother, and of the letters, only those have been preserved which were written when both were old men.

The tale is, that one day at a mess-table, an officer

"Mr Urban, I was in misery, and he helped me   To whom, then, shall I declare the humanity of this son of Mars but to you; or through whom can I convey my high sense of gratitude to him so well as you, who are the eye, the ear, and the tongue, of the world.

"If this youth is of the family above mentioned, *vere in illo virtus emicat majorum.* I have been a loyal volunteer, and am now your humble servant,   W. H. JOHNSTON."

amused himself by turning into ridicule the fellow he had seen preaching in the streets. Lieutenant Ouseley, presenting his card, said, " The person you are ridiculing is my brother. Meet me in the morning." They did meet, and Ralph received the fire of his antagonist twice without drawing his trigger. Then he called upon him to apologise. The seconds told him to do so. When it was done, Ralph said, " It is well you did it, or you would have been as dead as that! " aiming at a dog and putting the bullet through him, which, it is said, he never failed to do with anything he did aim at.

If the man of the world could so risk his life at the call of a conventional law of honour, how much more would Gideon feel that he should not count his life dear to him if he might fulfil the ministry of blessing which his Lord had committed to his charge!

CHAPTER VII.

THE residence of Mr Ouseley in Sligo introduced him to William Hamilton, then Superintendent of the Circuit, a man in the history of Methodism in Ireland who left his memory deeply impressed, as a very distinct mark, on the minds of all that knew him. Incurably droll, yet high-minded and warm of heart, he was constantly making people smile at his fancies, and often shocked those who had any culture by the roughness of his speech. But he never failed to gain and to hold a high place in their esteem, as one who served God and his generation with no wavering mind. It is evident, also, that he acquired that kind of intellectual ascendancy which comes by making men hear things which they can never forget, and making them see things in a light in which they never saw them before.

In Sligo, also, Mr Ouseley would often hear of a name which probably would be known to him before he left Dunmore, but which would certainly be on the lips of every Methodist in and about Sligo, for the man was born there. This was Charles Graham, the first and greatest of his colleagues. A few years previously, in the town of Sligo, Dr Coke, whose soul burned to make missionaries, had asked Graham, then a farmer, and remarkably useful as a local preacher, if he could not preach in Irish. He replied, " No." The Doctor rather reproachfully remarked that " he could speak it." Graham said, " Yes," but asked if every good man who could talk English was capable of preaching in it. The Doctor was silenced, but Graham was set on fire.

He went to work, and soon had a sermon ready in Irish. The success of it was great. He shortly came into fellowship with Bartley Campbell, the Lough Derg Pilgrim, as he was called, one of those picturesque monuments of grace which are raised up in all great revivals. Bartley had actually found peace with God through faith in Christ while going through the most miserable superstitions of a " Station " to Patrick's Purgatory in Lough Derg. These two together coursed the country, and by their labours the Lord lighted a great flame. The Irish Conference sent Charles Graham to the South, and the work which was wrought by his instrumentality there has been told by his grand-nephew, the Rev. Graham Campbell, in the " Apostle of Kerry."

In one place Mr Ouseley would hear that " this is where the wake was held where Charles Graham and other wicked youths were beginning their old pranks when a local preacher, a relation of the deceased, checked them." " Perhaps," said they, resenting the interference of the Methodist, " we shall get to heaven as soon as yourself." " Perhaps you may," was the reply, " but unless you live the life of the righteous, your hope of heaven will be as vain as that of Balaam, who said, ' Let me die the death of the righteous, and let my last end be like his ;' but alas ! how did he die ?" Graham went home offended, but determined to find out all about Balaam, and so he searched his Bible with that view. He discovered that Balaam "loved the wages of unrighteousness," and that he was found among the slain after the battle. This was the beginning of the great change in him.

At another place Mr Ouseley would have many to remind him that this was where the priest sent for Charles Graham, and said, " Mr Graham, I have sent for you, because I pity you, to be spending your time in striving to pervert my people ; and you know that ours is the true Church, and out of the Church of Rome there is no salvation."

" I know no such thing," said Mr Graham ; " for if you can show me one in your parish who is not in the way to hell, I will join your Church at once."

" On the way to hell ! " said the priest.

" Yes," said Graham.

" Do you mean to say that my father is on the way to hell ? How can you make use of such expressions ? "

" I ask you, sir, is sin the way to hell ? "

The priest said, " Yes."

" Well, then," said Graham, "I do not know one in your parish who is not committing sin from day to day."

Before they parted, Graham took his turn at reproof. " I fear, sir, that God never sent you to preach the gospel ; for had He done so, you would profit the people."

Almost everywhere Mr Ouseley would hear of the

labours of Charles Graham ; many a spiritual child
of his telling a tale which would prepare his heart
to rejoice, the day he learned that he was to be
Graham's yoke-fellow.   Even forty years later than
the time when Mr Ouseley was traversing this
ground, no one could go among the Methodist
Societies scattered over it without hearing much
to confirm the words of Graham's own journal :
" Wherever I came, the people had little rest, for I
was either preaching, praying, or praising God continually."

At the meeting of the Irish Conference following
the Rebellion, Dr Coke, who presided, insisted upon
the formation of a general mission directed to the
Irish-speaking population.   Many feared that it
would not succeed, and above all, that pecuniary
means could never be found ; but the Doctor pledged
himself upon the latter point, and the measure was
decided on.   A good deal has been said in praise of
the wisdom of choosing such a time for the commencement of this effort.   The fact, however, is, that
the crisis made its own appeal; and as to human
wisdom in selecting the agents, we need not say anything about it.   James M'Quigg and Charles Graham,
standing above all the Conference as Irish speakers,
were designated beforehand by the finger of Providence.   Before the arrangements were completed, it
was felt to be desirable that a third should be associated with those two, respecting whose qualifications
all were agreed, and the other must be one who was
master of the Irish tongue.   Here William Hamilton
came in, and named Gideon Ouseley.   He never had
offered himself as a candidate, had not passed any

F

examination or district-meeting; and so independent and spontaneous had been his labours, that no one was entitled to say that he would really work in harness. But Hamilton and very many others knew him, and all felt that, in his spirit, and gifts, and fruit, he had a kind of credential rising far above what boards of examination could have given. He was at once designated as a colleague of Mr Graham, without, however, being formally accepted as a regular probationer; and a note was placed on the Minutes indicating that he was only tentatively employed. The tidings of this decision were a great joy to him. As to what relation to the Conference he might hold, or what pecuniary arrangements were involved, he cared nothing. All he saw was an open door set before him to go and preach the glad tidings of his blessed Master far and near. He said, " When I received from Mr John Kerr, Secretary of the Conference, a letter inviting me to go forth as a missionary with good Charles Graham, I was amazed, as I had no thought or expectation of such an occurrence. I accepted the invitation gladly as from the Lord, and thus was received, without the recommendation of any district-meeting or examination as to my doctrinal views; and without hesitation, I unreservedly rendered myself, my life, my all, to the Lord, to labour as He should help me."

Brave old William Hamilton all his lifelong dwelt with delight on the deed of that day. He survived long enough to hear that Gideon Ouseley had closed his earthly course; and then, though nearly fourscore, wrote a letter to the beloved widow of his beloved friend, which is so characteristic, that,

although many passages of it anticipate the future of
our history, we shall give it here at large, rather
than break it into pieces to appear in proper chrono-
logical order :—

"My dear Sister Ouseley,—I heard of Mr
Ouseley's death : I felt it to the quick, and said,
'Who next shall be summoned away ? My merciful
God, is it I? May my last end be like his!' His
work was done, and he had nothing to do but die;
and now he is where all the ship's company meet. My
heart has gone much after him since I heard of his
departure, and I think I will soon be with him.

"Few knew him better or loved him more than I
did. He came to me in Sligo shortly after his conversion, and settled there for a little time as a teacher.
I saw his soul was burning with love to God and
zeal for the conversion of the world. He seemed to
want room to work for God, and on the market-days
would go through the crowd crying to all, 'Turn ye,
turn ye, for why will ye die?' He had but crude
notions of the gospel plan of salvation when he came
to Sligo, having had no fellowship with godly people
in his own neighbourhood. But he was an apt
scholar, and soon learned the way of the Lord more
perfectly; and what he learned he told to others in
love, and pressed them all to come to the Lamb of
God that taketh away the sin of the world. He had
been a wild young man, like Colonel Gardiner, and
like him he could sing—

"'The world beheld the glorious change,
  And did Thy hand confess ;
My tongue broke out in unknown strains,
  And sang surprising grace.

> Great is the work, my neighbours cried,
>   And owned the power divine;
> Great is the work, my heart replied,
>   And be the glory Thine.'

" I believe his conversion was occasioned by reading that good book, Dr Young's 'Night Thoughts,' for God has made it a blessing to many.   While he remained in Sligo, I observed him closely, and saw there was something in him beyond what is common to young converts, and that God intended him for public usefulness ; and at the next Conference which I attended, in Dublin, there was one wanted to join Mr Graham as an Irish missionary.   I saw the opening was of God, and I had the pleasure of recommending my dear Brother Ouseley to fill that department of God's work, which he has done for a long time, without spot or wrinkle, or any such thing, to the glory of God, to his own credit, and to the profit of very many, to my knowledge.

" I believe he was never so delighted with any earthly thing as with my letter from the Conference, telling him that he was appointed to travel the kingdom with that man of God, and preach the gospel to every creature ; and surely he did the work of an evangelist most faithfully to the end.   I did not see him for some years after he went out (except when he touched on my Circuit from time to time), until God sent the missionary spirit on myself, one Sunday as I rode between Castleblaney and Keady. I then got a black cap, and ran out into the market-places, crying aloud, ' Come all of you here, come all of you here ! ' and soon after this I was joined with Mr Ouseley, for Mr Graham was called to his reward, and we were many years together throughout Ireland, and a true yoke-fellow he was.

" His Irish tongue was of great use in every place, and many of the Papists were enlightened and turned to the Lord, some of whom are now preaching the gospel, and others gone to glory. But the devil, seeing his kingdom shaking, often stirred the baser sort to oppose and raise disturbance. One time, preaching in the street in Granard, an old man with a grey head gathered up his handful of the dirt in the street and threw it over the crowd right into Mr Ouseley's face. When he got his mouth cleaned he cried out, 'Now, boys, did I deserve that?' 'No, no!' was the cry from all sides; and shortly after the same fellow came again and attempted the same thing; but the people fell upon him, and you would think they were trying to kick twenty devils out of him.

" At Portumna we were more in danger than in any other place by the priests and their people. They lay in wait in the road in a lonely place, and rose up out of the ditches like a swarm of bees on all sides, and pulling out their sticks, cried, 'Deliver!' I forced my way through them by help of the spurs; but they beat him greatly, and he lost his hat in the fray, and had to travel many miles without it on Christmas Eve.

" We were in Connaught in the time of the Rebellion, and they took the shoes off his horse at night to make pikes, and cut all the hair off my horse's mane and tail, and one ear off his head. But in Ennistimon we had bloodshed and battery, and narrowly escaped with our lives. The soldiers were our friends in all places. He was always in the front of the battle, and often in more danger than I was. The devil and his people seemed to hate him most of all; but many a human devil was seen after us both in almost every place. He feared nothing, so that he might finish the work his Master had given him to do; for he was no eye-servant, and needed no driving, and it was not easy to keep up with him. I never saw his like, and never shall until I see him in glory.

"He was a strong man, and put forth all his might in the Master's work. I believe the Master always said, 'Well done, thou good and faithful servant.' He wrote hardly any while I was with him; but when I was worn-out and sat down, he then took some time to the pen, and wrote a great deal; and I think his little works will circulate everywhere with good effect, and be a blessing to the rising generation in saving them from the errors of Popery. Children yet unborn shall read with delight and profit what he has left behind him for the edification of the sons of the mother-Church; for he seemed to be raised chiefly for their good; and now he rests from his labours, and his works do follow him.

"Farewell, then, man of God! I loved you much, and you loved William Hamilton; and while I think of our fellowship here below, I weep and sing—

> "'Happy soul, thy days are ended,
> All thy suffering days below;
> Go, by angel guards attended,
> To the sight of Jesus go.'

And you will wait my arrival, and hail me on the shore. God bless her who is left behind, and prepare her to be numbered with the saints in glory everlasting!"

CHAPTER VIII.

AT the time of their appointment together as missionaries specially to the Irish-speaking population, Mr Graham was forty-nine years of age, and Ouseley thirty-six—the one a veteran, and the other a well-practised volunteer. Instead of the senior directing his junior to join him at some point in their intended field of labour, Graham came to Sligo to meet his colleague. This was very probably due to the fact, that he thought Sligo would be the best point for his family to reside in, during the frequent terms of absence which he had in prospect, for it was not far from his native place. For a week or two subsequent to the Conference, Ouseley does not appear to have joined Mr Graham, and the journal of the latter states that he had to settle his temporal affairs. It may be possible that he had to go to Dunmore, for, had he been in Sligo, it is all but certain that he would have been found side by side with Mr Graham in preaching in the streets.

The latter had opened his commission even before he reached the town. His last station had been at Longford, and on returning thither from the Conference, he heard that a man was lying in prison, just about to be executed. Hastening to his cell, he found a priest with him, "saying prayers out of a book." He continues, "I knelt down, and said Amen to every good petition, but was silent when he prayed to saints and angels." When the priest had concluded his offices, Graham began to speak to the prisoner, earnestly directing him to the Lamb of God which taketh away the sin of the world. The priest said, "You should not have interfered;" but Graham quietly replied, "My dear sir, do not be displeased; every one should be willing to assist the dying;" and then, in the Irish tongue, he spoke to the prisoner of the Lord who had bought him and would forgive him. The poor man showed such interest and emotion that Graham was soon upon his knees, pouring out in the mother-tongue of the culprit an imploring cry for the salvation of his soul, for his conversion even then, at the eleventh hour. "The man cried aloud for mercy. I again directed him to Calvary, and he calmed down to peace of mind. The priest was confounded, but could not oppose." Mr Graham then expresses his strong hope with regard to the poor man, who " went to the drop with a firm step."

It may naturally occur to many that, in the present day, no priest would tolerate such an intrusion ; but, at the time of which we are speaking, their position made them less imperious. The Rebellion had only just been crushed, and so many of their number had been openly involved in it, whilst so few had entirely escaped suspicion of complicity, that in the presence of men of well-known loyalty they were somewhat timid. This perhaps

accounts for many features in the early history of the
Irish Methodist Missions, which appear marvellous
by modern light.

Fresh from this scene, Graham "took the street"
the next day, and there preached in English and
Irish, amid tears, whilst some smote their breasts,
others went down upon their knees, and some even
kissed the ground.   On his way to Sligo, he con-
versed in Irish with the people whom he met along
the road; and one of these fell upon his knees and
cried aloud to God for mercy to his soul.

With all his apparent fearlessness, it is manifest
that Graham had an inward struggle with himself
before he could muster courage to stand up in the
streets of Sligo.   It was almost his native place, and
was, besides, a considerable town.   But he took his
stand at the corner of two streets, where he could
command "both Church and Mass people."   Soon
he was surrounded by a gazing multitude.   His open,
manly bearing, and soft, musical, but commanding
voice, secured a hearing.   The Irish flowing from
that voice is said to have been strangely sweet, having an effect in the enunciation hardly ever recognised in any other speaker.   In either of the two
tongues spoken by him, his flow of words was overwhelming—that sort of speech which critics would
never call pulpit-eloquence, but which Christians
would always recognise as having evangelistic power.
After a week of village preaching, Graham was once
more in the streets on the following Sunday, but we
do not yet find Ouseley with him.   Some "son of
Belial" led up a pig by the ear, until its shrill voice
competed with his; then a soldier came forward and

began to bark like a dog; when he had been removed,
an oyster-man lifted up his voice and shouted " Shell-
wares ! "   But the evangelist had resources they
knew not of to fall back upon.   Waiting and per-
severing, he overcame all, and finally pealed forth
the truths of eternal solemnity in thunder " that
bore down all before it."

It is only on Saturday evening, August 11, 1799,
that we first catch sight of the two yoke-fellows
together, riding into Riverstown, a little place about
ten miles from Sligo, where the early labours of
Graham had been made a blessing to many, and
where, in subsequent times, the word of God has
often been very fruitful.   Saturday evening as it
was, Graham gathered a congregation and preached,
and afterwards met the Society.   The priest, sus-
pecting that the preachers might aim at his own
flock, took good care to warn them well on the
Sunday morning, and made preparation to give the
intruders a warm reception.   But no sooner were
his people out of mass than a well-mounted man of
middle height and powerful frame, with his right
eye closed and a black cap on, was in the midst of
the people sitting upon his horse, filling their ears
with the sounds, not of the priest's Latin or of
heretic English, but of the sweet orthodox speech of
the cabin fireside.   Before the priest and his friends
had succeeded in carrying out their plan of attack,
Mr Graham came up with a number of friends to
strengthen and protect Ouseley.   The attention of
the people had been so instantly and completely
gained, that all the priest attempted to do was to
draw them away; but for an hour and a half they

listened to the alternate addresses of the two evangelists, sometimes exclaiming, "It is the truth." Of course, the senior missionary, besides watching the people, was taking note of his junior colleague, and his record is, "Mr Ouseley is, I think, one of the best Irish preachers I ever heard."

Gideon Ouseley had now all that his heart longed for, so far as sphere and opportunities are concerned, which, of course, made it long only the more after the fruit to which they were but the means. Free from every call but that of the inward Voice, which said, "Preach all the words of this Life;" with a leader who fulfilled his ideal of an evangelist, and with the whole country before them to go where and how the finger of Providence might appear to point; with next to no money, and plenty of air; every fibre of his powerful frame seemed instinct with love and joy. There were sick souls in the land, and he had a commission to proclaim the great cure. There was plenty of poverty, and he knew where all the people might find unsearchable riches; and surveying the desolation before him and the resources above him, he moved forward with the double inspiration of a loud call and unlimited support.

The united labours commenced at Riverstown were continued for six years, during which the two brethren rode and preached, and often slept together, as if one spirit animated both their bodies. They were too busy to write in detail. The descriptions contained in their letters are general ones. For particulars of the earliest months of their course, we often draw upon Mr Campbell's Life of Graham. Many men have held a career watched with in-

terest by the great world, whose reputations are
already dead, and whose works never had life in them,
while the names of Graham and Ouseley are dear to
numbers of the happiest families in every country
whither the people of Ireland have been scattered,
and the memory of their work, if not now so glowing
as among their contemporaries, is becoming more
comprehensive and elevated every year.

They soon began to be heard of in England through
Dr Coke, who published extracts of their letters
addressed to himself; but this was slow compared
with the speed wherewith their fame travelled in
Ireland. Their appearance in fairs, markets, and
patrons; their preaching on horseback; their wonderful Irish; their courage, love, and mysterious power
over conscience; and especially the unheard-of
changes in heart and life wrought through their
preaching, became the theme of common conversation,
so that, swiftly as they travelled, they almost everywhere found some prepared by report to welcome,
and some to oppose them.

Shortly after leaving Riverstown, they met
groups of peasants, coming away from a holy well,
where they had been attending the " Patron; " that
is, the anniversary feast of the patron saint. Who
the saint was, and where the well stands, we are not
informed. In a climate so humid as that of the
west and south of Ireland, it hardly seems natural
that wells should be objects of devotion, and the
large number of holy wells which exist there seems
a confirmation of the traditions which trace the
early religion of those shores to an Oriental origin.
Wells were worth much in Phœnicia or Carthage; and

if the priests who developed into Druids came thence, probably they would carry well-worship with them as part of their ceremonial. With superstitions of that sort the friars have always made their peace, and preferred turning them to gain rather than turning the people from them.

As the shoeless creatures, who had been praying and making offerings, perhaps for the forgiveness of sins, perhaps for the recovery of a sick cow, straggled in little groups along the road, they would expect to exchange a courteous, " God save your honour! " with the gentlemen on horseback; but were probably surprised when the horses were reined up, and " broadcloth " began to talk to " frieze " in the kindliest tones and in the best Irish. They did not suspect heresy in that tongue; indeed, probably, they believed that Satan himself could never speak it. Therefore their ears were open. They were told of One who loved the like of them so much that He came from heaven to seek them, and that He would forgive all their iniquities and heal all their diseases.

They fell on their knees, smote their breasts, and with uplifted hands and streaming eyes called upon God. One cried out, " What must I do ? " " They would almost adore us," says Graham; " we had hard work to prevent them from kissing our feet." The missionaries prayed in the midst of them, and then proceeded towards the well. A hoary-headed man ran before them, and called upon the people to come and listen to the gospel. They gathered around, Graham preached, and all the while he was doing so a woman knelt down behind him, as did also the old man, and both cried piteously. The next Lord's day found them in the county of Leitrim, at Manorhamilton. On the Saturday evening, the priest went to the magistrate, who was also rector, representing that these men were come to the town to turn him out of his chapel. "If that be so," said the sagacious justice, "they will put me out of my church; and so I will order them to be taken up." Graham, however, sent two friends to inform his worship that they were not quite so bad. He says, "I preached in the morning, and met the class, which was like the opening of heaven,"—something better than turning men out of church or chapel. In the streets they were gladly listened to, and Graham called it, "a good day, from morning to night." Three days after we find them in a churchyard preaching to an attentive crowd. In the same evening Graham writes, "Mr Ouseley was assailed by a poor conceited sinner, but he was soon foiled. He then tried to prevent the people from hearing, but in vain. The poor creatures flocked to hear us, and entreated us to return. They were nearly all Romanists." A couple of days later, we find them assailed in some country place by what Graham calls a blaspheming Rabshakeh, who would fain have laid hands on them, and "told Mr Ouseley that, if he had a book, he would swear that there was neither God nor devil, heaven nor hell." After another few days, we find them back again in Sligo, where Ouseley is preaching to the fishwomen in the streets; and his comrade says, "I came forward to assist him, and was now delivered from that cursed shame which has long pursued me." Quaintly enough he remarks, "Persecution never intimidates me, but *fear* sometimes does." On the Sunday they took their stand by the old market-house, and they believed that many were then truly touched by the power of the Spirit. One gentleman, who lived opposite, came and begged them to make his house their home. On a succeeding Sunday, Graham says Ouseley stood at the market-place, and he accompanied him. The priests had resolved to make an end of the "black caps." While Graham spoke the immense crowd stood still, but when Ouseley began it was the signal for a general shout. They tied kettles to the tails of dogs, and drove them among the crowd. For the moment Ouseley was silenced, but rising above the din, the clear notes of Graham rang out in articulate thunder, "It is all in vain for the sons of Belial to endeavour by means like this to uphold the devil's kingdom, for the Lord Jesus has resolved on its ruin, and down it must come." The eyes and ears of the people were once more with the missionaries, who, in spite of a few disturbers, were allowed to proceed, and even to conclude the service by praying with the people in peace, and dismissing them with the benediction. All this time meetings in the chapels and in private houses showed that in the services out of doors many, both Protestants and Roman Catholics, had received impressions too deep to be concealed. Members were daily added to the societies.

One day, in a churchyard, as the Roman Catholics, according to the custom of the country, were lying or kneeling on the graves of deceased relatives, wailing with the conventional yet bitter cry, Ouseley knelt down among them, and began to pour forth in Irish a fervent prayer for eternal life; not as if reclaiming against an inexorable fate, but as appealing to a near but very loving Father. It is said that the people were affected as if something wonderful was about to come to pass. Both of the preachers addressed them in English and in Irish, and it was believed that the fruit of that day's message was very great.

At Boyle, in the county of Roscommon, the military officers, who generally were friends of the missionaries, turned violently against them. In those days, long before the establishment of the constabulary, the military were the only guardians of order in public movements such as theirs. As a rule, they discouraged riot and insisted on liberty. In the present case, however, encouraged by the officers, the mob attacked the missionaries with rotten eggs and other odious missiles. A "Scapularian," proud of his "Order," opened a controversy, but he soon called Graham the old devil, and Ouseley the young devil. Here also the clergymen of the Established Church joined in the general opposition.

Like John Wesley himself, Ouseley found, as his course went on, that such opposition from clergymen became less frequent; and whenever he met with one, as eventually he very often did, willing to countenance evangelistic work in any form, he greatly rejoiced. His own words as to his feelings in his earliest years of labour are: "The grace of God saved me from a sectarian spirit. I loved other Churches, not heeding peculiarities with which I could not agree, and availed myself of every opportunity of conversing with

persons belonging to them, on topics tending to our
mutual profit; but I loved Methodists with a special
love, as through their instrumentality I was brought
to know Christ as my Saviour."

During the autumn of 1799, we find Graham saying, in a letter to his son, "We do more in spreading
truth in one fair or market day than we do in weeks
or months in private places. In some markets, the
cries and tears and groans of the people are enough
to rend the heavens. The Lord is with us, indeed."
From a letter of his to Dr Coke, we find that they
soon passed over the whole breadth of the kingdom,
and touched the east coast. He tells how at Bal-
briggan a Roman Catholic woman came to them while
they were at breakfast, and they at once began
preaching to her the good tidings of the kingdom of
God. "The power of God fell on her and on us;
and we immediately left our breakfast and went to
prayer." At Drogheda, after preaching in the street,
they were summoned before the magistrate, said by
Mr Bonsall to have been Mr Ralph Smyth, the
Mayor. He gave them leave to preach in the Tholsel,
or Town Hall. He, the Sheriff, and some of the
clergymen attended. The crowd was immense, and
the Roman Catholics seemed deeply affected. The
Mayor said that they might preach wherever they
pleased. Mr Sillery, who had been mayor the year preceding, became their friend, and a son of his joined the
Methodist Society. The latter gentleman afterwards
entered the Church of England, and became Chaplain
to St Stephen's Hospital in Dublin. He was a
faithful minister of Christ throughout life, always
remained affectionately attached to Mr Ouseley, and

G

often attended Methodist chapels. In fact, he continued to meet in class a good while after his ordination.

Graham traces their way to Ardee, then to the
Poles, when he says, "Heaven, indeed, was opened
unto us."   Next they appear in Kingscourt, and
preach in the market-house to a vast number of
Catholics, who, he says, "were wonderfully affected."
He was so encouraged by the effect of distributing
"pamphlets," that he wished they had thousands to
give away.   Entering Bailieborough, they found it
was market-day, and the rain was falling.   Hoisting
their umbrellas, they rode straight into the midst of
the throng, and from the saddle began at once to
tell of the good tidings of great joy.   He says that
the Methodists of the town wished them out of the
street, but that they had their eyes opened when they
saw that the Word of the Lord, like thunder, awakened
the crowd.   A poor woman, a Roman Catholic, professed to have found mercy.   That night, at the
house where they lodged, two Catholics, servant man
and maid, were awakened.   The next day, they rode
fifteen miles in constant rain to the fair at Cavan ;
" but we stormed the little towns as we rode along,"
sounding a brief but loud call to repentance.   Reaching Cavan "as wet as we could be," they at once
went into the midst of the fair.   The rain poured
down, but "the fear and terror of the Lord fell on
the crowd immediately, and the poor creatures stood
with their heads uncovered, bathed in tears."   The
people followed them to Mr Smith's house, and
entreated that they would preach at night in the
court-house, which they did.   On the same day

they visited the prisoners in the gaol, making, as they say, a day's labour indeed. Best of all, Graham, who used vivid language, but was anything but a boaster, says, " I can give you but a faint idea of the power that attended the Word." At Killeshandra, some Methodists who met them were not a little surprised to see them preach on horseback.

Of the letters sent in the joint names of the two missionaries, the first that we have reason to suppose was written by Mr Ouseley is the following, which Mr Bonsall says is his. It bore date—

" SLIGO, *January* 6, 1800.

" REV. AND DEAR SIR,—I know you will be glad to hear from us. We spent the last month in Ballyshannon, Enniskillen, and their vicinities. We have preached two market-days and one Sabbath in the street of Ballyshannon, to vast congregations, who heard with the greatest attention. We met with no opposition; the rich and learned seemed astonished, standing at a distance, and hearing us denounce the judgments of heaven against the crimes of a guilty nation. The Roman Catholics attended us from place to place; nor could any person prevent them from coming out to hear us. The fame of Irish preaching has spread through all the country, as we speak some Irish every night. Numbers of convictions and conversions took place. I was astonished to find such a work without opposition or persecution. We have visited and preached in Ballintra (County Donegal); but the place we preached in was too small to hold the people. Next morning we prayed from house to house, and the Lord was so powerfully present, that the people were deeply affected, and cried aloud for mercy. From this we proceeded to Pettigo (County Fermanagh), and preached in the street, in what they call their great market. This was a blessed day to many; some could hardly restrain themselves from crying out in the open market. The Catholics were greatly struck, and followed us that night and next morning to Mr Scott's. We then came on to Ballinamallard and Enniskillen. The power of the Lord attended us, both in public and in private, so that our meetings continued some nights five and six hours, until we were worn out. I can give you but an imperfect account of this work. There were two Catholic girls converted in Sidare, at Mr Armstrong's; and last Monday night several souls were brought to God in one house. As soon as we recover a little, we shall go to the north again. ' O Lord our God, strengthen Thy poor servants for this great work ! ' "

In the spring of 1800 they became persuaded that Clones would be a better centre than Sligo, and accordingly prepared to remove. Before their departure Mr Ouseley wished to make a set attack upon the " dire apostasy." Graham says, " We determined to make another trial in the street, although the priests commanded great power in preventing the Catholics from hearing us. Yet, on this occasion, contrary to our expectations, we were attended by a crowd of Catholics, who stood quietly while Brother Ouseley proved to them that they were deceived, and had not the doctrines preached by St Paul in his

Epistle to the Romans, and that their priests were blind guides, and false prophets, and knaves, and took their money, but did them no good.* I exhorted after him, not minding sects or parties, but begged them at once to turn away their attention from creeds, and from church and chapel walls, and to look to Him, who could alone grant them what they all wanted, *real happiness*, which could only be found by faith in Christ. They heard with attention, and the power of the Lord attended the Word. The hearts of many were melted."

On the 1st of May, Graham started for their new destination, leaving Ouseley behind him for a little while. Though as fully occupied as usual during the interval in preaching and travelling, Graham says that he felt " great loneliness." Ouseley, on his part, was found on the Sunday, which occurred during their separation, in the streets of Sligo, preaching with Mr Banks, the Superintendent of the Circuit, beside him. He also soon proceeded northwards. They had not laboured in vain, for many holy lives and happy deaths in and around Sligo, from that day down to the present time, have borne a constant and accumulating testimony to the blessing with which God had crowned their labours.

It is from the journal of Mr Graham we learn that Ouseley, on his way to Clones, preached at Lisbellaw and Maguire's Bridge. No sooner had he arrived than they set off together to Smithborough. Preaching in the evening at Mr Mitchell's, they say there were many Seceders, who, as Graham phrases it,

---

* It is not to be concluded that Ouseley used these words, but that what he proved amounted to that.

had been "preached to death by long harangues."
Thence to Monaghan, the people flocking around them.
Some seemed stunned, some were bathed in tears;
but a clergyman tried to turn the scene into sport.
The people, however, soon changed their counten-
ances.   When the missionaries left, Roman Catholics
ran after them, and cried, "When will you come
again?"   Graham adds, "All the priests' cursings
and threatenings are not sufficient to prevent their
attendance."   The next day they were at Smithborough, preaching to a mixed multitude of all
denominations.   It would seem to have been in the
open air, for we are told "the rocks began to rend,"
and when they went into the house, they could not
be heard on account of the loud and bitter wail of
distress.   Mr Graham quaintly remarks, "I doubt not
that we left enough for priests and ministers to do
for a while."   One of the latter had challenged a
Methodist preacher to dispute on the subject of the
Decrees, but Graham says, "They have other subjects to dispute about now; a great number have
been truly converted to God."   And so, day by day,
continually in one place or another — Newbliss,
Ballybay, Clones, Cootehill—every considerable place
in that region, and many of which the names are
unknown to books.   At Cootehill the Presbyterian
church was granted to them to preach in—an early
sign of liberal feeling which since then has blessedly
increased.   About this time we find mention made
of a woman who was "struck" in the street.   It is
added also that her husband was "struck," and some
others.   These would appear to be cases in which
spiritual sorrow of mind was attended by physical

prostration, such as, in the extensive Revival in Ulster, in 1859, took place on a scale that excited much public attention. As the first twelve months of their labours approached its term, they began to look forward to Conference. They had both sown in tears and reaped in joy, and the final efforts of the year were still attended with blessing. At Belturbet we find " numbers of ladies and gentlemen " mentioned as of their audience, who were astonished to hear the people cry for mercy. It is not said that any of the great ones believed, but that they thought the missionaries would be a great blessing to the "country." Here also a love-feast was held, at which many strangers remained, and not a few conversions took place. We find our evangelists next at Ballyhaise, and on the 12th of July again at Clones preaching to a vast number of Orangemen. We do not make out where it was that they laboured on the next Sunday, but they were about to preach in the open air, and a multitude had flocked beforehand into the church. A week previously the clergyman had expressed a wish that the missionaries would come, for his preaching seemed to do the people no good, and he thought he had better give it up; but now, in his crowded church, a young man either fainted or was " struck." " Take him away," cried the minister, " I will have no irregularity in my church ; and if these strangers are my parishioners, I wonder that I never saw them here before. But if they are following these cavalry preachers, I wish they had remained at home in their own churches. Let no one say that I invited them."

The " cavalry preachers " were soon on the spot,

and delivered their message out of doors to some four thousand people.*

Not long afterwards, in some part of this district, they were invited by a clergyman to preach in his church. In the middle of July they turned their faces to Dublin, to meet the brethren in Conference, it being the first time for Ouseley. Glad were they to tell all the blessed things the Lord had wrought under their eyes, as well as to hear of His mercies to others of their fellow-labourers. Of course they preached everywhere on their road. At Cavan we find them assisted by the Rev. George Brown. At Oldcastle, Mr Henry, who became their host, declared " it gave him the greatest happiness to see so many poor ignorant Roman Catholics calling on God for mercy, and so broken down." It is said that some of them would remain on their knees for hours, without apparent weariness. From Oldcastle the missionaries made for Dublin, and there were refreshed in spirit, and caused all their brethren to rejoice by telling how mightily the Word of the Lord grew and prevailed. That year, the Irish Conference reported an increase of more than three thousand members, and the abounding testimony of the brethren whose Circuits had been visited by our two missionaries, showed that no small portion of this good fruit was due, directly or indirectly, to their blessed toil. But the numbers added to the Methodist Societies were only the proof, not the sum, of the total good done; for very many to whom God had made them a blessing never became Methodists,

---

* I give the numbers as I find them, not forgetting how greatly over-estimated they generally are in such cases.

but spread divine life in other branches of the Church. This remark does not apply only to the case of our two missionaries, but also to that of their fellow-labourers generally. One of the tokens in which they have always been accustomed to see the good hand of their Master with them, has been that their success did not mean the barrenness or decay of other branches of the Church. On the contrary, they found, as an almost invariable rule, that wherever the message delivered by them was blessed to the souls of many, other denominations were quickened and became more useful. To Methodists it would not be a sign that they were a branch on the stem, if, when themselves flourishing, there was not a manifest rising of the sap and fatness of the root into the neighbouring branches. Rather they would take this as a mark of being a " sect," a cutting separated from the tree and left to grow alone. When they hear themselves called a " sect," schism, heresy, or the like, they may not enjoy it; but it does not hurt them. They will not be called to give account for the words of other men, but if they began to give such names to those who hold the one Lord, the one faith, the one baptism, because they "follow not with us," it would then be their turn to face the accountability.

CHAPTER IX.

WHEN Graham and Ouseley again set their faces toward Clones, their field of labour had been defined by the Conference as the province of Ulster, with the counties of Louth and Meath. So greatly had the results of the General Mission of the year preceding, as carried out by themselves and Mr M'Quigg, encouraged the Conference, that six men were now set apart for this particular kind of evangelistic labour. The south and east, roughly speaking, were assigned to Messrs Kane and Webb, and the central counties to Messrs M'Quigg and Bell.

On the 1st of August we find Graham and Ouseley in the Tholsel at Drogheda, calling an attentive throng to repentance. Next day they were at Ardee, Graham being ill, and Ouseley at work in the street. At Kingscourt, among many Roman Catholics, one intelligent young man was smitten with such deep conviction of sin that he cried aloud, and continued so to do. Among other things he said, " I am full of fire." They ceased not to plead in prayer for him till his sorrow was turned to peace, " and oh, his expression of gratitude for ever having heard those servants of the Lord!" At Shercock they had the Protestant clergyman to hear them. A Roman Catholic shopkeeper said that the man who would pin his faith to the sleeve of any individual, would deserve to be lost; and his wife told them that they had heard of them, and had been afraid that they would not come. From place to place they pursued their course, almost everywhere some signs of awakening and conversion following.

At Kilmore, the scene of the labours of the blessed Bishop Bedell, Graham has the following entry: " The Lord be praised, this country is all on fire. Travelling preachers, local preachers, leaders and hearers, are flaming with zeal for the glory of God."

Fields that once had been sown with the good seed of the kingdom, are often those where, after a lapse of years, the blades shoot up vigorously when a new spring sets in. This has been proved in different parts of France, when, on the spots where truth had flourished in the days of the Reformation, the efforts of modern evangelisation have proved very fruitful. In both England and Scotland, also, it has sometimes been found that where one great Revival had occurred, subsequent ones took place. The work of Bishop Bedell was of the kind that never dies. The friend of Diodati, who enriched the Italian language with a good version of the Word of God, though for centuries Rome prevented it from being any boon to the Italian people ; and of Paolo Sarpi, the historian of the Council of Triest, Bedell knew the gospel of Christ in its original fountains, and the Church of Rome, in full bloom south of the Alps; and he rightly judged that the greatest gift that he could

bestow on the people of Ireland was the Book of God
in their own tongue.   His was a memory from which
Ouseley gratefully drew inspiration.   A labourer in
a humbler sphere, and of a rougher mould, he was
nevertheless continuing the effort to give the gospel
to Ireland in the language the people could understand.

It was Ouseley's brother-missionary, James M'Quigg,
who was the first editor of the Irish Bible for the
British and Foreign Bible Society.   He is said to
have been an admirable Irish scholar, and Mr Reilly calls him " an able and acute preacher."   He
carried the Bible through two editions ; and, at least
in the latter instance, collated it with Bedell's original manuscript.   His career in the work of the
General Mission was short ; and many years after
retiring from it, he died, while preparing to carry a
third edition of the Irish Bible through the press.

The efforts of the missionaries in the town of
Clones, upon their return, were not suffered without
opposition.   Graham's journal contains the following account :—

" On our return from the Dublin Conference in
the month of August, we found the *rulers* of Clones
took counsel together that we should no more preach
in the street; but we resolved to go on as usual.
Some of our friends thought it right that we should
speak to the magistrate and explain our position.
We did so, but all in vain.   He resolved to carry
out his threats."   After a lengthened conflict in the
street the scene thus ended : " We then went to Mr
Ouseley's door, the people following us.   Mr Ouseley
ascended a block, and began to preach.   The rector

cried out, 'Call out the army.' The captain appeared, the drums beat to arms, and the men were
drawn up. Immediately some of the yeomen ran
for their firearms. The magistrate, seeing that this
might lead to blood, ordered the soldiers back, and
ran up to Mr Ouseley and pulled him down from the
block, when I started up to finish my sermon.
Then he thought to pull me down, but he found to
his confusion that I was a little too *heavy* and
stiff, and not so easily moved. I finished, and pronounced the benediction, and dismissed the congregation."

The following evidently refers to a subsequent
occasion, on which Ouseley was alone. Mr Bonsall
gives the narrative as he had it from himself. In
the year 1800, the Rector of Clones, who was also
Dean of Clonmacnoise, and the curate, who was a
magistrate, united in prohibiting Mr Ouseley from
preaching in the street when he was about to do so.
While he was reading a portion of Scripture, both
the clergymen came up and ordered him to desist.
He gently remonstrated with them, but they threatened to arrest him if he did not immediately comply.
He replied that, as he broke no law, human or
divine, and caused neither disturbance nor obstruc-
tion, he must beg them not to interrupt him. They
withdrew, but soon returned with a guard of soldiers,
who took him to the guard-house. The crowd,
swelled in numbers, followed and stood before the
place. "Being more favoured by the soldiers than
the divines," he went to one of the windows and
continued his discourse to the people, but the rector
insisted that he should be removed to the back of

the house. He was detained till evening, and then released without any application on his part. Mr Campbell alludes, but in general and reserved terms, to the traditions of the neighbourhood as to the subsequent lot of the two persecuting clergymen.

Graham tells of a case about this time, somewhere in the Ballinamallard Circuit, when Mr Armstrong, the preacher of the Circuit, was in company with Ouseley and himself. They met a wedding-party near to a chapel, in which the priest was waiting for it. They began affectionately to speak to the young couple, urging them to seek true union with the Lord Jesus Christ. Then Ouseley alighted from his horse and knelt on the ground to pray with the bride and bridegroom. Of course the other two joined him. So the three preachers, as Mr Campbell describes it, holding the reins in their hands, with the wedding-party kneeling on the road around them, prayed earnestly, while tears flowed, and the impatient priest peeped from behind the half-opened chapel door.

Mr Armstrong, just mentioned, wrote about this time to Dr Coke, who published the letter in the " Methodist Magazine " for 1801 (p. 542), giving some account of the work of God, as he had himself witnessed it in the course of this year. He said that, as the field was large, the time short, and he kept no journal, his account could not be a very full one. He had belonged to the Methodists for about thirty-one years, but had never seen a year like this one, for a deep-spreading work. When preaching, he had often been forced to stop, not being able to make his voice heard by reason of cries coming from the people.

" We often wrestled till the break of day." He takes care to say that his colleagues were more laborious and successful than himself, and complains that at some of the love-feasts his enjoyment was spoiled because the penitents would not quietly listen while others related what God had done for them, but would break out and cry aloud. During one of these meetings, Graham and Ouseley made their appearance. All order, he says, was laid aside. " The spirit of deep conviction seized on the people; it was like the Day of Pentecost." He proceeds to describe their success in Cavan, Pettigo, Kesh, Lowtherstown, Trillick, and Dromore, and he concludes by urging Dr Coke to get the missionaries to come oftener to his Circuit.

It was about this time that, on one of their visits to Lisbellaw, they were first beheld by one who still survives, cherishing a thankful memory of them, and hoping soon to join them in a better country. The venerable John Nelson was then a boy at school, and the master gave his pupils a holiday to go and hear the " cavalry preachers." They were much talked about, as well as stared at. The question was, " Who, or what could they be?" A number of people gathered around the schoolmaster to ask his opinion. It was delivered with such authority that at least John Nelson thought it must be right. " They are two discarded priests, who have taken to this way for a living."

This reminds me of what I heard the late Mr Hearne, of Ballina, tell of one of their most respected contemporaries, in the Irish Conference, the Rev. Charles Mayne. An old lady in a country town, being invited to go and hear him preach, was told that he was the brother of Judge Mayne. " Dear me," she exclaimed, " is he now ? a brother of Judge Mayne ! And what could have brought him to that ? I suppose it must have been the drink."

At Charlemont some of the officers resolved to have fun out of the " Black Caps," but most of them soon felt ashamed. One, however, said, " I charge you not to preach in the street any more. Your doctrine is very good, but you make such a —— noise that the town is annoyed." Ouseley replied, " We do make a noise, but ours is a hallowed noise." At Loughall two men in authority declared that, if they came there, they would send them to —— ; but neither the parson nor Colonel C—— could stand the power with which they spoke. At Armagh they say that all came to hear, except the rich. At Portadown they had a numerous and attentive audience. A Roman Catholic woman, at Bluestones, declared that she had been in company with twelve priests, but had never heard this way of salvation before. At Keady a man cried, " The other clergy may throw their caps at them." One day in December of this year, Graham writes from Enniskillen to his son, exulting in what he had witnessed that day. He says that Mr Stewart, the Circuit preacher, mounted his horse, took his stand with them, and did valiantly. He had never seen the prejudices of Enniskillen conquered before, but he thought this was one of the best days he ever had witnessed. " The numbers converted in the last few weeks had been astonishing ; many of the Roman Catholics since we left Clones."

The secret of this good man's public power may in part be learned by an entry in his journal made about this time at the house of Mr M'Donald near Enniskillen. "All glory to God! He met me here in a manner that I can hardly describe. So much of His love and power did He let down into my soul, that nature could hardly sustain itself. I for some moments thought I should have fainted; nor was I sure but that the Lord was about to call me from the body. O Lord! give me grace and wisdom to guard this sacred treasure." At Lowtherstown some of the officers threatened to duck the missionaries, or bayonet them, if they did not desist; but they were neither ducked nor bayoneted. Ouseley about this time met with a serious loss, for his horse died. There was, however, a Mr Little of Redhill, who had been converted through the instrumentality of the missionaries, and whose house had in consequence become the home of the Methodist preachers; and he made up the loss by making Ouseley a present of a good horse.

Once, when they were preaching in Cavan, it is stated that the Roman Catholics showed great concern, even alarm, when told that "neither salt, nor water, nor oil, nor beads, would ever save them." One of these men cried out, "It cost me half-a-guinea for wine and spirits at the last confession." It is not to be supposed that the wine and spirits were the confessor's fee—that would be paid by all the penitents alike; but the wine and spirits mark a superior style of privilege. Probably this person had been the host of the priests, who were in the habit of announcing from the altar that, on such and such

H

days, they would hold " Stations " at the house of so-and-so,—those selected generally being the most comfortable ones in their respective neighbourhoods. To these the people from around came, and were confessed and absolved by the priests. After this was over, the evening was given up to hospitality. The host on such an occasion was bound to entertain to the very best of his power. Carleton minutely describes one such " Station," and any one who has had the honour of an invitation to "dine with the clergy," which occasionally was extended to neighbouring Protestants, and sometimes was embraced with avidity, can speak to the truthfulness of the substantial points of his sketch.

It is about this time that Mr Campbell fixes the date of the conversion of Terry M'Gowan, the cock-fighter, one which, in the phrase of the people, became " the talk of the country-side." Terry lived near Maguire's Bridge, and one market-day, making for the cockpit, he entered the town with a game-cock under his swallow-tail coat. On turning a corner, he found two men before him on horseback with black caps. They were making the street resound with the accents of his mother-tongue. Terry stood and listened, eyes and all. They talked of the great and terrible day, when sin shall be all uncovered, and the righteous shall shine like the sun at the Lord's right hand. Then they called loudly on every sinner there to lose no time, but surrender at once to the Lord Jesus Christ before it was too late. Terry knew not what a finger had touched him. The cockpit had gone clean out of his mind, and he thought that the judgment-day was fast coming. He wanted to lift up both hands and call upon God, and the one which had been keeping guard, under his coat-tail, forgot its charge. The two hands went up together to present the publican's prayer, and the game-cock was gone. "Terry prayed and wept, and cried aloud again and again," entreating for that mercy which he heard God would grant, and for the sake of that Jesus who, he knew, died for men. There, upon the street, He, whose mercy endureth for ever, heard the cry of poor Terry, and blessed his soul. A peace and gladness, such as before that moment he never knew, were shed abroad in his heart, and his spirit began to rejoice in God his Saviour. Home he went bounding, to tell wife and children the strange way in which he had been made a winner that day. They heard, but did not understand. He made them all go down upon their knees to give thanks to God for the deliverance He had granted to him. His wife told one of the children to go to the house of a neighbour, and beg them to hasten away for the priest, because Terry had come home from the market out of his mind. In the poor woman's idea, the duty of the priest in this case would be to charm away the madness; or, if he owned that he could not do that, to advise what must be done with the madman. When the priest arrived, he inquired what was the matter.

"Never better in my life," said Terry.

"Nonsense," replied his reverence; but he soon saw further into the case than the poor wife had done. "Did you hear the Blackcaps?"

"I did, thank God."

"So I thought. Those fellows would turn the

world mad. Well, now, Terry, just mind your own business, and go to your duty next Sunday."

"I will, if your reverence will do one thing for me."

"What is that, Terry?"

"It is to come with me to Maguire's Bridge, to get the Lord to *undo* what He did for me there this day."

"What did He do for you?"

"He said to me there, 'Terry M'Gowan, your sins, which were many, are all forgiven you.'"

This was more than the priest could stand. It was as if his business had been taken out of his hands, and claimed for a higher tribunal.

"I give you up as a lost case," he said to Terry, and took his leave.

Thus left to his new-found way, Terry went on, led of the Lord, from strength to strength. After a while, he began to go about holding prayer-meetings; and, plain man as he was, he was made a blessing to many. When his end drew nigh, the "neighbours" made great efforts to get the priest admitted to his dying bed; but no. The Protestant clergyman came to give Terry the Lord's Supper, but so fearful was he lest the people should think that he had any notion that the elements could be changed by the word of man, or placed any confidence in old forms, that he entreated the minister, instead of reading prayers out of a book, to pray extempore. After he had prevailed upon him to do this twice, he said that now he must pray himself, as he wanted "a fuller manifestation of the countenance of God." He did pray, and it seemed as if the Lord had descended, and filled the place with His glory. It is said that, ever afterwards, the clergyman thanked God for that day. Mr Campbell, a good many years ago, went out of his way to see a daughter of Terry's in the county of Fermanagh, whom he found aged and in affliction, but very happy in God.

In the "Methodist Magazine" for 1802, at page 40, we find a letter to Dr Coke, written before the Conference of 1801, by Mr Thomas Davis, the Superintendent of the Clones Circuit, describing the work of God as he had seen it in his own sphere during the year. He had feared, in returning from the previous Conference, that the second year would not be like the preceding one; but it had proved better and better. The power which had accompanied the Word had often brought him a refreshing view of St Peter preaching to the multitude. The first Sunday after Conference, as he preached, numbers were melted down and sought mercy with prayers and tears, and the meeting lasted from four in the afternoon till eleven at night. In going round his Circuit, he had more than once taken from twenty to fifty new members into the Societies at a time. At the love-feasts, they had often to go out into the fields, and sometimes held them in storms of wind and rain. He says that his constitution is much hurt, but his consolation is, that, in the course of the year, God has added 746 members to the Societies in his Circuit. What he says of Graham and Ouseley we must give in full :—

"Permit me, dear sir, to say something of the Irish missionaries, Messrs Graham and Ouseley. The mighty power of God accompanied their word with such demonstrative evidence as I have never known, or indeed very rarely heard of. I have been

present in fairs and markets while these two blessed men of
God, with burning zeal and apostolic ardour, pointed hundreds
and thousands to the Lamb of God that taketh away the sin of
the world. And I have seen the immediate fruit of their labour,
the aged and the young falling prostrate in the most public
places of concourse, cut to the heart, and refusing to be comforted
until they knew Jesus and the power of His resurrection. I
have known scores of these poor penitents stand up and witness
a good confession ; and, blessed be God, hundreds of men now
stand and adorn the gospel of Christ Jesus. These two men
have been the most indefatigable in their labours of love to
perishing sinners of any that I have yet known. From four to
six hours they would preach, exhort, and pray, and next day
perhaps ride a journey, and encounter the same labour of love.
Thus—

> " ' They scorned their feeble flesh to spare,
>   Regardless of its swift decline.'

"My dear sir, I am wanting both in memory and language to
set forth the wonders I have seen wrought by the mighty power
of the Holy Spirit. When I look at the usefulness of these two
dear men, I am humbled to the dust ; and again, when I view
them, with shattered frames and wrecked constitutions, stepping
into the grave, I am truly affected. But it is God's own work,
and He is able to raise up labourers, and qualify them for the
greatest tasks."

Once more they turned their faces towards the
Conference with glad hearts. Their brethren from
the different Circuits which they had visited in their
journeys would tell them what gracious things the
Lord had wrought, not only during their own presence,
but in fruits manifesting themselves when they had
passed from off the ground. Success had attended
the labours of their brethren in the two other mission
tracts, though not in an equal degree. Indeed, in
that year prosperity had been granted to the Circuits of the Irish Connexion generally, so that, with

exceeding great joy, the Conference was able to record an increase in the Societies of close upon five thousand members, making, with that of the preceding year, more than eight thousand in all. The Conference records its belief that the Irish Mission, in both south and west, had been successful in a very encouraging degree. As to that in the north, with which our narrative is concerned, it says that the success has been " very considerable among the Roman Catholics, and its usefulness in stirring up Protestants almost unbounded," and that, in conjunction with the labours of the regular preachers, it had been the means of the conversion of " vast numbers."

CHAPTER X.

THE field appointed to our two fellow-labourers
by the Conference of 1801 was "the Province of
Ulster."

Mr George Brown, of the Boyle Circuit, a minister
of whom it is said by Smith, in his "History of
Methodism in Ireland," that he was, "living and
dying, a bright pattern of Christian simplicity, and
of that perfect love which casteth out fear," wrote to
Dr Coke in August 1801 :—

"Yesterday I received your favour, and send you an account
of the revival in the Cavan Circuit briefly as follows. When I
returned from the Conference in July 1800, I found some had
obtained a consciousness of the pardoning mercy of God in the
time of our absence by means of the local preachers and lively
zealous class-leaders. Our love-feasts were crowned with
wonderful outpourings of the Spirit of grace. Silent tears
flowed freely. Some were constrained to cry out for mercy,
and very few of them went away until their sorrow was turned
into joy unspeakable. Poor backsliders were restored, and a
few obtained the direct witness of a full sanctification.

"Two young men had met in order to fight a duel, but were
prevented by means of a wall falling on one of the spectators
and crushing him to death. Some months after this, they were

converted by means of the Irish missionaries, and joined the Society. They now walk in love as dear comrades in the way to Zion, and are as zealous for God as they had been in all manner of wickedness before. At a prayer-meeting which the Irish missionaries held in one of our new places, fifteen persons were converted. As I could not neglect my stated places of preaching, I spent very little time with our dear missionaries last year. Mr Ouseley was three nights with us. In that time, twenty-four persons, I believe, found redemption in the blood of the Lamb, among whom were two Roman Catholics, and another was deeply convinced ; he is now converted, and has withstood the priest to his face. Two more of them in the same neighbourhood were convinced, and set at liberty, while my wife prayed with them in Irish. We must confess that the Lord has crowned the labours of the regular preachers in the several Circuits with very great success. Nevertheless, under His blessing, I cannot but attribute our late extraordinary revivals in the north to the missionaries. They, sir, have provoked us to jealousy, and made us ashamed to stand still, whilst they laboured, with all their powers, by day and by night.

"I have the pleasure of informing you, that we added 226 to our number last year, and left 101 on trial ; 192 professed justification, and as 14 of these found mercy since Mr Douglas and I left them, you will see that the good work is still going on. All glory be to God and the Lamb for ever ! Last Sunday morning, after preaching near Carrick-on-Shannon, I spoke to the men, and my wife to the women ; at which time four females received the witness of adopting love. If we continue humble, steadfast, and faithful, keeping the unity of the Spirit in the bonds of peace, harmony, and love, Satan's tottering kingdom shall fall before Him who sits on the right of the Majesty on high until all His enemies are made His footstool."

Though the appointed circle of our evangelists, embracing the nine counties of Ulster, appeared large, we suddenly find them in the south of Ireland. Mr Langtree, at page 115 of his narrative, describes a visit to Tipperary, stating that he himself took his place with them on horseback in the streets of Clonmel, where they were violently opposed by the mob, but preached with fearless fidelity. A sort of madman was set up to preach in derision, but did little harm. Next day, when the missionaries again appeared, the disturbers advanced, blowing a horn. Some influential members of the Society of Friends went to a magistrate applying for protection, which they obtained. On the third day, when again in the streets, some women assailed them with bitter and wicked words, but were overcome by a powerful appeal of Mr Ouseley. Then the men began picking up stones and dirt to pelt them, but they were seized by the soldiers, and carried off to prison. As the preachers left the town, they were once more attacked, though little hurt.

From a letter of Mr Graham to Dr Coke, published in the "Methodist Magazine" of 1802, p. 472, it appears that before they started on this journey, which lasted eighteen weeks, he was spitting blood ; but in the course of it he had not been confined to bed except for five days, and that with heavy colds, of which he made light. He exults in the fact that the priests cannot any longer prevent the people from coming to hear. Some Methodists, he finds, think, if the downfall of Babylon is not accomplished at once, it will not come at all; but he hopes, after they have been seven times round the island, the walls will come tumbling down. His " seven times " need a more patient interpretation than even he was prepared to give them.

He goes on to state, that, even in places where

they expected nothing but persecution, they saw
the people weeping and praying in the streets. In
the city of Limerick, and around it, the Lord was
very manifestly with them; "a mighty fire has been
kindled, and continues burning." In Kerry, the
scene of former labours of Graham, they had much
in which to rejoice, and no opposition till they
reached the town of Tralee. "Here you would have
imagined that hell was let loose. Though my voice
is pretty loud, I could not be heard. Such shouting
of men, women, and children, I think I never heard
before; and although we had four or five magistrates
on our side, and officers and yeomen, and many
Protestants, it did not avail." Nevertheless, they
preached in the court-house to many hundreds, yet
under the protection of a guard of soldiers. One of
the Roman Catholics went up to three priests and
said, "Your people are in the dark, and so you
would have it."

Entering the county of Cork, they found at
Skibbereen a good reception, and the people seemed
to be prepared of the Lord. In the market they
were heard gladly, and the next day being Sunday,
the poor .people flocked about them in hundreds.
While they were preaching, a priest came up and
tried cavalry-preaching after his manner, "riding
furiously through the crowd, lashing with his whip
on every hand." The people ran, tumbling one over another. He then called them to the chapel and lectured
them; but a Roman Catholic gentleman lectured him,
and said he would write to the bishop and have him
discarded. The preachers held their ground, and
preached on "after the hurry was over," the Catholics

hearing in both street and chapel with hearts greatly broken down, and some of them saying " they could follow us through the world."

At Bantry, Mr Graham thought that Satan was very destitute of friends, for no one molested them but one old woman making a great noise.

When in full and happy activity at Bandon, they heard that Mrs Graham was dying, and set out for Monaghan, preaching by the way at Cork, Kinsale, and many other places; and yet in five and a half days riding 176 Irish miles, which make about 230 English. On arriving at Monaghan, happily they found Mrs Graham recovering. They soon revisited the south, making a tour of twelve weeks. Private letters, written by different persons, describing the effects of their preaching, are quoted at length by Mr Campbell.

One writer from Bandon says that the flame has spread through the Western Circuits; that in their own they have an increase of two hundred members. Another from Cork tells his friends that poor and rich, profane and moral, scoffer and inquirer, Papist and Protestant, indiscriminately fell beneath the mighty power of God; and that in ten days one hundred and twenty persons had been converted. Another, speaking of the region to the west of Bandon, says that never did any one now living see such a day at Ballydehob; no less than sixty found peace with God, in Dunmanway thirty, and in other places twenty-nine.

In the year 1802, Graham and Ouseley were appointed to labour in Leinster, Ulster, and all Munster, excepting the county of Clare, which was attached to the Connaught Mission under Messrs Kane and Allen.

In July of this year Mr Ouseley appears to have begun to keep a hasty journal. He describes their travelling from Dublin to Mr Fox's, talking to the people and distributing papers, and lifting up a voice of warning in every place through which they passed. The following day they rode thirty miles to Cootehill, once more, in every town and village along the road, calling upon the people to prepare to meet the Lord. In one small village, as Ouseley talked with the people, and gave them his papers, they fell on their knees upon the road; and he, sitting on his horse, prayed with them. When he left, they "poured blessings after me;" but he went on, reflecting, what a change would come when the priest should see the papers and sour their minds.

On the 24th of July he speaks of preaching in Brother Wyley's "haggard" (stackyard). At a prayer-meeting subsequently held in the house, his attention was arrested by the prayer of one of the leaders, which was remarkably sensible, and accompanied by deep feeling on the part of the people. It proved that this man was one who had come to mock the first time they visited this part of the country, but was "struck," and now was a useful leader of a class.

Soon after he writes, at Brother Whitley's at Goley, that he met with a lately-married couple, who had been Roman Catholics, and whose hearts were overflowing with gratitude to God for His goodness to their souls. When the young man brought home his bride, his mother fully expected to get her to

accompany her to mass, and by this means gradually
to cure her son of his "swaddling," as the term was.
But, instead of this, the young couple commenced
holding family prayer. The mother removed her bed
out of the house into the barn, that " she should not
be hearkening to their heretical prayers;" but she
afterwards compromised by prevailing upon them to
have prayers during the time that she milked the
cow.

On the 26th of the same month, after describing
his labours in Monaghan, he says, " As I rode to and
from the market, I met many to speak to of the
things of God. How delightful to be found in this
duty particularly! I feel God is greatly pleased
with it. My soul is made so very happy when I
diligently perform it; so true is the scripture, He
that watereth others shall also be watered himself."

On the 29th, at the funeral of Mrs Gregston, who
living had adorned the gospel, and dying had rejoiced
in its salvation, while Graham was preaching, Ouseley
went up to a group of people who held themselves
aloof. One young man broke out into blasphemy.
When rebuked, he threatened to ill-use Mr Ouseley;
and the next day he came up to him and renewed the
attack with frightful oaths and threats. Ouseley
says he had not been so abused for five or six
years, "but a servant, acting as a master directs,
must expect no better treatment than the master."

On August the 4th he says :—

"We rode into the market at Aughnacloy, and truly a vast
congregation surrounded us. The people heard with deep attention, and with many sighs and tears. I do think instead of

being more embittered, the Catholics are still more pleased the more they hear. I hope that many will pluck up resolution, and give them market, street, and fair preaching; and thus the light will spread and prevail in spite of all the powers of earth and hell. Here I gave some tracts, which they gladly received."

That same evening they preached in a field. On the 5th of August—

" We rode to the fair at Middletown. When we came in, and took our stand and put on our caps, a vast crowd came around us. As one of us preached, a man, half-drunk, stood in the crowd and listened for a while, but then began to make a disturbance, and to challenge our authority for preaching, telling the people it was the devil's preaching. I bid him to be quiet for a while, and spoke in an affectionate way to him; but he went away grumbling. It seems he was a degraded, drunken priest, that thus came forward to defend the faith, as he supposed; but we proceeded, and for the most part all the people were deeply attentive, till a magistrate came, just as we were concluding, to stop us. We had some reasoning with him. He insisted that he would stop us, or that he would disperse the crowd. I replied, If it were a ballad-singer, he would not be heeded, and that we were ready to go to jail for the truth. He rode away, and we, after a little while, did so too. Along the way home we had much conversation with several Catholics."

On the 8th of August he thus writes :—

" I went out early this morning to meet a class. Every heart seemed to feel the work of the Lord. I was greatly blessed among them. After breakfast, we went to Rockcorry, where we met Brother Barber. Here a great congregation came together. The house was quite thronged, and the power of the Lord was blessedly among the people. Some souls were born again, and, in short, every heart seemed powerfully to feel the operation of the Divine Spirit. After preaching, I went to visit a friend in the town, and the other preachers rode on before me on the way to Monaghan. As I rode along in company with some of our friends, we came to the Roman Catholic chapel, which is near the roadside. Here many were sitting and lying on the grass, waiting for the priest. When I came amongst them, I began to speak to them mildly of the things of God. They received it with much cordiality, and several began to draw near. One opposer cried out to them to beware of me, and after a little he came forward with the multitude, and immediately wanted to enter into some dispute with me about doctrinal points. I gently told them all, that I did not want to contend about points, but as a friend to incite them to goodness and love. Many of them were well pleased, and desired me not to fear. I spoke to him till he was quite puzzled in everything. Whilst yet we were speaking, up came the priest all in a fury. The people got before him, and bid him go away. So he went into the chapel, and began to ring the bell, but many of them stood to hear us speaking. I was about going, some of them beginning to express anger. A woman took my mare by the bridle, saying I should not leave that till I would clear up the point. Others said I spoke what was right, and no man should touch me. However, when I saw contention among them, I moved on. It seems that the opposer was a schoolmaster. As I was just departing, out came the priest scolding, and a great many with him. He began to beat the people, and to call me names ; but I did not heed him, and quietly rode away. They still contended among themselves, some saying that I was right and a good man, and others that I was a deceiver; so that they gave each other the lie."

On August the 23d he thus writes :—

" We went to Friend Anderson's. Before dinner I walked out, and went into one of the Friend's houses, where I met a young girl who was a Catholic, spinning at her wheel. I began to speak to her, and the Lord so applied the word to her heart, that her tears began to flow down. I called them to prayer, and she and several wept sore, but she roared aloud. The family of the next house, hearing the cry, ran out ; and among these was another Catholic or two, but one of them also was bathed in tears while yet we prayed together. At night again the people assembled, including several Catholics, and truly we had a very blessed time ; all seemed keenly to feel the Divine power. When we were leaving this, the poor Catholic girls, particularly, wept together. The one that was first struck was very fond of dances, and used to curse, but now she seemed resolved to turn to the Lord. Her neighbours began to say that her parents would kill her, and what not ; but when she told her mother how the Lord had touched and turned her heart, the mother herself said she also would go to hear us, and would not hurt her."

On August the 25th he writes :—

" We rode into the fair of Killeshandra. We were surrounded by multitudes of poor Catholics, who seemed exceedingly glad to see us once more, and now heard us with flowing tears. It seemed as if their prejudice were fled. O Lord, hasten their deliverance ! At night we preached at Friend Johnston's, about five miles from the fair, and had a happy meeting. Here I met a very bigoted and self-wise Catholic. At first he was very perverse, but after I had given him one of my little addresses to a Catholic, and reasoned with him, he went for his wife and for other Catholics, till we spoke, and sang, and prayed with them. How gentleness and patience do win upon these ! They went away very thankful, and I saw them at some of our meetings after that, with their tears flowing."

After mentioning good meetings at Widow Hodging's and Friend Trotter's, he says, on September the 3d :—

" We rode to Ballyconnel market, and had to pass some rivers with some difficulty and danger, they were so full from the rain the day before. The people in the market gave us a very attentive hearing. The hearts of many poor Catholics were broken, and their tears flowed. They seemed well pleased. We stopped at a friend's house, dried off the perspiration, and after a little refreshment rode out to the country. As I was riding off through the market, the people again came round me ; and I spoke to them to their great satisfaction. This evening turned out very wet. We dined at Friend Anderson's, and at night the house filled with

I

people. We had a very blessed time. The two Catholic girls that were awakened the last time we were in this part of the country were to-night greatly melted, and professed to have received the pardoning love of God. They came also the next morning to see us, and both seemed very happy and very loving."

On the 4th, after preaching at Swanlinbar, they rode to Furnaceland, and there we find the following words :—

"Closed the week's labour, and lay down weary and worn, yet happy in God. And what on earth can equal this ? What king can boast such true, substantial, and solid happiness ? Ye are kings, saith the apostle ; yes, and more than kings ; happier than any, and moving in a grander sphere ; ambassadors for Christ to immortal souls."

On the 7th we have the following :—

"We came to Froree. The power of the Lord greatly appeared to reach the hearts of the people, while Brother Graham preached from Revelation iii. 20, ' Behold, I stand at the door and knock ; ' —also at prayer. A Roman Catholic that had been convinced when we were in this country before, and had received happiness from God, brought out his wife to-night to hear us. She cried and wept sore ; and after a while the Lord made her happy in His love. Oh, with what joy the husband and she returned to their little hut !"

On the 13th :—

"We preached here to the market-people, and had a blessed, attentive hearing, with the tears flowing. I gave out papers, and the people were well pleased. In general, when we were distributing such among them, they ran for them so greedily as almost to crush us against one another, and the horses so, that we were often afraid the horses would hurt both them and us."

On the 17th :—

"This morning, I went to see an old Catholic man, who had

been convinced of sin some time ago, and met in class for a while ; but through evil reasonings, he cast away his confidence and fell into a deep melancholy, became unable to do any business, and, as it were, insensible and inconsolable. As I approached his hut, I heard him muttering something in his little room. When I came in, his wife called him out. He came, and a wretched sight was he to behold, all emaciated, dejected, and self-neglected. He said little or nothing, but chattering to himself, sat down by the fire. I spoke a little in Irish and English, and then sang an Irish hymn. While I was singing, I observed him stealing a look at me through his fingers, which covered his face. He seemed pleased and astonished, and the tears began to fall down his cheeks as I sang. After that, I spoke to him. He replied, he had no hope. He said, he could not be saved ; he had no heart, his heart was gone. He said, he could not pray at all ; though he might stir his lips, his heart would not pray. I called him to kneel down, which he did ; and while prayer was made many came in, and the power of the Lord began to reach the people's hearts, so that the house was filled with noise and mourning. He, poor man, wept bitterly for a time, and then broke out into a most pathetic prayer—a prayer that reached every heart. His poor wife also wept sore. After prayer I again spoke to him. He said, still he had no heart ; that there was no good in him. 'But,' said he, 'though I myself should be lost, I wish all the world would believe on the Lord Jesus Christ, and go to heaven.' Then I asked him, would he be satisfied to be parted from the Lord Jesus. He burst into tears, and cried, 'Oh, no, no —no, no !' So I left him, and hope I shall see him in glory. After this I rode off to Derrykihane, to the Quarterly Meeting (love-feast). The people were wellnigh gathered. We held the meeting in a field. There was some softening power while Brother Graham preached from Rev. xix. 9, 'Blessed are they which are called to the marriage supper of the Lamb.' At the love-feast we had some sweet gales, as it were, only for a few moments, and then again all seemed cold and unusually dry. Thus we continued for two or three hours, while the people were hearing and speaking their experiences. I was looking on, not without some degree of pain. I saw a young woman at a distance, pensive-looking. I went round to her, and began to speak to her. Her heart began to give way. I brought her into the midst of the people, sang a hymn, and the tears began to flow from them on every side. I then called on all that felt distress to draw near. Many came, and we kneeled down ; and while prayer was made, God heard and sent down His power, and then indeed many began to cry for mercy. The field was wet, which was not known when we began ; yet the people lay on their faces even in the wet without regarding it, and cried, and prayed on. I had to roll my pocket-handkerchief into a lump and put it under my knees ; and yet the wet reached over it through my small-clothes and stockings. The Lord mercifully set several souls at liberty. To His name be the glory. 'Tis His Spirit alone, and not the exertions of man—though often He seconds and blesses such—that can reach an immortal soul."

He does not name the place where, on the 21st of this month, they held a love-feast in a field with several Roman Catholics present. At night they held another meeting, and about half-a-dozen Roman Catholics were crying for mercy at the same time. One man who had been awakened when they had visited the neighbourhood previously, but had been led back by his wife and friends, now " roared for the disquietude of his heart." A little Catholic maid, who had been converted a few months previously, was sitting, with her sister lying across her knees, crying and faint. After a while, the Lord set her at liberty ; and also another Catholic woman. On September the 3d, he states that while Brother Graham preached, his voice could hardly be heard for sighs and cries. In the evening of the same day at Lisslean House, though it poured with rain, the crowd was such that it was impossible to kneel ; but the feeling of those present appears to have been remarkable even for the meetings of Graham and Ouseley. On the 6th, at Drumclamp, high on the hills of Tyrone, near Castlederg, after the meeting, Ouseley says, "We were wet all through with perspiration; the very lining of my sleeves was as if my coat had been in water." The next day, in Omagh, Protestants and Catholics heard with flowing tears, crying, "It is all right, all true." And the day after, at Fintona, "almost all the market came round us." On the Sunday they heard the Rector of Fintona, the Rev. Mr Athill, preach a sermon, which was to the point, was spirit and life.

In November 1802 ("Methodist Magazine," 1803, page 375), the Chairman of the Clones District, Mr Steward, wrote to Dr Coke, stating that there were seventy-two members of the Methodist Society in the district who had been Roman Catholics, though the priests employed every art to terrify them, such as cursing, ringing the bell, and quenching the candle. Only a week previously a young man had been seized, and after various attempts at persuasion, the priests cried out, "Speaking will not do," and began to cast salt and water upon him, at the same time repeating the words, "Go out, Graham;" but the exorcism failed, and Mr Steward hopes that the young man will continue to the end. He also states his intention of specially inviting the Roman Catholic converts to the next love-feast, and presenting each with a copy of the Word of God in the presence of the assembled brethren, as a token of their love to their souls.

In November we find them amidst the charming

scenery of Wicklow, visiting among other places the residence of the Tighe family, long connected with traditions of piety and goodness. John Wesley was painted, preaching in the demesne, in a pleasant picture which belonged to the late Mr Farmer, and still is at Gunnersbury House.

On November the 26th he writes : "Left Dublin for Rosanna. As we were riding through Newton-Kennedy, I saw a number of people assembled at a door, where it seems they were drinking. I rode up to them, and took out a few tracts, spoke to them in a gentle manner concerning eternal things, and gave them the tracts. They were greatly pleased, and returned me thanks; but an old man came forward, nearly drunk, and, dreadfully blaspheming because the other Catholics should listen to me at all, he cursed me with many abusive names. The rest pulled him away. I rode on a little further in the street, pulled out more tracts, and called the inhabitants to come to me. So they ran, and I gave them the tracts. The old fellow, seeing this, came forward again, uttering horrid curses. I rode away, and then he returned to the ale-house, cursing the swaddlers, Protestants, and especially the Orange-men. It seems that two of the latter were drinking in the house, and hearing, and not having patience, one of them stood up and knocked him down. Some other of the Catholics took his part, and a bloody battle ensued, in which the Catholics suffered and had to run away. What a pity that people called Christians do not understand the true nature of Christianity ! for then they would not quarrel, but love and serve each other, like the children of God and disciples of the Lord Jesus. It was pretty late when we arrived at Rosanna in company with Brother Howe.

"27th.—This night Brother Graham preached in Mrs Tighe's house, and had a good time, though they seemed very still and hardy.

"28th.—This Sabbath morning I preached again in this house from Matthew vi. 9, ' Our Father which art in 'heaven.' The Lord gave much freedom, and a great power appeared to reach every heart; all faces were wet with weeping. Even the children —a sweet flock, which Mrs Tighe charitably supports and educates here—were melted into floods of tears. From hence we rode into Wicklow, and after church, as the congregation came pouring into the streets, we sat on horseback. Brother Graham preached an awful sermon, and I exhorted till covered with perspiration. The people heard with the greatest solemnity, and at night the house was filled, and the Lord was with us. The people appeared to drink in the Word, and I trust many powerfully felt.

"29th.—We again preached in the house, which was unusually filled; and I trust good was done, for many appeared to feel very deeply.

"30th.—We returned to Rosanna again. They all were glad to see us. Mrs Tighe was very kind and attentive. This day and night we had two other meetings here. The people seemed much moved. The servants, some of whom were backsliders, cried out in the bitterness of their distress.

"December 1st.—The Rev. Thomas Kelly preached an excellent gospel sermon on the new birth, and we prayed, and had a sweet, melting, lively meeting.

" 2d.—We held a prayer-meeting. The power of God was much felt, so that some cried out with flowing tears. I spoke to the Catholics about this place. They were shy, but acquiesced in the things spoken. Oh, how they fear their teachers; yea, more than they fear God!"

At Roundwood a man said he would go all the way to Wicklow, next Sunday, to hear them. At Newton-Mount-Kennedy they rode up and down, with their caps on, till the people gathered. Then they returned to Rosanna, where they preached in the morning of the Lord's Day, and then "off to Wicklow." Speaking of the tears which flowed at the meeting here on the Monday, Mr Ouseley expresses his gratification at seeing so much feeling in a town; "for in towns, generally, people are so hardened that little impression is made, or if made, it soon disappears." He judged by symptoms among the less restrained inhabitants of solitary houses or small villages. At the market at Rathdrum they had a kindly multitude of Catholic hearers; and some months later, he met one in Athy, who had been awakened there.

The next name mentioned is one that has taken its place in the permanent respect of Irish Methodists, because of the useful life and blessed death of one of the members of the family, Fossey Tackaberry, who became a minister, and of whom a memoir was written by the Rev. Robert Huston.

" 7th December.—We came to Friend Tackaberry's. When I had just got into the little parlour, and stood a short time, a young woman came in, and looked earnestly at me, then went down and looked at Mr Graham, and then said to her mother, 'That man above is him that I remember to have seen in my dream. I saw two,' said she, 'but I recognised his face particularly; and methought that he did me good, and that many were blessed.' So it was. That night I preached, and God so blessed the Word that there was a cry and a shaking. One Catholic girl cried out, and professed to have got some comfort. I heard that she joined the Society afterwards. The family of the house were much blessed, and I trust much good was done.

"8th December.—This morning we had a most blessed meeting at morning prayer. From this we rode into Arklow Street, one of those towns where there was a dreadful battle with the rebels. Many came to hear us, and heard with patience. From this we came near the seaside to the rock. Many came out, and some from Arklow, and we had a powerful breaking. To God be all the praise.

"9th December.—We rode into Arklow market, and took our stand in a convenient place. Some of the Catholic women and fishermen were cursing us; and, when we began to preach, some of them began to be rude; but some of the soldiers slapped them in the face. Another of them was going to strip off his coat to fight, but he was soon glad to be gone; so that we had a peaceable hearing, and the tears flowed from some. A young clergyman stood a while, and conceiving that our doctrine would drive to despair, he wanted the churchwarden to help him to stop us; but the churchwarden would not. Then he applied to others to little purpose; then, with an officer, he went to the colonel to obtain aid. The colonel told him he would not have anything to do with us, and advised him to do so too. Then, when none would help him, he sent us word by a friend not to come again, or that we would not get off so well. I wrote to him a gentle, explanatory letter, as I believed him to be a well-intentioned man from some accounts I had of him, and enclosed a couple of the little papers I had been giving out amongst the people. I heard that a Catholic woman was so deeply convinced of sin that day that she could not rest, and was eager that we should come back again. On the whole, I hope good seed has been sown. This night we preached at Sister Fearn's. We had a blessed time. The Catholic girl lives here, and was now again greatly moved. A man said, after hearing, that there was no use in delaying any longer, and that for his part he would begin and serve the Lord. We had much praying, and I trust it will not be forgotten.

"10th.—Came to Redna. As I was passing through the village of Aghrim, I rode up to the people's doors, spoke to them here and there, gave them some little tracts, and invited them to preaching. As I went along the road, I called at a house to invite them. The man shut the door, and said he would have nothing to do with any such. He was a Catholic, and rather decent-looking. I gently bid him not shut the door, and spoke a few things to him in Catholic expressions, and a little Irish. He got quite calm and good-natured. He said it was all true, and gave me his blessing with the tears in his eyes. What a blessing is patience and gentleness in a gospel minister! This night, many came out; the Lord was very present. The people around here were rather wild, ignorant, careless ones; but the Holy One this night thawed down their cold hearts, and an appearance of good was among them. Some said, they found comfort and love.

" 11th.—We came to Hacketstown, expecting to find a market, but there was none. We preached in the house this night.

" 12th [Sunday].—This morning again, and after mass, the street being full of Catholics, we went out to the cross where the people stood. Brother Graham is unwell, and I felt very weak; so that my whole frame trembled as if fear had assaulted me. My feet were scarce able to carry me, till I came to the place. They cleared the way for us very quietly, and so soon as I gave out my text, Galatians vi. 14, ' God forbid that I should glory,' I got quite strong. They listened with the deepest attention, but a few ran away. As I was speaking, I saw the congregation moving and looking frightened, yet unwilling to go away. Their priest, it seems, was coming toward us, but he quietly passed by; and so all was easy. When I came to explain the nature of the Cross, as it respected our self-denial and every duty on our part, and the benefits flowing to us through Christ crucified on the part of God, who thus poureth His benefits upon us; and also when I showed the inutility of any other cross, or sign of the cross, the people stood amazed, their faces turned pale, and the tears came down gushing. Brother Graham exhorted after, and all heard as if for life. Then we retired with the heavy weight departed, and our minds eased after thus bearing our cross, in declaring the counsel of God amongst such crowds of uncultivated beings, where a little before war and destruction had been. This night again we preached in the house, and had a lively meeting, so that we were wet with perspiration. I hope good was done in this place. Brother and Sister Condell were very kind to us. The Lord bless them for ever! I had an account after, from this little town, that the priest greatly persecuted the people that had been to hear us." . . .

"15th.—We came to Gorey. When the people saw the men with the black caps on horseback, they ran in. crowds, and we preached to them in the underpart of the Market House. They were very attentive, and at night again the Court House was well filled, and with a decent-looking congregation, such as one would imagine to be calculated to do good—neither too grand nor too mean; for the great folks seldom stoop to the religion of the Cross, and the rabble are so used to wickedness and blindness, that they disregard it. I preached from 1 John ii. 12, 'I write unto you, little children, because your sins are forgiven.' The tears flowed down many faces, and some lifted up the voice, and cried out whilst we were at prayer. I thought it a pity we had not time to stay a night or two more with them." . . .

"18th.—We preached in the street of Ferns. The people here seem as if they had no souls, they are so very careless. When Brother Graham, after singing, began to preach, there was a good number; but he had not been long speaking till the most of them dropped off, walking away quite insensible.

After he had done, I roared out against the ungodly town in such a way that I greatly strained myself; but we left our warning with them in the name of the Lord. From thence we rode on, after preaching, into the market of Newtownbarry. Here the people surrounded us in multitudes, and heard with flowing tears and quietness. I gave them some tracts, for which they were very thankful. I was now very hoarse indeed. I did not get over the effect of this day's exertion for many days.

"19th.—This, Sabbath, morning, the preaching-room was well filled with attentive hearers. Brother Graham preached from Rev. xxii. 17, 'And the Spirit and the Bride say, Come.' The power of the Lord greatly attended His Word, so that every heart was penetrated, and some fell on their knees; so that we had to cease preaching, and go to prayer. We had a sweet time. After church I preached in the street to a numerous audience, from a clause in the Creed, 'I believe in the communion of saints,' wherein I endeavoured to lead the people to look at the character of both saint and sinner; the communion of each, and their end. All was peace and tranquillity. They said, the great man of the town said he would stop us; but he happened to ride by us, heard for a little, and then quietly rode away. This night, again, I preached to a very crowded house. We had a good time, and I hope good was done. We had many Catholics out this night. I heard of one and her daughters, whose husband is a thoughtless Protestant. I went out to their house, and was well received by them all. I prayed with them, after much conversation, and all seemed very powerfully affected, and promised to turn from sin to the Lord." . . .

" 25th.—This morning, we had a very blessed meeting, and after breakfast rode away for Ross. As we went along, we met, near the town, some of the people coming from the mass. They were very mad and bitter, particularly against Brother Graham, thinking that he had been formerly a priest. Some of them crossed themselves so soon as they saw him, and some more cursed. We met several parcels of them on our way to Ross. I spoke mostly to them all, and they were very thankful. None were insolent, excepting two or three drunken creatures; but a few soft words made them silent, and, to appearance, ashamed. This night, we preached at the house in Ross, and the Word seemed to go with power. A girl, after she went home, met the clergyman in the house, and burst out into bitter crying, saying, 'O sir, you have known me so long, and why did you not speak to me, and tell me my danger?' She cried most of the night." . . .

" 28th.—We went to the streets of Kilkenny, it being the market-day. As we were singing, the people ran forward; and after a little, some drunken ones of them began to make a noise; but none being present to suppress it in the bud, it became almost general, and they gave the word, one to another, to keep it up; so that they entirely drowned Brother Graham's voice, notwithstanding his exertions. They began to throw some dirt, and then to crowd in upon us. The horses began to plunge, so we had to alight. Some gentlemen came up, and one of them took a stick, and chased them away a little, and then very mildly advised us to desist, and leave them, as they would not hear. We thanked them, mounted our horses, and rode away, the multitude running and hallooing after us, and flinging odd stones; but we missed the right road, and had to turn back, and we again came amongst them. They set up a shout, and after a little began to shower stones and dirt upon us and our horses, crying out, ' Will you ever come here to preach again?' We turned into the barrack, and so escaped the fulness of their fury. Brother Graham escaped unhurt, but I got several bruises. One stone particularly hit me on the chin, though it did no further damage than raise a lump; the others made my flesh black, but, to God be the praise, I received no material injury. The town mayor came, and some of the officers walked with us, till we got near the outskirts of the town; and hardly could the people be kept from murdering us on the spot, in his, the mayor's, presence; for they perceived he had no armed man nor any weapon with him; but we rode off, and while I was paying the turnpike, some of them from behind a ditch aimed at me with stones, one of which struck me on the back of my head, but yet not so as to hurt me. I rode away rejoicing, and feeling the words of the apostle, ' that I may know Him, and the fellowship of His sufferings.' I felt also real pity for their blindness, and thus judged. The poor things believed they had the devils among them, and they considered that they ought to kill them whilst they had them. I wrote afterwards to the Catholic bishop a complaint. I fear he did not heed it, but a day is at hand. We rode into Loughlin Bridge, and preached there that night, and had a lively, refreshing time.

"29th.—We rode into Athy, and this night preached in the house. The power of the Lord attended His Word, and some began to cry out; and others were very much disgusted. One of these I reasoned with after, and he took it in good part. He was a Calvinist young man, and thought we were endeavouring to work on the passions of the people mechanically, and by our own exertions; but after a little conversation, he saw things in another view, and saw that no rational exertion could be blamed when an immortal soul was the subject in question."

"16th January 1803 [Sunday].—In the street, after prayers, the Catholic people came forward and kicked a football, expecting to cause a riot, and hurt or hinder us; but the Deputy Sovereign took a stick, and ran after some of them. He took the ball, and cut it, and we had peace for a while. It seems the priest here set them mad against us, so that they would hurt us if they could. A great number of them stood afar off, and still made a noise. Some of the Orangemen, seeing it, went together, and moved towards them. When they saw it, they ran away in such confusion as to be tumbling over each other; so we had no more noise with them, and some heard very attentively. At night, again, the house was well filled, and the power of God was amongst the people. Several Catholic girls particularly came out to hear, and were deeply affected." . . .

"20th.—Preached in the market to a great and attentive crowd, mostly Catholics. The markets, or streets, but chiefly the markets, are the only places where we can get a good hearing from these. They are so much afraid of their priests that, even on the Sabbath-day, they will scarcely stand even in the streets, lest the priest should come on them.

"21st.—We intended to have gone this morning, but Brother Graham had to keep his bed, being very sick. This night, I preached in the house. The Lord powerfully reached the hearts of many. There was a stranger present, a Roman Catholic young man. It was the first time he had heard preaching. He was greatly affected, and after preaching came with me to a friend's house, where I spoke and prayed with him. I met him again before I went to bed, and the poor fellow wanted to give me a bottle of wine, the best mark of his friendship. 'Oh,' said he, 'our priests do not half mind us, nor tell us the right truth. They are like a shepherd that would lazily stand on a hill, and just cast a look over the sheep on the plains, but would not come nigh them.'" . . .

"23d [Sunday].—I met the class in the morning. After prayers, when the people were coming from church and mass, I rode along into the street, Brother Graham being too feeble. After singing, and numbers having come forward, I gave out my text, Galatians vi. 14, 'God forbid that I should glory.' The people began to hear with great attention, and wonderful power seemed to reach us all; so that our tears began to flow down together. But some were quite displeased. One came up and insultingly asked, What the —— college I came from? One of the army—an officer, I suppose—turned him away, and another of the soldiers gave him a kick.

K

Then he walked off. Another said, ' How dare he stand to talk to us? or catch us, and we coming out of our chapel? But we will soon tear him down.' ' No,' said a soldier that overheard him; ' not while we are in town.' Another came cursing and bravadoing. He had once been a rebel of some influence; but he perceived that he could not get on as he would wish, so he walked away up the street. A soldier followed him, and when he considered it far enough away, so as not to disturb the congregation with him, he hastened up to him, attacked and beat him, and told him why he did it. However, the congregation perceived it, and many ran up. So I closed the discourse, and gave out in the street that I would preach this night from Matthew xvi. 18, ' And I say also unto thee, That thou art Peter.' After ceasing in the street we repaired to the preaching-house. Brother Graham preached, and I prayed, and we had a good time. At night the house was quite filled with people. I preached according to promise, and truly we had a very solemn, melting, watering time; whilst I chiefly insisted and proved negatively that man could not be, but Christ Himself was, the Rock, the Foundation, the chief Corner-Stone; and that the true Church was those in whom Christ was received by the Holy Ghost—those who were born again, and had Christ formed in them the hope of glory. After this we had a very blessed prayer-meeting. About eight o'clock, many were present; and I gave them an exhortation, and at prayer every heart was melting. After all the labours of the day, I cannot say I felt much weariness; so doth the Lord support me, thanks to His name! And what is still more astonishing, at every meeting I am generally wet with perspiration, and yet I am not worn out."

They traversed the midland districts of Ireland, and their course was a simple repetition of the same labours, interruptions, and encouragements. They were frequently joined by the Circuit preachers; and at Clara we find both Mr Wood and Mr Lougheed in the street with them. After speaking of meetings at Moate, and of the conversion of a Roman Catholic servant maid, Mr Ouseley says, " How good it is to go into the kitchen, and instruct the poor neglected servants ! "

On the 19th of February, at Athlone, he writes : " We rode into Athlone. After we got in, it began to rain ; but, hoping it would not be heavy, we rode into the market to preach. When we were going to fix our horses, for the purpose of speaking, the rain began to fall as a torrent. However, after a little, it abated; and the people perceiving we were preachers, began to be rather insolent. But when we began to speak, they came running; and the force of truth was such that they stood amazed, and were quite charmed. I spoke till covered with perspiration, and after me came Brothers Graham and Wood. They stood as satisfied in all the rain as if they were in a preaching-house. A carriage was passing by, full of ladies, and one of them put out her head, and was not at all ashamed to put out her tongue, and make wry faces, as a mark of her dislike to have the gospel preached; but the poor sent their thousand blessings with us as we were going away. Even those who were at first insolent, and the drunkards, did the same. I believe that the rain, in spite of the umbrellas, wet some of us through our clothes."

A few days later, at "Friend Watson's," he began to speak to a girl about fifteen, the child of Methodist parents, who having been morally brought up, knew of no harm she had done, and seemed altogether careless. He told her how our Lord had taught, that we must be born again ; and, after. a while, the child sought for mercy, and while he prayed for her she was made happy.. We find them riding, on a very blustery Saturday, into some market that is not named, where they sought the most sheltered place, and preached to the people. On the next day, after having preached indoors, they found the people in the street very un-willing to hear ; for the priest had collected their papers and burned them, and warned the people at their peril not to go near them. Whereupon Mr Ouseley thought it well to try something that would make them feel. Giving out the text, " Howbeit, in vain do they worship me, teaching for doctrines the com-mandments of men," he made his voice reach the people, at least, in the houses on both sides of the street, and discussed the doctrines of Romanism ; such as supererogation, purgatory, masses, anointings, prayers for the dead, and transubstantiation, con-trasting them with the teaching of Holy Scripture, and insisting upon the great doctrines of salvation, upon repentance and faith in Christ, and the cleansing of the conscience and the heart, upon love to God and love to man, evidenced in keeping the commandments of God, and a holy life. He afterwards heard that this sermon had been very useful even to some Pro-testants who had a great leaning to Romanism.

On returning to the north, they pursued their
course as usual. Under the date of March the 28th,
he writes at Mrs Robinson's :—

"29th.—We rode to the Quarterly Meeting of
Smithborough. As we rode along, Brother Barber
showed me a little cabin, where had dwelt a poor
woman, a Catholic, who when sick a few days before
her death (which happened about three weeks since),
desired those around her to send for one of the
Methodists to come and speak to her. They asked
her, Would she not have the priest to anoint her?
She answered, 'No, I don't want him.' Brother
Barber, having heard it, went to see her. She was
very weak. He asked her, Did she know anything
of repentance? 'Yes,' replied she; 'and more
than repentance. The Lord God has pardoned all
my sins, and filled my heart with His love. Glory to
His name!' Being astonished at such an answer
from a poor Catholic, and, as he thought, an ignorant
woman, he asked her, How did she obtain all this?
She again replied, 'The Lord Himself hath done it
for His mercy's sake.' He found that she had heard
the gospel preached—perhaps in the streets also, as
we preached very often in the streets of Monaghan,
convenient to where she lived—and she had been at
some prayer-meetings. I hope many, very many of
these poor creatures shall reap eternal advantage
from the street-preaching, though now we know it
not. He asked her, Would he pray with her? 'No,'
said she, 'but sing; I wish to sing, or hear His praises
sung.' She died in a few days. This occurrence, I
think, produced new emotions and encouragements
in my heart to go on, to cry aloud and spare not, to

speak everywhere, and not cease or slack my hands at all. I preached in the open air, to a congregation that we could not get a house to contain, from Matthew xiv. 35, 36, 'And when the men of that place had knowledge of Him.' Our children in the gospel, and friends in this country, were rejoiced once more to see us. We had a very powerful and blessed watering season ; and the presence of the Holy One was greatly manifested all along in the love-feast. Towards the close we had a prayer-meeting, some crying for mercy, and some set at liberty."

The last entries in his journal, for this twelve-month, are :—

"April 11th.—We rode into and preached in the market of Dungannon to an exceedingly large and deeply attentive multitude, but we were interrupted by a recruiting party, whose sergeant had led them, by the direction of an officer, as he said, to the very horses' heads, and there continued a while with fife and drum ; but after a while he was called off, and then we got leave to go on peaceably, and to finish with satisfaction to ourselves and the people. We preached in the house at night, and the Lord visited us with His sweet blissful showers from on high."

"14th [Sunday].—I met the class in the morning. Brother Graham preached at about ten, I preached in the street at about two, and he in the house in the evening. This was a Sabbath of blessings within and abroad, but I think we had the most blessed and powerful time in the streets ; and I always am of opinion that God is more honoured, and mankind more profited, by occasional out-preaching than by house-preaching.

I wish all the preachers would duly consider this. Though it is a cross, yet it can bear to be looked back at again. And *how* in the great day! After these exertions for the past week, we both were nearly worn down; but, oh, how gracious is our God, who so soon revives us again!

"15th.—We had a great congregation at Brother Mark's, among whom were several Catholics. The day was fine—a clean, open place—and the Lord gave us a good time."

CHAPTER XI.

On the 30th of April 1803, Mr Graham relates to Dr Coke a new experience which had befallen him and his comrade, while on a tour of six weeks in the north. In the market of Stewardstown they could hardly restrain the poor Roman Catholics from making a collection, and displeased them by declining their offer. In May of the same year Mr Ouseley writes from Oldcastle ("Methodist Magazine," for 1803, p. 423), confessing that, from weakness and hoarseness, he had been afraid of the labours of the Sabbath in Cookstown; but he found that Roman Catholics had come three or four miles to hear, and, when he commenced to preach, the power of God seemed to reach every heart. Thence he went to Coal Island, preached in the rain, and again in the house to crowds; and at the close was stronger than in the morning. The next day, in the Charlemont Circuit, he was feeble, but his Master gave him success.

In passing through Cavan, he learned that a man was about to be executed. "I visited the prisoner with two of our Church ministers, and, when they left,

I still continued with him; and while he was hanging, I lifted up my voice, and exhorted the people, both in English and Irish."

At this time Mr Graham was laid up of influenza.

The journal of Mr Ouseley for 1804 is fragmentary, being little more than notes of where they went, and what they did.

" 4th August.—I looked at the town, and upon going through the poor part, the words of my Redeemer came into my mind with some force, ' To the poor the gospel is preached.' Passing through, I spoke to some, who heard with gratitude; and that evening I preached in a place where my voice could be heard by two little streets or lanes of these poor benighted Catholics. Many of them came out and heard. Some walked by, careless. The Word seemed blunted, and as if ineffectual, rather evaporating than fastening on the people; yet some few did weep. A drunken soldier disturbed us, which distracted the attention of the hearers for a good while; yet I trust good was done; for the next morning, going through the street again, I found the people very friendly. Spoke a little to them again, for which they appeared very thankful.

" 5th.—This evening, early, came into the market of Newtownbarry. We rode into a convenient part, and hundreds flocked around us. The Word seemed to reach them with power. Brother Graham preached from Psalm ix. 17, ' The wicked shall be turned into hell,' &c. When he finished, I began; and then a colonel came and requested that we should remove to another part. We did so. The people followed us, and I spoke from part of the Catholic " Christian

Doctrine," that, without faith, hope, charity, and good works, we cannot be saved. As I enlarged on this point, we all began to weep together. The spirit of grace and supplications was poured out on the whole congregation. An old poor Romanist came up to me, weeping aloud, and grasped my hand in his, and prayed, and poured out his flowing tears. He followed us down to our lodgings, and again wept in an agony. My poor heart was revived and watered, my hope invigorated, that we would have a great work. My gratitude to my God greatly increased, and prayer to Him that thus He would be with us, and then, what could stand before us? Such a time in the streets among Romanists I did not see (that I can remember) these four years; with such greediness did they run for our papers. I hope this day will never be forgotten."

On the 26th of March 1804 he wrote to Mr Butterworth, the well-known member of Parliament, speaking gratefully of a pamphlet issued by the Rev. Joseph Benson under the title of "The Inspector of Methodism Inspected." The Rev. Dr Hayes, Rector of Killashandra, and a Fellow of Trinity College, Dublin, had published an attack upon the missionaries, entitled "Methodism Inspected." The charges he brought against Methodism were that it taught the doctrine of assurance, or the conscious experience of the pardoning love of God by the operation of the Holy Spirit upon the mind, that the missionaries preached in the street on horseback, and wore "black coifs, or skullcaps, like the Puritans formerly," and by so doing courted persecution, and cast that which was holy unto dogs. The "Christian Observer" took up those accusations, both against Methodism and the missionaries, and this drew out the reply from the pen of Mr Benson. Graham and Ouseley felt that, even upon earth, they had powerful friends; and the latter gratefully says that the " Inspector Inspected " was much approved, even by the clergy.

In the same letter he speaks of Mr Graham's health as declining, but, as to himself, states that the Lord seems to have given him bones of iron and brass. His greatest trial appears to have been violent perspiration in preaching, but he had not been a single day confined to bed, and was better and stronger than before he set out on his mission five years previously. Weary at night, he was as fresh in the morning as ever. He then proceeds to say that the Catholics are more friendly than ever. " In the markets they crowd around us, because there they cannot be watched by the priests. They are ready to trample upon one another in striving to get the tracts." The priests in Munster are much more hostile than those in Connaught. In Limerick, on a market-day, he went through the streets, having his pockets full of papers, standing now here and now there, reading with an audible voice an Irish hymn, or some striking paragraph, speaking for a few minutes, giving away his papers; and so passing on, he was received with looks of kindness and love. In a little town he rode up to door after door, and gave them the papers. Mr Graham writing about this time, also to Mr Butterworth (" Methodist Magazine" for 1805, p. 383), reports the re-establishment of his health, and states that in the little town of Boyle one hundred persons had been brought to the knowledge of God.   During the winter they had preached in the markets, in frost, and hail, and rain, and found magistrates and officers more favourable than in previous years.   "Many wonder we are alive, considering the labour we go through."   A letter given by Mr Langtree (page 143), relates among other striking incidents of a visit to Drogheda, that they had a special sermon preached by Ouseley to beggars in the Tholsel.   His text was Dives and Lazarus.   The beggars stood next to the preachers, and a vast crowd outside.   Such showers of tears, he says, had not been shed in any other of their meetings.   They then made the beggars pass into the Tholsel, giving a penny or a halfpenny to each one ; but they were seized with a panic, some one having suggested that they were being caught in order to be sent on board a ship in the harbour.   "The children began to squall, the men to bustle, and the women to have the heart-beat, all wanting to get out."   However, when they were at last let go, they parted from the missionaries, blessing them.   Mr Ouseley proceeds to mention happy labour at Carlow, bearing repeated testimony to the usefulness of Mr Averell and Lorenzo Dow.

Hitherto the missionary life of Mr Ouseley had been prosecuted in such close connection with his well-beloved Charles Graham, that the two seemed to be not only associated but identified.   They had coursed all Ireland through, as perhaps no two men ever did before, travelling uncounted thousands of miles. The same hospitable homes had bidden them welcome, and the same execrations driven them away. The same missiles had whizzed about their ears, and the same blessings lighted on their heads. They called the converts gathered out of the world " our " children, and the converts hailed them almost as if they had been one and the same person. The words of Mr Campbell, "We never heard of a jealousy, or a jar, between them," are to be taken strictly. It does not appear that any one ever did. When they were separated at the Conference of 1805, many thought that, after the exposures of the past six years, they were both far spent, especially Mr Graham. Even he, however, had yet nearly twenty years of fruitful toil before him, and Ouseley thirty-four. Neither of them had been worn down by study or labour before their frames reached full maturity; hence damages were soon repaired.

During the six years, the Methodist Societies in Ireland had increased from 16,277 members to 23,321. The calamities of the Rebellion had prepared the people to hear and feel the Word, and the Lord had blessed the preachers generally with a large measure of His Holy Spirit. It is remarkable with what cordiality, not to say fervour, the ministers on the regular Circuits welcomed the occasional visits of the missionaries, rejoicing in the power they had over the people, and setting themselves to gather in and permanently shepherd those impressed by their preaching. We do not mean that none disliked such departures from " regular " Methodist routine, as their proceedings involved ; for there will always be men who cannot distinguish between the extraordinary and the irregular, just as, on the other hand, there will always be men who think that, because they are irregular they are extraordinary. In the years of which we are speaking, however, we find no trace of coldness on the part of any one.

CHAPTER XII.

At the Conference of 1805 the two yoke-fellows were separated, and Mr Ouseley was sent forth in connection with his dear old friend William Hamilton, whose letter in a former chapter throws clear light both on the spirit of their joint labours and on its general features. Mr Graham was appointed with a new colleague, Mr Andrew Taylor, and four other missionaries were employed. Mr Langtree mentions the trial of a man named Caulfield, from Granard, for throwing dirt in Mr Ouseley's face. He was convicted and imprisoned. The morning after the trial, Mr Ouseley was expected to preach, at six o'clock, in the chapel; but Mr Langtree, an hour earlier, heard singing in the street, and found him surrounded by a number of labourers, who were standing with their spades waiting to be hired. He was preaching to them in their own tongue, and after doing so, went to his congregation in the chapel; and he adds, " Often, in the course of a day's ride with him, have I witnessed the same aptness to teach." The same author quotes a letter of Mr Ouseley, rejoicing in the appearance of a revival in

Dublin, and especially upon the manifest blessing resting on the labours of Lorenzo Dow, of whom he speaks as "rude in speech, yet not in knowledge," and says that even St Paul might have been seen ranging through vast countries, poor-looking and sometimes ragged and starved in appearance; and he doubts whether, if he came to Ireland, and the people did not know who he was, they would all receive him, even though they saw the work of God prospering in his hands. In a letter from Granard, on the 8th of March 1806, addressed to Dr Coke, and signed by both the missionaries, they mention that, after preaching at Cootehill, a man came to speak to them privately, stating that he and his wife had gone to confession the day previously, but that the priest would not receive the dues, "unless they added a hank of yarn." He also stated that the wife of a neighbour having died in childbirth, her husband and he went to the priest to get him "to do the rites of divinity for her," that is, to say five masses for the repose of her soul. The husband, not having paid as promptly as the priest thought right, he called out to him in the open congregation, and said he would excommunicate him if he did not pay him five-and-fivepence quickly. After the poor fellow had received counsel, he went down on his knees, and requested the prayers and blessings of the missionaries.

In 1806, Dr Adam Clarke wrote at great length to Mr Ouseley, stating that, in the Committee of the British and Foreign Bible Society, the utility of printing the Scriptures in the Irish language had been seriously discussed, some alleging that it was altogether unnecessary, and supporting their opinion by letters from clergymen and other persons of authority. One sentence is very striking, "I am satisfied that any language in a civilised country, that has to cope with another at the same place, must soon perish if the Scriptures do not exist in it." The vitality of the Keltic language among the small population of Wales, immediately joining the great population of England, as contrasted with the rapidity of its disappearance in the more numerous population of Ireland, separated by sea from England, is one of the most striking illustrations of the effect of the Bible and preaching on the life of a language. In a Roman Catholic country, the want of the Bible in the house, and of the mother-tongue in worship, leaves a new language, if it has superior prestige, an open field for speedy victory. We need not say what the reply of Mr Ouseley would be to such an inquiry. Dr Clarke had also raised some questions as to the legends and superstitions of Ireland, and Mr Ouseley gave his opinion very decidedly that, in substance, they were more ancient than the introduction of Christianity into the country, and were, really, but variations of the previously existing heathenism.

The following incidents, furnished by the Rev. James Tobias, belong partly to a later period, but are inserted together : " About the year 1805, when Mr Ouseley was associated with William Hamilton, also of racy speech, he visited Enniscorthy, which was then included in the Wicklow Circuit, and on a market-day preached, the upper step of the stone stairs of the market-house being his

L

pulpit. In his discourse, which was pretty quietly listened to, he—to use a phrase of his own—'gently opened up the errors of Popery,' closing with a promise to return, and preach there again on the next market-day. All his gentleness, however, did not avail. Some of his sayings reached the ears of the priests, and their ire was aroused; and his friends in the town learned that so strong a feeling had been excited against him as to make it dangerous for him to fulfil his intention. When he arrived in the town, the friends sought to dissuade him from the attempt; but his answer was, ' Children, what would you have me do? Is it not my Master's work? Am I not pledged to do it? Would you break my heart by hindering me?' Opposition was then given up; and some of them, with fear and trembling, but with many prayers, accompanied him to the ground. He took his stand, put off his hat, assumed his black velvet cap, and, after a few moments spent in silent prayer, commenced to sing. People began to gather round him, and, during the singing of a few verses, were quiet, and apparently attentive, but soon began to be restless and noisy. He then commenced to pray, and quietness for a short time followed; but presently, as the crowd increased, it became uneasy, and even turbulent. He closed his prayer, and began to preach; but evidently his audience were not disposed to hear him. Before many sentences had been uttered, missiles began to fly—at first, not of a very destructive character, being refuse vegetables, potatoes, turnips, &c.; but before long, harder materials were thrown—brickbats and stones, some of which reached him and inflicted slight wounds. He stopped, and, after a pause, cried out, 'Boys dear, what's the matter with you to-day? Won't you let an old man talk to you a little?' 'We don't want to hear a word out of your old head,' was the prompt reply from one in the crowd. 'But I want to tell you what, I think, you would like to hear.' 'No, we'll like nothing you can tell us.' 'How do you know? I want to tell you a story about one you all say you respect and love.' 'Who's that?' 'The blessed Virgin.' 'Och, and what do *you* know about the blessed Virgin?' 'More than you think; and I'm sure you'll be pleased with what I have to tell you, if you'll only listen to me.' 'Come, then,' said another voice, 'let us hear what he has to say about the Holy Mother.' And there was a lull, and the missionary began : 'There was once a young couple to be married, belonging to a little town called Cana. It's away in that country where our blessed Saviour spent a great part of His life among us ; and the decent people whose children were to be married thought it right to invite the blessed Virgin to the wedding-feast, and her blessed Son too, and some of His disciples ; and they all thought it right to come. As they sat at table, the Virgin Mother thought she saw that the wine provided for the entertainment began to run short, and she was troubled lest the decent young people should be shamed before their neighbours ; and so she whispered to her blessed Son, "They have no wine." "Don't let that trouble you, ma'am," said He. And in a minute or two after, she, knowing well what was in His good heart, said to one of the servants that was passing behind them, "Whatsoever He saith unto

you, do it." Accordingly, by-and-by, our blessed Lord
said to another of them —I suppose they had passed
the word among themselves—"Fill those large water-
pots with water.". (There were six of them standing
in a corner of the room, and they held nearly three
gallons apiece, for the people of those countries
use a great deal of water every day.) And, re-
membering the words of the Holy Virgin, they did
His bidding, and came back, and said, "Sir, they are
full to the brim." "Take some, then, to the master,
at the head of the table," He said. And they did so,
and the master tasted it, and, lo and behold you! it
was wine, and the best of wine too! And there was
plenty of it for the feast, ay, and, it may be, some
left to help the young couple setting up house-keep-
ing. And all that, you see, came of the servants
taking the advice of the blessed Virgin, and doing
what she bid them. Now, if she was here among us
this day, she would give just the same advice to
every one of us, " Whatsoever *He* saith to you, do
it;" and with good reason too, for well she knows
there is nothing but love in His heart to us, and
nothing but wisdom comes from His lips. And now
I'll tell you some of the things He says to us. He
says, " Strive to enter in at the strait gate ; for many,
I say unto you, will strive to enter in, and shall not
be able." ' And straightway the preacher briefly, but
clearly and forcibly, expounded the nature of the gate
of life, its straitness, and the dread necessity for
pressing into it, winding up with the Virgin's
counsel, ' Whatsoever He saith unto you, do it.' In
like manner he explained, and pressed upon his
hearers, some other of the weighty words of our

divine Lord,—'Except a man be born of water and of the Spirit, he cannot enter into the kingdom of God;' and, 'If any man will come after me, let him deny himself, and take up his cross daily, and follow me,'—enforcing his exhortation in each instance by the Virgin's counsel to the servants at Cana. 'But no,' at last he broke forth, 'no; with all the love and reverence you pretend for the blessed Virgin, you won't take her advice, but will listen willingly to any drunken schoolmaster that will wheedle you into a public-house, and put mischief and wickedness into your heads.' Here he was interrupted by a voice, which seemed to be that of an old man, exclaiming, 'True for you, true for ye! If you were tellin' lies all the days of your life, it's the truth you're tellin' now.' And so the preacher got leave to finish his discourse with not a little of good effect.

"When he was travelling in the north of Ireland one day, about the year 1814 or 1815, in company with the Rev. Henry Deery, as they jogged along on horseback, they heard the voices of young girls blithely singing, and through an open doorway at the roadside saw a group of them in the house, employed in 'scutching' flax [*i.e.*, stripping off the husk from the fibre; the former, falling in fragments to the ground, is termed 'shows,' or 'shaws']. Ouseley pulled up, saying, 'Brother Deery, there's work for us here; take hold of my reins;' and, quickly alighting, entered the house, taking off his hat, and saying, 'God save you, children.' 'Save you kindly, sir,' was the cheerful response. 'What is this you're doing?' 'Scutching flax, sir.' 'Scutching flax! what's that for?' 'Ah, don't you know what flax is, sir? Sure, it's what your shirt is made of.' ' What my shirt is made of! how can that be?' 'Don't you see, sir?' said one of the elder girls, holding up a ' strick ' (or ' strike ')—in plain language, a bunch of flax—which had been partially *scutched*, and showing Mr Ouseley the fibre. ' That's what we do spin into yarn, and the weavers make the yarn into the kind of cloth your shirt is made of.' ' Oh, I see, I see!' said Mr Ouseley ; ' thank you, my dear. And what is all this lying about the floor?' pointing to the heap of chaff which lay at the feet of each of the workers. ' Them's the shows, sir.' ' Shows, my dear! and what will you make of them?' ' Make of them, sir?'—and there was a little laugh among the girls. ' Why, nobody could make anything of them.' ' And weren't they a part of the flax a while ago?' asked he. ' To be sure, sir; but they're good for nothing now, except to be burnt; and a bad fire they make.' ' Oh, I understand, I understand,' said the preacher; and then very solemnly went on : ' And, children dear, just so will the Lord Jesus Christ ' (and here every head was bowed) ' come one day with all His holy angels, and He will *scutch* the world, and He will gather together all that is good, every one that is fit for His kingdom, and take them to Himself; and the rest—the shows, the chaff—He will cast into unquenchable fire !' ' The Lord save us !' was whispered around. ' Amen !' said the preacher; ' let us pray.' All were promptly on their knees, while Mr Ouseley, in fervent petitions, pleaded for the salvation of the young workers. Rising up, he blessed them in the name of the Lord, mounted his horse, and rode away, leaving them hardly sure that an angel had not visited them."

About this time the name of Threshers was adopted by those who represented the party of chronic disorder in the country. Mr Ouseley relates in a letter to Mr Langtree, that as he came through the mountains, he was told by the people where he had preached that they were afraid of the Threshers, and that the preachers could not come any more; but " next morning, when the people came together, four or five houses were open to receive us." Thence, without tasting food, he went off to another place and gathered the people, who wept vehemently; and as he was arranging for places where the preachers from Sligo could stay upon their visit, one Roman Catholic cried out, " Come, sir, two days in the week to my house, and welcome indeed." He says, " On Tuesday last I preached in a fair in the mountains, among the Threshers, and they gave me thousands of blessings." In another letter he mentions that he was getting the young people and children to commit the Holy Scriptures to memory. One boy had repeated part of a chapter, who did not yet know his letters. In a place where ten or twelve Romanists had joined the Society, the priest, a great drunkard, came threatening to curse them, and to make the hair fall off their heads, and when they were dying he would refuse them the " seal of Christ." But when Ouseley came round and ran into their cabins, the poor things sprang towards him with their eyes dancing with joy and affection. As he preached, " Oh, the priest, the priest!" cried one in Irish," why is he hindering us from all this comfort

and sweetness?" The next morning, a large barn
was filled, and it seemed like heaven upon earth.
One after another cried out for mercy, and found
peace with God. As they were about in equal
numbers Protestants and Catholics, one said that
"God is giving us one about of each sort."

The following "wondrous thing," as he calls it,
is in striking contrast with all his own experience.
We never find him having visions or manifestations of any particular kind whatever. Mr Langtree, in
printing the letter, states that on the 30th of June
1834, before doing so, he showed it to Mr Ouseley,
who perfectly remembered the whole narrative, stating that the matter made a great noise in the
country. Some people declared it could not have
been St Peter, but an evil spirit, for "why should
he come to a Protestant, and not to ourselves." The
priest, however, who was warned, had preached an
alarming sermon; and others said, "Be that as it
may, we have got one good sermon by it, at any
rate." The tale he tells his friend is as follows:—

"Matthew Rogers, of whom I think I made mention in a letter before, told me that on the night in
which he was struggling for salvation (a night or
two after I was last round), he came out of his bed,
and for an hour or two he was in an agony of
prayer, his family being asleep. While yet he
prayed, with his face to the ground, he saw a light
suddenly shining, and conceiving the house had
taken fire, he lifted himself up to see where; but to
his astonishment the house was full of light, and two
personages stood by him, one like our Saviour nailed
to the cross, looking upward, and two straps tied

under His chin, binding a crown of thorns on His head. The other, accosting him, said, ' Be not afraid; we are not bad spirits, but good : my name is Peter; I am come with the Lord. Only pray on, and no harm will happen unto you. Go to the Priest Gilboy, and tell him to quit his drinking whisky, and to preach to the people. The priests are destroying, and not doing by their people as they ought.' He replied, having lost all fear, 'Is it not fitter for some of his own flock to warn him than me ? ' To which the apparition answered, ' You will have to go yourself.' Rogers again replied, ' But he will not believe me.' Then said he, ' Go, and I will give you a token that he will know, and he will believe you. Tell him that he was lately in a passion, pursuing a person who had vexed him ; and when passing over a bridge, his horse stumbled, and threw him over the battlement : he was in danger of being killed, but the Lord pitied and saved him at that time that he might repent; therefore, go and warn him.' In an instant, while he yet wished to speak more, all vanished. The person on the cross did not speak at all. Rogers is counted a steady, sensible, respectable man. He did warn the priest, who attempted not to deny the token given him, but said he would die if he would quit the whisky ; and hoped St Peter would not be angry if he should take a little."

Shortly afterwards, he cries, in the same breath, " More good news : the Romanists have bought the Testaments as fast as the Protestants ; " and then says, " The Threshers have come upon the poor mare, but they have only taken off her four shoes, and the hair of her tail." A Romanist from Killala, who had

heard him preach on the oil and purgatory, came to
consult him, took home a Testament, and told him
that the priests had been hearing him, though they
kept out of sight.   Mr Graham Campbell mentions
having visited an old woman of eighty-five, in the
county of Wexford, sixty-seven years after the period
of which we are now writing.   She had been passing
through the street of Newtownbarry, where Hamilton
and Ouseley were preaching.   The latter was singing
a hymn to the air of Tara's Hall, which attracted her,
and she came that evening to hear Mr Ouseley's
sermon, and went home to blame her mistress for
having "informed the preacher on her," for she
declared, "He showed me all that ever I did."
Finding, however, that her mistress was innocent, she
was convinced that the message had come from God,
and through a long lapse of years she adorned the profession of the gospel, and in extreme old age rejoiced
in hope of the glory of God.

Mr Reilly, alluding to the labours of his future
colleague about this time, mentions a fact which may
stand side by side with that of the "scutchers"
related by Mr Tobias.   One fine summer's day, Mr
Ouseley saw some men cutting peat.   He said, "What
are you doing, boys?"   "We are cutting turf, sir,"
was the reply.   "Sure, you don't require it this fine
weather?"   "No, sir, we don't want it now, but we
will want it in the cold days of winter, and in the
long nights."   "And won't it be time enough to cut
it when you want it, and let the winter provide for
itself?"   "Oh, *muisha*, sir, it would be too late
then."   It will be readily seen that he had been
working for a text, and having now got it, would

proceed with his sermon. Mr Reilly adds the following fact at the same time, though to us it appears
to belong to a later date :—

"A gentleman in Dublin told him that once, when
under great anxiety for the salvation of an eminent
friend of his, he had in vain applied to several clergymen to accompany him on a visit, with a view to
speaking to the nobleman in question about his soul.
One day he said to himself, 'I had a promise from
B—— that he would come with me, but six months
have elapsed, and he has not fulfilled his promise.
He is like every one else, afraid of his lordship. Oh,
will nobody come with me to see my dear lord? I
will go to Gideon Ouseley. He is in town, and
he'll come with me.' The gentleman went to Mr
Ouseley, and carried him off to the house of the noble
lord. The object of their visit being intimated by
the gentleman, Mr Ouseley affectionately urged home
upon his lordship the indispensable necessity of preparation for the eternal world. 'Mr Ouseley,' he
replied, 'public business must be attended to, and
we have no time for these things.' 'But, my lord,'
said Gideon, 'we must find time to die, and we
must be prepared for that event.' The reply was,
'And what am I to do, Mr Ouseley?' 'There's
the New Testament, which contains the will of the
Lord Jesus Christ, and tells you what you are to do,
my lord.' 'But, Mr Ouseley, though there are
many things in that book which I can understand,
and do admire, I must confess there are other things
which I cannot agree with.' 'Ah, my lord, that
will never do. What if your lordship had a
case submitted to you for an opinion, and after

your opinion had been drawn up with the utmost care and legal accuracy, the person should say, " Why, my lord, there's part of this—a large part—good; but with other parts I can't agree." What would you say, my lord? ' ' Ah, I perceive your meaning. We must receive the whole of it as a revelation from God.' ' Exactly so, my lord. Take up that Book, believe what it says, and do what it commands, and you will, my lord, be prepared by His mercy for the hour of death and for the day when the Great Judge shall appear.' " Mr Reilly adds that " as he reasoned of righteousness, temperance, and judgment to come, Felix trembled "—the great man expressed his feelings of gratitude, and invited the two friends to dinner. Mr Ouseley sought faithfully to impress him with the realities of the world upon the threshold of which it was said he was standing; but whether any beneficial results followed is not known.

Mr Reilly further mentions that a favourite name for Mr Ouseley among the country-folk was *Sheedd-no-var,* which he translates as " the silk of men; " it seems to express the strong feeling of personal affection with which they always regarded him, when not excited against him by some hostile influences. The intense love he bore to them was expressed in his every tone and movement, and could not fail of making its impression on their hearts. It is said that sometimes during his sermons the congregation would simultaneously rise from their seats, as by a sudden impulse, and, all falling down, cry out, with earnest tears, seeking for mercy. In the neighbourhood of Ballina and

Sligo, two helpers are mentioned, differing from his ordinary Methodist fellow-labourers : one, the curate of Easky, a village in the county of Sligo, not far from Ballina, who is spoken of as labouring very zealously, and having Ouseley and Hamilton at meetings in his church; and the other, the Rev. Mr Caldwell, of Sligo, a minister of the Presbyterian Church, who, after he had himself experienced a great change, would help him in his field-meetings and prayer-meetings, remaining for hours together praying with the penitents, as they sought mercy.

In 1807, Hamilton and Ouseley were appointed to the counties of Sligo, Mayo, and Galway, ground on which they were not strangers. The population was thin, the Protestants few, and the important places lay far apart. From the remote corners of Erris, a typical highland tract on the coast of Mayo, to the comparatively civilised regions in the east of Galway, Roscommon, and Sligo, they could be tracked by tales of risks, escapes, and happy conversions.

While labouring with great success in the neighbourhood of Ballina, Mr Ouseley published a series of letters to Dr Bellew, the Roman Catholic bishop of Ardnaree, as the ancient portion of the same town on the Sligo side of the Moy is called. These tracts appear to have been the commencement of his polemical publications. They were called forth by the violence to which he and his fellow-labourers as well as their converts were subject. He evidently thinks that the influence exerted by Bishop Bellew was rather a stimulating than a moderating one; for he plainly says, after alleging many acts of violence, that they were mainly due to the bishop; and among cases of cursing, mentions, " You cursed a friar for begging in the parish." After much controversial matter, he comes to particulars, making statements which illustrate, not only the point immediately in hand, but the condition of the country generally. " Some of the poor in your diocese," he says, " lest the curse of the clergy should light on them, were compelled to go as public spectacles, bare-headed and bare-footed, in the cold from their own houses, and along through the streets to the chapel, and there to walk on their bare knees from the door, through the chapel, and from one chapel to another—some in Crossmolina, by Priest Hughes; some here lately, by Priest Walsh; and some in other places — not for any of the monstrous crimes daily committed against God, but for having with sighs and tears heard us preach the gospel of Christ. I remember Priest Grady, of Ballymote, about nine years ago, when I preached to the people there, brought in the same manner a number of these poor creatures, bare-headed and bare-footed, through the streets, as public spectacles, and then made them kneel down to ask his pardon, and God's, for having heard His Holy Word." He further states, that " Priest Flannagan, at Ballycastle, in the barony of Tyrawly, not long before, took oath publicly on the Book of God, that no Protestant would ever enter the kingdom of heaven. He took a second oath, that the Protestant Testament, which he had in his hand, was a false one. He also took a Testament from a Romanist young man, and had it locked up.

" The Priest Gilboy, of Migavnagh, in the same barony, in his drunkenness and in the presence of Protestants, swore by the hand of God that we were false prophets. At a public funeral, when a young man had reproved one for swearing, the same priest prayed most earnestly that his seven curses, the curse of God, and bad luck, might alight on any one that would listen to him or to us. Priest Hopkins, helper of Priest Hughes of Crossmolina, declared that any one who would·listen to Ouseley would be bound to the devil in the flames of hell for ever. Priest Walsh, of Ardnaree, beat some people with a stick in the streets on the Sabbath-day, because they had been to hear for themselves. Priest Kelly, of Ballysakeeny, came into the house of a Protestant, drunk and roaring forth curses, and asked the owner of the house if he did not let some of the Methodists into his house. He beat a young man of his own flock severely for living with a Protestant, in a village where we preached; and declared upon his honour, and again upon his honour, that he would banish the fellow, and not let any priest receive him, on account of his having heard these false prophets.

" On the 22d of November last, as I was preaching in the street in the town of Tuam to a large flock as solemn as death, and was explaining out of a Roman bishop's book (Challoner's 'Meditations') the nature and necessity of true faith, into the crowd runs a young man—Priest Hughes, just from Maynooth—crying out, 'O Catholics! O Catholics! why are you listening to this devil? Follow me!'"

In the midst of all this, writing to his friend Mr

Langtree, he says that instead of feeling disheartened by such opposition, he was full of courage and thanksgiving. He speaks of one village where twelve persons had lately found peace, four of them being Romanists. "When I am away, the priest threatens, curses, and exhorts them to hear me no more; but when I last came back, they broke their cords like Samson, weeping and praying—young men, men, women, and children. Last Thursday a priest came and called out to one of the hearers, 'Polly, you are here again, hearing the preacher; Polly, I will cut you off, I will drive you from my flock, I will excommunicate you; and John Willis, and Thady Twohy, and John, and all of you; so I will.' 'Well, sir,' said Polly, 'so you can, I am sure; but I hope you cannot drive us from God!' He walked off, and next day sent his man to gather corn from them all; but they all refused, and would not give him a grain." Mr Ouseley then relates how the little daughter of one of them, having found peace in a class-meeting, stood up and said, "Oh, if you but felt what I feel; oh, if you would but get the love of God, you would never be afraid of the priest again!"

Mr Hamilton, writing also to Langtree, says, "Last Christmas we were waylaid and robbed of our books. Ouseley was hurt, and lost his hat in the fray. He had to ride seven miles before he got one. It happened near Eyrecourt on the Shannon. We had preached there that day, and had a battle with the priest and his people. The priest beat my horse greatly, and the people dragged him down the street, and I on his back; but the soldiers got me into the barrack-yard. Ouseley was hurt there too. The soldiers then got arms, loaded their pieces, fixed their bayonets, marched out before us, and formed square about us both in the street, until we preached to the market-people. They then put us safe out of the town, but never thought our persecutors had got before us, and lay concealed until we came up; and then they surrounded us with horrid shouting, as if Scullabogue Barn had been on fire. At another time, a big priest and I were in holds of each other. He had been going to pull my Ouseley down. I could easily have injured him, for he was very drunk."

The Rev. John Duncan says, " Frank Shannon was returning home one market-day from Ballina, when he was attracted by the voice of Ouseley preaching in the street, in Irish. It had a charm for the ear of Frank, and he and his wife pushed their way through the crowd to get near the preacher. After listening for a while, the wife, not altogether relishing his home thrusts, plucked her husband's coat, and asked him to leave. ' Wait till we hear him out,' was the reply. The preacher became more pointed and earnest. A second and third effort from the wife to draw Frank off met with the reply, ' Wait till he's done.' The gospel truths heard on that occasion made a lodgement in a mind exceedingly dark, and previously wholly destitute of the fear of God; and Frank went home a convinced sinner. It was the turning-point in his life. Mr Ouseley soon found his way to Ballinagar, Frank's neighbourhood, five miles from Ballina. He was entertained in the house of a man far better off than Shannon, and there preached ' the disease and the

M

cure,' as he was wont to express it.   Several received
the truth, and were formed into a class.   Of these
Frank was one of the first.   He entered into the
liberty of God's children, and at once took his stand
with them.   From that time until his death, the
class-meeting was a service he greatly loved, and from
which he never willingly absented himself.   And this,
with his unceasing prayer, helped to nourish his deep
piety, and his unwavering stability, for half a century.

"The man in whose house Mr Ouseley preached,
unwilling either to bear the reproach or the expense,
gave him, by his manner, to feel this; and Mr
Ouseley, one night, after preaching, when announcing for his next visit to that place, said, pointing
to Frank Shannon, 'Frank, I'll stop and preach
in your house.'   'Ah, sir,' said Frank, 'I would
be delighted to have you in my house; but what
shall I do for a bed?   The only one myself and
my wife have to lie on is straw.'   'Can you give
me straw and a blanket?' asked the missionary.
'I can, sir,' said Frank gladly.   'Then I'll be
with you, please God, this night month,' said
Ouseley.   'Ah, then, sir, it's myself will have a
cead mille falthe (*Anglicè,* "a hundred thousand
welcomes") for you.'   'And sure enough,' said
Frank, with an air of triumph, when telling me
this (about 1841 or 1842), 'he came, and preached,
and held the prayer-meeting, and met the class, *and
slept on the straw,* and put up with my poor fare;
and he continued to come regularly until he left the
mission, and he often came since.   And,' added the
good man, 'I have never been a month since without
a preacher.   I have sometimes had the servants of

God two together. Frequently, I have had them once a fortnight, and oftener. And, best of all, I have my wife converted, all my children converted, and their houses the preachers' home. And now, glory be to God, all my grandchildren who are capable of it are converted ' (for we were at the time favoured with a gracious visitation of saving power), ' and my highest wish, next to beholding my glorious Lord, is to see my spiritual father, Gideon Ouseley, in heaven.' This was said with weeping eyes, and with an earnestness and pathos which showed that the hope of the aged pilgrim was full of immortality.

" While the property and family of the man whose house Mr Ouseley forsook all melted away, Frank Shannon became comfortable as a small farmer, reared and educated his family, lived a blessing in the neighbourhood, died in the triumph of faith, and has left his offspring behind him following in his steps."

Both ministers of the Ballina Circuit were entertained periodically in Frank's house, when Mr Duncan was stationed there. Mr Duncan says, " The house of the old man was what some would call a very humble one; but it was clean and comfortable, and happy too, for it was sanctified by a deep and all-pervading piety. . . . He was familiar with the Holy Bible, for which he had the profoundest reverence, and would often quote it in conversation. He was a man of much prayer, and would often leave his work to plead with God beneath the hedges of his fields, or in one of the outhouses. He blessed God for the possession of that ' perfect peace ' which ' casteth out fear.' All who knew him respected him. The godless would say, ' Yes, Frank is a good man ; ' but those who knew him best would say, ' He is a holy man.' ".

In 1809, for the first time, Ouseley speaks of serious illness. By lying in a room with a damp floor, he contracted cold and ague, but seems to have been able, after a few days, to resume work. At this time he was labouring chiefly in the county of Clare, a hard and stony ground, with a few scattered handfuls of Protestants, and immense distances to travel. Hamilton and he sought out, not only the little groups of Protestants, but it is the impression of Mr Nelson that over the whole extent of that large county, Mr Ouseley did not leave a single Protestant family that he did not find out and visit. The most secluded tracts on the wild coast beaten by the Atlantic, the mountains and the bogs, were all traversed in search of even one lost sheep. The accommodation obtainable would sometimes be in a cottage, sometimes in a cabin, sometimes in a hovel. With the single exception of the case we have just cited, we have no hint from him of the sort of place he had to sleep in, or the sort of fare he enjoyed. But Mr Reilly tells us that when Ouseley gave him his " plan " for travelling, there was one place which he never failed to mark with this note, " Sleep in the loft ! " and this was not the cabin of some wretched labourer, but of one who was called by Mr Reilly a wealthy farmer. The loft indicated was the choice portion of the house, because the only dry one. It consisted of a bit of boarded floor, between the rafters over part of the kitchen. It was reached by a step-ladder, and one could not stand upright in it. The old couple made it their bedroom, and in spite of Ouseley's recommendation to Reilly, the latter never procured admission to it but once. The preacher's room was a back one, with an earthen floor, and a small window choked with nettles and hemlock. The walls were covered with sepulchral green, and the earthen floor was so damp that " when I entered," says Reilly, " at any time, my feet sank into it; and when I entered my bed, I thought of my grave." On this ground, the brave and faithful William Hamilton was soon disabled, and yet he lived to mourn over the death of his beloved Gideon Ouseley. The next colleague of the latter, Mr William Rutledge, carried into the work a frame unequal to its hardships. He lived long enough to record of his leader, " Why, Mr Ouseley preaches more on his horse's back, as he rides along his way, than in all his sermons." Before Rutledge had spent an entire year in missionary labour, he was laid low; and this, of course, threw additional care and work on Ouseley, who toiled on.

From Clare, crossing the broad Shannon into Tipperary, Mr Ouseley penetrated to the town of Borrissokane. In writing to Dr Coke, he says that when he entered it alone, "last Christmas twelvemonth, there were no Methodists in the place but one, and he a Baptist; nor did I know a single person in it. I was told it was a most wicked place, in which many efforts to preach the gospel had been baffled." Three persons are mentioned, Messrs Hackett, Holland, and Reid, as having been kindly and seriously disposed. Here the preaching of Mr Ouseley was attended with a power from on high, remarkable even for him. On Easter Monday, 1810, accompanied by the Rev. Adam Averell, he took down the names of sixty persons as admitted on trial into the Methodist Society. One day, while he was standing upon a table in the street preaching to a crowd, a youth, called Thomas Ballard, heard him and cried, "What must I do to be saved?" He lived and died a faithful Christian minister, and left sons behind him to follow in the father's steps. Both Nelson and Reilly speak with deep and reverential feeling of the manifestations of the converting power of God in Borrissokane and its neighbourhood at this time, and the years succeeding. The permanent walk of the converts yielded an accumulating testimony to the reality of the work.

Mr Edward Rigby, now a City Missionary (in London), says, "It is more than sixty years since I first heard Mr Ouseley. I see him now as distinctly —his gestures, his fire, his pathos, his smile, his benignity, his powerful persuasiveness and tact, and his peculiar shake of the hand—as ever I did. If ever heart went with hand to a brother or sister, it did so in Gideon Ouseley's shake. . . . My early days were passed in Enniscorthy, on the beautiful, blood-stained river Slaney, which flows beneath Vinegar Hill, notorious for the murder of Protestants in 1798. When very young I was taken to the Methodist preaching, in a large attic, a chair being the pulpit, and frequently the preacher was a bandsman in full military uniform. It was always too small for the gatherings which followed ' the men in black caps and long gaiters.' Before and after the erection of the chapel, opened in or about 1810 by the Rev. Adam Averell, Messrs Graham and Ouseley preached on Sunday mornings and evenings in large corn-stores, still standing, opposite the new and pretty

Wesleyan chapel near the castle, the old chapel being converted into a foundry. The services in the stores were usually preceded by outdoor services in some part of the town. I was known as a singer, and was looked for in outdoor services. Mr Ouseley used to say, with his coaxing smile, 'Now, Edward, my lad, let your voice be heard.' In 1814 I sang in the church, with several others. Mr Ouseley had preached at ten o'clock in the chapel, and went thence to the church. When the service was over, I was told by an old friend, now in heaven, to hasten to the corner of Church Street, as Mr Ouseley was going to preach. I joined the crowd. He read the hymn,

> 'When I survey the wondrous cross,'

first in English and then in Irish. Whilst reading it in Irish, the crowd greatly increased; whatever noise there had been before, ceased; and the people all remained to the end. His text was Acts x. 34, 35. The sermon was short, but pithy, with a modest touch of controversy. He dwelt chiefly on Peter's teaching, and quoted the Rhemish Testament; and described the character of God as set forth in the Bible, both Douay and Authorised, and finally the acceptance and approval by Him of the righteousness indicated. The interchanges between the English and the Irish languages, kept the hearers perfectly quiet. At that time there was a good deal of Irish spoken in the neighbourhood, but it has totally disappeared. Half the audience were Romanists.

" In 1815, Mr Ouseley and Mr Taylor met in the town, and preached in the chapel and streets. The soldiers were invited to the chapel, and it was filled, and persons stood outside to hear. One of Mr Ouseley's texts was Psalm xl. 2. He described pits, dark, dismal, and yawning; and in describing hell, he leaned over the pulpit, and looked down, as into perdition, and quoted several scriptures as descriptive of its horrors and duration, which occasioned much feeling.

"When I was a schoolboy, in 1808 or 1809, on a market-day, it poured with rain when school was dismissed for dinner at noon. We were all in haste because of the rain, but were met by schoolfellows who reported that the 'black caps and saddle-bags' were preaching in Irish at the market-house. It lay on my way home, and at that time neither young nor old cared as much for a shower of rain as people do now, and an umbrella was a novelty, there being hardly one in twenty miles, in the humbler walks of life. There was a great crowd, and great attention and much feeling were evinced while Mr Graham was speaking; and at the close of his address, Mr Ouseley began most pathetically, when a woman near me began to weep. After a few words, he gave out his text, laying a strong emphasis on particular words. It was Isaiah lv. 1, read first in English, and then in Irish. While he was making powerful appeals, the priest, who lodged over the way, crossed the street, enveloped in a huge greatcoat with several folding capes, and bustled into the midst of the assembly. He listened for a while, and then peremptorily ordered his flock to leave. No one stirred, as the preacher did not cease. The priest then undid his outer garment, and produced a large whip, with the thong of which he belaboured every one near him, and away went men, women, and boys, like a flock of summer flies fanned away by a handkerchief, only to return again when the handkerchief has been restored to the pocket. The priest, when the people ran away, held up the whip, and threatened Mr Ouseley, saying, that ' but for the law, I would serve you the same.' Having so delivered himself, he hastened back to his quarters ; and the people, with equal haste, returned to hear the end of the discourse. There was preaching in the stores on the following Sunday, and crowds attended.

"On another occasion, Mr Ouseley was accompanied to Enniscorthy by one who both spoke the Irish tongue, and had the voice of a Boanerges. They preached in the market-place on market-day, and on Sunday at noon, when the people were leaving last mass. Two priests looked on from a distance, but did nothing, although two hundred of their people stood listening to persuasive truth. On Monday morning, at ten o'clock, both stood on the market-house steps, and preached ; and, while they were doing so, a man who affected to be drunk began to sing a vulgar song and perform antics, but was soon sent adrift by Mr Williams, a Methodist—a man always ready to protect those who needed it, and more feared than loved by those who hated Protestantism.

"At another time, Mr Ouseley paid us a hurried visit, preaching in the street and the chapel, and leading special prayer-meetings. It was the first time I ever saw the ' penitent form,' but I then saw not a few happy results. At this visit, when Mr Ouseley was just giving out his text in the market-place, from Isaiah iii. 10, 11, ' Say ye to the righteous,' &c., two men began to quarrel. A strong emphasis was laid by the preacher on the words ' say ' and ' woe,' and some others, and the oddness of the thing attracted the quarrellers as well as others, and there was an end to the quarrel, and the discourse was listened to with the desired result. The hymn, ' And am I only born to die?' was sung with great fervour, and a prayer-meeting in the chapel afterward was well attended. This was a refreshing season. The last time I was in Enniscorthy, I inquired if the same could be done in the market-place as used to be, and the answer was, ' The preacher would be likely to lose his life.' Such is the change with that of the population."

CHAPTER XIII.

LABOURS IN CONNECTION WITH MESSRS NELSON, REILLY, AND OTHERS.

In 1810, John Nelson and William Reilly were appointed to share with Ouseley his hard lot and endless toils in Clare. The former still survives in hale and happy old age, a noble specimen of the men who did God's work side by side with Ouseley. The latter, in his biography, has left permanent records illustrating the character of Gideon. He first met him as his colleague on a Sunday evening, on the western bank of the Shannon at Killaloe. Already that day the young missionary had ridden some thirty-one miles, and preached, and had now to preach again before the veteran. After his sermon, Mr Ouseley gave an address, in which Reilly—deeply affected himself, and witnessing the power which moved the people — heard him relate the circumstances of his conversion, nineteen years before, when the Lord had taken away his intolerable burden of sin and guilt on " that Sunday morning; " and then, said Ouseley, three months afterwards, " my great Prince, who sits upon the throne, said, ' Behold, I make all things new.' "

Mr Reilly relates how he soon found out that he had

" to follow or move onwards," with a man possessing

> " A soul inured to pain,
>   To hardship, grief, and loss.
>   Bold to take up, firm to sustain,
>   The consecrated cross."

He had heard so much of Mr Ouseley, that he imagined that such a public man could not possibly find time to visit small places, or form or shepherd little Societies; but it proved to be far otherwise. In their long rides, every town through which they passed heard Gideon's deep voice roll out, in both English and Irish, the message of grace for all. One day, after they had travelled far to Ennistimond, where he preached with vehemence, they rode on five miles farther; and neither of them tasted anything until after the labours of the evening meeting closed about nine o'clock. This was always the case at that particular spot. The only pretence of a window in the house was one polygon piece of a broken pane stuck in a green sod. The next day they reached a place still more remote, where they were received by two women, the men being away at work. No sooner had they sat down in the cabin than Ouseley began to sing a hymn of thanksgiving for preserving and redeeming mercies. The two women went off to the fields, and bringing some sheaves of oats—because the time of potatoes was not yet, and the old ones were all gone—they toasted the grain over the fire, and then the missionaries literally saw the " two women grinding at the mill." Even at that time, and indeed much later, the hand-mill of the East was still represented in the *quern* of the farthest West, the shores of Coromandel and those of Connaught displaying the old unity of human want and supply, though half of Asia and the entire breadth of inventive Europe, with its new-fangled mills, lay between them.

Mr Reilly, one day riding alone to a preaching-place in a tongue of land called the "West," bounded by the Atlantic and the Shannon, found wilds succeeded by sterner wilds, till bare mountains, terrific cliffs, and the lone ocean were all the eye could see. He exclaimed, " O Mr Ouseley! Mr Ouseley! how did you find out this retreat?" At last a neat cot cropped up on the moor, disclosing the precious grains for which Ouseley had prospected. The family had already received the good word, and with them and a few neighbours Mr Reilly enjoyed the communion of the Church in the wilderness. The next day, as the young preacher rode along, with the peaks of Kerry and the estuary of the Shannon in full view, a vivid, evangelistic life was thrown into the picture, of which the natural framework was so magnificent, by the image of George Whitfield, who, a hundred years before, had landed in that little town of Carrigaholt on the right.

Speaking of his own leader, Mr Reilly says, " Some of the most hallowed reminiscences associated with the character of that saintly man, are those in which I witnessed his pure and fervent devotion. He made it a rule, when he travelled in company—and sometimes we were several weeks together—that when we retired we should alternately pray with and for each other, and for the work in which we were engaged. But his devout breathings, when alone, which I often overheard, were most affecting. It was difficult on such occasions to determine whether the love of lost men or the love of Christ predominated. "My gracious Master, my gracious Master," had generally the accompaniment, "Oh, poor lost sinners! oh, my deluded countrymen! O Lord, save my country!" He then quotes from Mr Noble, a later fellow-helper of Mr Ouseley, and his own son in the faith: "How often have I known this blessed man, when all the family with whom he lodged had retired to rest—how often have I known him to spend hours together, wrestling with God in ardent, mighty prayer for the conversion of lost souls; and he would plead with God in great earnestness, 'If Thy presence go not with me, carry us not up hence.'"

Study went with prayer. His sermons were so free that many would think them impromptu, whereas they were only extempore. The substance had been well thought out, the expression was as God gave it. On horseback, where he very often read, his favourite books, according to Mr Reilly, were old divines, or Gallagher's Irish Sermons, the Decrees of the Council of Trent in Latin, or the Greek Testament. In houses where he was entertained, he soon retired to apply himself to reading and writing.

One day, in Limerick, Mr Thomas Tracey accompanied him in a round of applications for subscriptions towards the building of some chapel. Mr Ouseley was constantly speaking to the persons with whom they met on points connected with the new birth. In the evening his sermon was on that subject. Mr Tracey said, "I always wondered how Mr Ouseley could get time to study his sermons; now, I am not surprised."

Such a student, if not unprepared, was not hampered by his preparation : free to take advantage of every incident and every inspiration, he was also apt to do so. The Rev. William Ferguson, whose venerable figure adorned the Irish Conference long after Ouseley had been laid asleep, tells us (as related, at length, by Mr Reilly) how on one occasion, in Limerick, he heard Ouseley preach in the barracks of the Sligo Militia, while under the window rolled the Shannon, from near the head of which river most of his hearers had come. Speaking on the words, " The simple passeth on, and is punished," he defined the simple as a man without the knowledge of God, and a stranger to the wisdom from above. He may be very acute in transacting the business of this life—an able statesman, a profound philosopher, an eminent artist, or a distinguished scholar —but he passes on, according to the course of this world, and dies unconverted. . . . His punishment —the place—the company—the duration. On the last point he said, " If you were to count a thousand years for every drop of water that ever flowed in the Shannon from Drumshambo to the sea, it would be a point compared with the eternity through which you will have to endure the wrath of God."

In company he was as much an evangelist as in the saddle or pulpit. Mr Reilly describes an evening party in Borrissokane, where Mr Ouseley, turning to the lady on one hand, whom he knew, quietly inquired respecting the one upon the other hand, " Is this lady born again?" The first replied, " She is of age: ask her." And the result was an almost instantaneous conversion, and a blessed influence upon the whole company. Again quoting from Mr Noble, he relates a case where Mr Ouseley had stopped to water his horse at a stream in the county of Wicklow, and saw a young woman standing at her father's door. He went up to her, took her by the hand, spoke to her for a few moments about her soul, and parting, prayed that the blessing of the Lord might rest upon her. Two years subsequently, after preaching, a young man came up to him and invited him to his house. On arriving the next evening, the hostess said to him, " Mr Ouseley, I believe you do not know me." " No, my dear, I don't." Recalling the scene at the door of the house by the stream, she said, " I am the person you spoke to on that occasion. Up to that period I had known nothing of the way of salvation through the Lord Jesus Christ ; but your observations resulted in my conversion. I am now married ; the young man who invited you is my husband, and is a class-leader. The Lord is with us, and is blessing us ; and we rejoice to see under our roof my father in the gospel."

In small towns, before preaching indoors, he would select an hour when the labouring men were sauntering about before supper ; and, getting under a tree, if possible with seats round it, would begin singing the plaintive air of " Molly Asthore " to a hymn in Irish or English. In larger towns, on the other hand, keeping to the saddle, he would place himself before a shop window, if possible that of an apothecary, and, above all, of a Roman Catholic, for both of these circumstances helped to deter the mob from throwing stones. In county towns he aimed at being present during the assizes, and by this time his name was so generally known, that, in the language of Mr Reilly, lawyers, magistrates, jurors, yeomen, and the lower orders crowded into his outdoor congregations.   The field-meetings—sometimes by barns, and occasionally on the lawn beside a mansion—were among his most favourite scenes of labour.   One of the latter is dwelt upon by Mr Reilly, evidently with reminiscences of very remarkable blessing.   It was held near Borrissokane, in the grounds of Mr Wilson of Ballineven, and attended by thousands from all parts of Lower Ormond.   After Mr Clegg had preached, came Mr Ouseley, and " Oh, with what effect! "   To house the converts over his wide field, he undertook the erection of chapels in eight separate towns.

In the spring of 1811, we find his first mention of Connemara in a letter to Dr Coke, where he speaks of dining with a priest of " rather good information," at the house of a gentleman who had for two years forsaken the mass.   He and the priest had a controversial, yet perfectly friendly, conversation.   He preached to three families, and some Papists, all of whom were in tears.   The gentleman showed the tenacity of company incident to such remote localities, and did not leave him until twelve o'clock at night, which, for him, when doing anything else but pleading among penitents seeking mercy, seems to have been an hour unknown.   He ends by saying, " They wished to lay an embargo on me, but I came away in the midst of a great storm, as I must, as it were, fly from place to place."   In the same year, alluding to the centre of his work in Tipperary, Borrissokane, he tells Dr Coke, " We have more than 150, perhaps nearly 200, in Society; and six blessed class-leaders."

N

About the same time, speaking of Clare, he says, "It is
the worst ground for the gospel I ever met with ;
but even there we have sons and daughters born
to God." He was soon greatly rejoiced by a remit-
tance from Mr Averell, then in England, amounting
to no less than £400, towards the building of the
various chapels which he had in hand. Mr Reilly
gives an interesting account of the way in which this
money was procured. One Saturday evening, preaching in the city of Galway, in a room like a cellar, in
a miserable back lane chiefly occupied with herring-
stores, he saw in the congregation an elderly gentleman whose appearance impressed him. At the close,
the stranger introduced himself as Mr Maberly of
London, and said, "Mr Reilly, this will never do.
The Methodists of Galway must have a fit place for
the worship of God. I am not a Methodist, I am a
Dissenter ; but on my return to London, I will speak
to some of my friends, and I hope I shall get something to assist you in building a suitable chapel."
Mr Maberly, who belonged, as Mr Reilly believes, to
the Congregational body, procured £250, and gave it
to Mr Averell, then attending the London Conference. The latter procured £150 more, and so was
enabled to send Ouseley what, at that time, seemed a
very large amount.

It was in some of the tours of which we are now
speaking that one was converted, who proved to be
fruit of rare value. James Horne, then a soldier,
soon became a public exhorter, and gave such proof
of gifts and grace that his discharge was procured,
and eventually he ran a noble race in the West Indies
as a missionary, and had a son who became a missionary in Western Africa.

Mr Ouseley used to relate the following illustrations of his manner in dealing with Roman Catholics. He reports as an eyewitness. Conversing with a Romanist, Mr Ouseley learns that he has been at confession; "And what good do you get from that, my child?" "Och, and I get plenty, your riverence. I get absolution, and everything is put right for my soul." "And how long does it last, my child?" "Och, and shure enough, not long; for I'm soon back to my ould ways, and I'm in need of absolution again." "And so, my child, you're no better. Your old sin has still the old power over you. You're not cured. Don't you see that? You're not cured. Now, suppose you had the falling sickness, and that you had tried every way you could think of for a cure; but you're no better—rather worse. One day a man comes to your village, and sends word round by the bellman that he has a never-failing cure for the falling sickness. 'Och,' you think, 'I may be cured after all!' and you're very glad, and away you go to him, with your money; and you find him with a robe and a ribbon upon him; and he asks you a lot of questions; then he says some words in a strange tongue, and waves his hands over you, and tells you you're cured. That would make you happy, Asthore, and you'd pay him his fee; and as you went home, your heart would be light, and you'd be saying, 'I'm cured—I'm cured at last!' But just as you're reaching your house, the old fit comes on, and you fall down at your own door. Would you call that a cure?" "Troth no, your riverence." "Wouldn't you be ready to run back, and call the man a cheat, and require him to restore your money?" And then he would preach Jesus, the Saviour from both guilt and sin, until the wondering dupe was brought to understand the difference between the imposture and the healing power of the truth as it is in Jesus.

As he was preaching in a fair, " a furious mob of roughs " came, intent on mischief. Some friends tried to form a " close circle " round him for his protection ; and this indication of intended defence increased the violent excitement of the advancing mob. Mr Ouseley immediately, with loud voice, addressed those nearest him—" Make way for the gintlemen ; " and then with perfect courtesy of manner, looking at the surprised roughs, he said, " Come forward, gintlemen, I want to speak to you on important business." This reception was so unexpected, and the mode of address so novel, that they were quite disarmed, and their leader hushed them to quiet, and quite respectfully approached the preacher. " You know Father O'Shaughnessy, the parish priest ? " " Yes, your riverence." " Will you carry a message to him for me ? " " To be sure, your riverence." " Well, take Gideon Ouseley's compliments to the reverend father, and ask him, Can he make a fly ? not the fly that they put on the fishing-hook ; but one of those little things buzzing about our ears." " It's no use, your riverence," said two or three at once ; " shure, we know he couldn't." " What ! is it Father O'Shaughnessy, the parish priest, cannot make one of these little flies ? " " Och, and shure, he could do nothing of the kind ! " several voices good-humouredly shouted. " Ah, then, gintlemen, if you're sure he couldn't make a little fly out of a bit of clay, how could he make the blessed Saviour out of a bit of bread ? "

"True for your riverence," several said gravely. So he proceeded to show the absurdity and impossibility of Transubstantiation; and they heard him quietly and attentively to the end. The late Rev. John Greer, who furnished the narrative, added, "I regret that I cannot give any idea, in writing, of the rich Connaught brogue in which these things were spoken, or the expressive action and gestures with which they were accompanied, and by which he adapted himself to the Romanists, gained their attention, and often their affection and confidence as well."

He was preaching on purgatory, in Sligo, and Mr Greer was present. Some time before, Dr Doyle, one of the popular Roman Catholic bishops, had published his view that purgatory was paradise. "My Roman Catholic brethren," said Mr Ouseley, "you have heard much about purgatory, and it has cost you a great deal. Perhaps the priest never told you where it is." "Arrah, sure he didn't," was the immediate response. "Well, listen, and I'll tell you. You know Dr Doyle? Well, Dr Doyle says paradise is purgatory. Aren't you sure *he's* right? Then, we'll take for granted he is. You know the blessed apostle St Paul says paradise is in the third heavens. And sure *the apostle* must be right. Then, we'll take for granted they are both right. If paradise is purgatory, and paradise is in the third heavens, *ergo*, purgatory is in the third heavens! Now, ye fools, go and sell your yarn, your cattle, and your pigs, and give your money to the priest, to bring your friends out of the third heavens!"

In Larne he was showing forth the duty of the
people searching the Scriptures for themselves, and
expatiated on the commendation of the Bereans by
the inspired historian (Acts xvii. 11), and illustrated his subject from a recent travelling experience.
"I was coming here from Carrickfergus in a gig.
Taking for granted that I knew the road well enough,
I drove right on, passing many people going to
market.   After a while, I began to doubt whether I
was right; and meeting a gentleman on horseback,
I said to him, 'How far is it to Larne?' 'This is
not the way,' said he; 'you are two miles past where
you should have turned to the left up the hill. Come
back with me, and I'll show you the right way.'
Then striking his forehead with his·hand, he shouted,
'You ould fool, why didn't you inquire in time?' So
you go on from day to day, thinking you are going
right to heaven; but you're in the wrong way.   The
great God has told you the right way in His blessed
Bible.   The priest says you mustn't read it; but if
you don't inquire, you'll find you're wrong, as I did.
Never mind the priest.   Inquire of God in His own
blessed Book, and He will teach you the way you
should go; and the blessed Jesus will tell you, 'I am
the way, and the truth, and the life.'"

Mr Greer adds, "Is the subject of Transubstantiation introduced, and is especial emphasis placed on,
'This is my body'? He has many a reply. He would
quote similar forms of expression, such as, 'This cup is
the new testament—I am the true vine—I am the door
—I am the way—The bright and the morning star—
John the Baptist is Elias—The tares are the children
of the wicked one—Herod, that fox.' And he would

require from his opponent the equally literal interpretation of all these, with that of, ' This is my body.'
He would remind his opponent that, according to the
teachings of the Church of Rome, there was no *true
sacrifice* for sin until Friday, the day after the institution of the Eucharist ; therefore, there could be no
proper sacrifice in *it*, and therefore no proper sacrifice
' in any after-Eucharist for ever.' Also, he would
ask him, If (as he would admit) Christ held the bread
in His own hands, and ate it with His own mouth—
was that not Christ holding His own body in His own
fingers, and putting Himself, even His whole body,
into His own mouth, and swallowing Himself?" *

In 1811, a Rev. Mr Thayer, who professed to be an
ex-Presbyterian minister converted to Romanism, in
America, issued boastful challenges to all Protestant
champions, promising to disprove, either privately or
publicly, anything they might allege. Ouseley wrote
to him, stating his own difficulties, and requesting
the proofs so loudly promised. Thayer judged it
well not to reply, and this fact becoming known,
he said publicly in the chapel in Limerick that Mr
Ouseley's letter was not worthy of an answer. The
latter, after waiting six months, said it was hardly
honourable to promise to pay on demand, and when
requested to do so, return for answer, "I do not
think it worth while to pay ; it is too trifling." He
again wrote, pressing for an answer, but in vain.
After this he expanded his letter, and published it
in a large pamphlet. It struck the attention of the
community, was eagerly read by all classes, was
vaunted by the Protestants as a triumph, and Thayer

* These retorts are repeated in some of his publications.

never offered battle again. His own partisans did
not meet the exultations of their opponents with any
counter-claim to the honours of the field. We have
no means of judging the correctness of an opinion,
reported by Mr Reilly as that of a gentleman in
Limerick, to the effect that the death of Thayer,
which occurred not long after, was hastened by mor-
tification at his defeat. However, with the bulk of the
Protestant population, Ouseley from this time forth
became a favourite champion. His tract was, at various
times, modified and added to, until at last it expanded
into his "Old Christianity," a volume of between four
hundred and five hundred pages, several editions of
which were sold, and to the reading of which very many
useful men traced their release from Romanism. It
is one of those works which only a man of the people,
living among and for them, can write. Questions
of doctrine, which in other hands would be abstract
and remote from common feeling, are handled as
matters of fireside debate, acutely, homely, and
eagerly. Every now and then he moves under
restraint, as if he were bound to talk like a book;
but soon falls into his natural tone of a popular dis-
putant, with home-thrusts, clever illustrations, and
absurd dilemmas. The force of the attack lies in
his perfect knowledge of Romanism, as a working
system, combined with a thorough study of some of
its most important doctrinal standards, in his reverent
and passionate love for old Christianity as revealed in
the New Testament, and in his fearless purpose of
pressing home the truth, as taught in that blessed
book, against any logical fence, and any amount of
prescription or human authority. It owes not a little,

also, to the fact that it is all attack; for he feels that the Reformed faith is not on its defence, standing as it does in the old ways, and that a defensive position is for those who add dogma to dogma and cult to cult. Its perfect representation of the modes of attack and reply common in the controversies of the country, added more to its local effectiveness than it detracted from its adaptation to other spheres, while the freshness and individuality of treatment took it out of the range of commonplace provincial polemics.

In May 1812, in the town of Ennis, as Mr Ouseley was returning at night from the stable, where he had been looking after his own horse and that of Mr Reilly, he was watched by some fellows, one of whom, taking aim at his head, threw a stone with all his force. It struck the handle of his umbrella and glanced off, but laid open his thumb "from the tip to the joint." He calmly said, "Thank you, you have drawn my blood at last." At Mr Lloyd's, where the two colleagues went, it was proposed to pursue the assailants; but Ouseley rejoiced that he was counted worthy to suffer, and would not hear of it.

A few days afterwards, when a fine young carpenter was standing on a wall by the river Fergus, about to plunge in and bathe, a stone under his feet rolled round, and he fell on his stomach. Inflammation set in, and in a few days he died. His comrades told, and immediately it was whispered round the town, that he was the man who had aimed a stone at the head of the " servant of God."

At the house of Mr Hardy, of Killimore, a tall, intelligent man, Father Glin, joined the company;

but finding two Methodist preachers, soon said it
would be well to have a convention from all the
states of Christendom to settle the faith of the world,
and not to allow every tinker or tailor who pleased
to set up and interpret the Word of God. Ouseley
replied that such a thing would be very desirable.
After the priest had alleged that such an assembly
must be infallible, the other told him that he did not
believe in their infallibility, but found the disproof
of it in their existing system, many points of which
were erroneous.

"What part?" demanded Father Glin.

"I shall begin," rejoined Ouseley, "with Extreme
Unction, which is no Christian sacrament, even
according to your own definition."

"Oh, my dear sir, was it not taught by St James
as having been instituted by Jesus Christ?"

"No, sir. You are aware that, in order to be a
sacrament, it should have been instituted by Christ;
but the Council of Trent is so far at a loss, that three
hundred bishops, with the Pope at their head, could
not find a single word of our Lord to sanction its
institution."

He quoted the language of the Council to the effect
that Extreme Unction had been hinted at by our
Lord, but recommended and promulgated by St
James.

"Thus you build the doctrine on an insinuation.
Besides, you say it is necessary to salvation, and
at the same time not necessary; for it is forbidden
to such as have not come to the use of reason, and
if one is about to die under the sentence of the law,
he cannot receive this sacrament. Therefore, you

cannot believe it to be Divine, when you say it is necessary and not necessary." *

Father Glin changed the subject. They passed on to that of Half Communion, to the doctrine of Intention, and that of the Real Presence; and when pressed on the latter point, he exclaimed, " My dear sir, if you saw all the books I saw when at college in France on that one subject, you would be afraid to speak a word about it all the days of your life."

" My dear sir," replied Ouseley, " there are things which a child can tell as well as an archbishop. For instance, how many panes are there in that window?"

" Pooh," said Father Glin, " that is a physical fact. Any one can tell that."

" Is it not equally a physical fact that John the Baptist was not the son of the Virgin Mary?"

" Very true, indeed, sir."

" Why was he not her son?"

" Because John the Baptist was not born of the Virgin Mary."

" Could any man that had never been born of her, by any power become her son?"

" Certainly not."

---

* Doubtless he quoted the words of the first Canon of Sess. VII.: " *Si quis dixerit sacramenta novæ legis non fuisse omnia a Jesu Christo Domino nostro instituta, . . . Anathema sit.*"—" If any man saith that the sacraments of the new law were not all instituted by our Lord Jesus Christ, . . . let him be Anathema." The passage by comparing which with this he proved the inconsistency of the Council would clearly be the language of Caput I., under the head of " Extreme Unction," Sess. XIV.: " A Christo Domino nostro apud Marcum quidem insinuatum per Jacobum autem apostolum ac Domini fratrem fidelibus commendatum ac promulgatum."—" Hinted at by Christ our Lord in Mark, but commended and promulgated by the apostle James, the brother of our Lord."

" Could anything that never was born of her be-come her son?"

" Indeed, I think not."

" I have you now," cried Ouseley, and proceeded to argue that corn could not become the son of the Virgin Mary; and so for two hours the debate ran on.

Next morning the priest called at the house, and said to the son of Mr Hardy, " Why, Master James, these Methodist preachers are queer fellows. I did not think they were such men." The young gentle-man asked, " But what did you think of your own argument, Father Glin?"

" If it were not for a bit of bread, I would never celebrate mass as long as I live."

We hardly find any mention of presentiments in the mind of Gideon Ouseley, but one case is given by Mr Reilly. As they approached the town of Loughrea, one Saturday, with the intention of preaching in the market, Ouseley suddenly reined up his horse, and said, " I feel as if the atmosphere were crowded with devils. We'll be attacked in the town." Before entering, he rode up to the house of a magistrate to ask for protection, but the gentleman was not at home. Meeting a sergeant in the army, he requested him to walk with them through the street. It was so thronged that they were obliged to ride single file. As soon as Mr Ouseley appeared, a hideous yell was set up; such a yell as, in an Irish mob, means blood. Execrations and missiles were hurled against him. At length they reached the guardhouse where a sentry stood. Here Ouseley halted, turning his back to the guardhouse and facing the crowd. They pelted him with whatever came to hand, till the sentry, being struck by a big cabbage, levelled his musket, and the crowd flinched.   The fellow who hit the soldier was caught, and meanwhile the missionaries rode off unhurt ; but the mob attacked the guardhouse, and would have torn it down had not their comrade been liberated.   Two or three versions of this affair have been published at different times, but we follow the statement of the eyewitness, Mr Reilly.

Prosecuting this same tour, Mr Reilly had the pleasure of visiting Dunmore in company with his friend, and of being introduced to his father and mother.   Going on to Holly Mount and to Castlebar, they there learned from Clare that the house of a gentleman, who had become a Protestant after hearing Mr Ouseley, had been set on fire, and burned, farmyard and all, while the family escaped by flying in their night-dresses to the fields.   At Newport, an attempt to preach was defeated by the violence of the mob.   In Westport, Priest Judge assailed Mr Ouseley while preaching to a crowd in the market.   At his instigation, a man struck him with a hard black peat, rendered all the harder by being frozen, which almost knocked him down, and left a severe bruise on the whole of the right side of his face.   All the rest of the people were quiet, if not friendly.

In Ballina, a big potato, flung at him, hit Mr Bruce, who stood by his side.   One man deliberately took aim with stones, another supplying him.   One passed under the arm of Mr Ouseley, as he had it uplifted in speaking, and broke the window of Mr Lundy's house, before which he was standing.   Both the men were seized, and one was sentenced to two months' imprisonment.   In company with Mr Bruce, he proceeded through the mountains to the wilds of Erris. Mr Bruce's narrative is found at full in Reilly, and we shall give only the substance. At the house of Major Bingham, where they stayed for three days, Mr Ouseley preached repeatedly, besides employing his invariable personal and private endeavours for the benefit of all in the house. On the Sunday they proceeded to Binghamstown, where they found a number of people strolling on the shore, or standing in groups. Father Jordan had just gone into the shebeen-house, after mass, "to take his grog." With his gallant host on one side, and Mr Bruce on the other, Ouseley commenced singing an Irish hymn. The people gathered, and when he began to address them from the saddle in their own tongue, attention was fixed; and after a while, tears began to roll, and sobs to be heard. Forth came Father Jordan from the cabin, and brandishing his stick, commenced to drive the people away. Ouseley remonstrated, and a desultory discussion followed. Father Jordan soon relinquished this contest, and again applied himself to the stick. "Do not be surprised, my good people," said Ouseley, "at what he is doing. He has sworn on the holy evangelists to prevent you from hearing me." The priest denied this, but said he was doing his duty. "Oh," said Mr Ouseley, "you need not tell me; I know your oath as well as you do yourself." Then drawing a book out of his pocket, he read, no doubt, the *Forma Juramenti*, appointed after the Council of Trent; and to the annoyance of the priest, translated it into both English and Irish. Mr O'Donnell, a Roman Catholic gentleman, who had previously heard Mr Bruce, cried out, " We must hear what the gentleman has to say. We will wait and hear for ourselves." " Go home," said Father Jordan, " you have heard mass, and that is enough for you." The squire answered in a way more suited to the character of Father Jordan than to his office, and brought down upon him the ridicule of all who were present. The major then suggested a movement across a little stream, from the other side of which Ouseley continued to preach. Among those present stood one who afterwards was known as the Rev. John Feeley, but was then a zealous Roman Catholic, and a student for the priesthood. While Ouseley held the people in rapt attention, Father Jordan beat an old kettle to drown his voice, and Mr Feeley said he was assisted in this by an itinerant tinker.

Returning from Erris, Ouseley again met Reilly, and once more passing through Dunmore, he preached by the inn at the corner of a street to a great crowd; and Mr Reilly says that such a torrent of Irish eloquence he never listened to. The sermon lasted an hour. On reaching his father's house, the old man heard that some one in the crowd had interrupted, and he was ready to sally forth " to chastise the ruffian who dared, in his own town, to disturb his beloved Gideon."

At this time his brother Ralph was in the Peninsula, beginning to win medals and stars; but even they were not earned by feather-bed service, any more than the less worldly honours that were gathering around the head of Gideon.

CHAPTER XIV.

IN the year 1813, Dr Coke for the last time presided at the Irish Conference, and being on the point of sailing on his final voyage towards India, his heart was full of the claims and prospects of that grandest of his missions. The correspondence of Mr Ouseley shows that, years previously to this time, his own thoughts had turned in the same direction, and that he would willingly have gone forth to labour for the great East. He had some idea that his relative, then Major Ouseley, afterwards Sir Gore, might be able to open his way. When Dr Coke in the Conference asked who was willing to go with him, Gideon not only offered himself, but pressed his brethren to send him, even with tears. They, however, wisely judged that he had already found his sphere; and however strong might have been his desire at the time, he would seem to have perfectly acquiesced in their decision.

He was now appointed to the counties of Antrim and Londonderry, with Arthur Noble as his colleague. Some dozen years before this time, when Graham and Ouseley visited Fintona, in the county of Tyrone, a boy of fifteen years was among the crowd who listened to the men with black caps, and Bibles in their hands. Ouseley was the preacher, and his text was, " For the great day of His wrath is come, and who shall be able to stand ? " The boy was moved by the preacher's appearance, by his fervour, and his tears ; who having concluded, just as his horse was moving away through the crowd, again lifted up his voice, and cried aloud, " O Fintona! Fintona! remember that, on the great day, you will recall to mind that a man, sitting on his horse in the street, warned you to prepare to meet your God." The boy was overwhelmed. In secret he sought the Lord, and found His saving mercy; and now he came to take his place beside " the man sitting on his horse," and to be his helper for several years, in many a hard but happy day.

We have no clear tracing of the range of his labours in the years immediately following the Conference of 1813. But the reader already knows enough to feel that he can, for himself, draw the outline of Ouseley's daily course, by that exercise of the imagination which does not invent fiction, but presents facts to the mind though not presented to the senses. We soon find traces of him far down in the South ; for, as before, his nominal sphere was only part of his real one. In his case a very wide expression was really one of the most exact—" The kingdom at large." That was the field to which he felt called, and though every now and then some brethren wished to confine him to a " regular sphere," every token told that he was no more made for one fixed round than other men are made for anything else.

o

The controversy which, for several years, agitated and finally divided the Methodist Societies in Ireland, on the administration of the sacraments among themselves, had now come to a crisis. Mr Ouseley, though himself no particular promoter of the change, took a firm and active part on the side of the bulk of the people and the Conference. To abate the evil effects of the division, he wrote, spoke, and, if possible, laboured more than ever. One duty, incidentally arising out of the strife, was a mission to England to procure funds for the support of places, and labourers sorely tried and pressed.

One of his few surviving colleagues dates his first knowledge of him in the year 1815—the Rev. John Armstrong, now past fourscore years of age, with warm complexion and white hair, and a voice which, strong as it might have been at twenty-five, seldom pronounces the name of Gideon Ouseley but with a thrill, very often preceding it with such words as, "the sainted," "the blessed," or "that man of God." Sixty years have passed since he received the letter signed Gideon Ouseley, telling him, as an accepted candidate for the ministry, to proceed to Ballimena, and join Mr Noble. The first time the young man met his revered superintendent, he asked him for his "plan." "I have no plan to give you, my son; the country is before you; go into every open door, and, if permitted, preach, or exhort, and pray, proclaiming the grand truths of our holy Christianity: and while you thus preach with Divine power, and the love of God burning in your heart, you will never want hearers."

The Rev. J. Poole, of Canada, writes, relating

how, in 1816, in the town of Gorey, Ouseley illustrated a point he was pressing home, by saying,
that Ralph Ouseley, the soldier, when recovering
from what seemed to have been mortal wounds,
wrote telling his sister Peggy, who, on reading the
letter, wept bitterly, because of the love she bore to
her brother Ralph. But when she heard from the
preachers that the Lord Jesus Christ was wounded
for her transgressions, and bruised for her iniquities,
not a tear did she shed; and why? Because her
heart was hardened through unbelief. The people
had no idea of who the soldier Ralph, or the sister
Peggy, were. The wound alluded to in this reminiscence of Mr Poole was probably one received by
Colonel Ouseley in leading his Portuguese regiment
in a night attack, late in 1813, when he carried a
formidable position against immense odds, but was
borne off the field with a bayonet wound in the
breast, and a bullet through the body.

Mr Poole goes on to say that, at another meeting
of Ouseley's in 1818, in Carnew, on the borders of
Wicklow and Wexford, "his sermon left such an
impression on my mind as five-and-fifty years have
not erased." The people so thronged that they trod
one upon another, and two or three were seated on
each step of the pulpit. "While the preacher was
speaking of the indwelling of the Holy Ghost, such
a power rested on the people as I never witnessed
before or since." He was obliged to conclude his
sermon, and attempted to get among the people to
direct the penitents to Christ, but those on the
pulpit-steps could not move, and he had to climb
over the other side. He directed mourners to look to

Christ, that they might receive remission of their sins.
When he came to the Rev. Mr Ffrith, the curate of
the parish, he said, "Kneel down, my son in the
gospel, and I will pray that the Holy Ghost may
come upon you. God will make of you an able
minister of the New Testament." Mr Ffrith, as far
as was possible for the crowd, bent down, and
Ouseley, placing his hands on his head, prayed.
That night he stayed with the curate, of whom it
became reported that Ouseley had made a Methodist.
The rector, Mr Ponsonby, who lived in a castle at
some distance, resolved to remove him ; but several
of the nobility and gentry, who happened to reside
in the parish, held him in such esteem that they told
the rector, if he was dismissed, they would go to the
next parish. The curate testified boldly to the great
spiritual good he believed that God had sent to him
through the agency of the old evangelist.

This is one of many cases of his sons in the
gospel labouring among the clergy of the Established
Church. By the time we are now speaking of, the
number of deeply pious men in their ranks was
rapidly increasing ; and we find, as his course runs
on, that almost every year seems to witness a growing intercourse on his part with devoted men in all
ranks of the ministry of that Church, from the curate
to the bishop.

In the spring of 1817 he landed at Liverpool, and
visited several parts of England ; but we have much
clearer traces of a subsequent visit in 1818, from
letters to Mrs Ouseley which have been preserved.
In this case he was not alone, but had brought his
faithful mare with him ; and after the tour had pro-

ceeded for a length of time, he says in one of his letters, that it was of great advantage that he had done so. He was collecting money for the Irish Societies thrown into distress by the results of the division, and now and then notes how many pounds he had got here and there, but only in a word or two,—dwelling almost exclusively on the work of God, the congregations, the prayer-meetings, the conversions. We may here remark that one of his phrases, in which he habitually described his twofold proceedings while collecting money, was, " I offer people what they do not like to receive, and ask them for what they do not like to part with."

He did not admire some of the English towns, but the preachers and people won his heart. Whatever objection his Connaught brogue and idioms, and his manner, heedless of the conventionalities of either church or meeting-house, might raise up against him, seem to have been forgotten—except with the few who can never overlook such things—under the influence of the overwhelming religious power attending his appeal to the heart and conscience. The places in which the greatest spiritual effects appear to have followed his labours were Leeds and Hull. Two gentlemen, then youths, in the former town, afterwards connected with the press in London, have told me of the results they then beheld. One, still among us, my venerable friend Mr Gawtress, says he never witnessed such a revival of religion. He recalls to this day the cases of some of the most heedless people in the town, belonging to different ranks, who were converted; and, in particular, remarks upon the stability of the converts as contrasted with the prophecies ventured upon by many at the time. The other was the late Mr James Nichols, the learned printer of Hoxton Square, who repeatedly bore a precisely similar testimony in conversation with myself. He printed the second edition of Ouseley's " Letter to Priest Fitzsimmons of Ballymena," which was at this time his nominal home.

York and Howden are both mentioned in Ouseley's letters as places in which he saw good done, more particularly the former. But in Hull, he was evidently more and more rejoiced; and thirty years afterwards, some of the best Methodists in that town used to speak with gratitude of his labours. He dates one letter from the home of the noble Mrs Bealey of Radcliffe Close. Chester and Liverpool are spoken of with satisfaction, and in the latter place, the "vast and grand" Brunswick Chapel evidently struck him, in contrast with his mountain and village congregations. He does find time just to mention that on his way to spend a night with Dr Adam Clarke, at St Helens, the forewheel of the coach flew off, and his right wrist was a little strained by the fall; "but I can now write." Though I find no mention of Halifax in his own papers, a visit of his to that town, in 1817, is mentioned in the " Methodist Magazine" for 1840. "His ministry was owned of God in a peculiar manner, and a blessed revival of religion commenced." A long letter, addressed to him from the Rev. Marshall Claxton, dated Shrewsbury, 1818, describes with great joy the result of his labours there : " Poor, dull, dead Shrewsbury has come in remembrance before God."

In a letter from Wolverhampton, he mentions

Bunbury, Aston, and Nantwich as among the places where he had laboured. He tells of a young woman who ran away from him when she first met him at Nantwich, but afterwards walked five miles to hear him, and five miles back. The Rev. John Burdsall, in writing the obituary of Mrs Wolstencroft, of Manchester, in the "Methodist Magazine" for 1831, states that she was converted through the influence of the private conversations of Mr Ouseley, while a guest at her father's house, on his visit to Nantwich. At Wellington, he found what he calls a "cold society," but "the Lord awoke many." Notwithstanding the associations of Mrs Fletcher's old chapel, he found Madeley a poor village, and at Broseley was glad that the people gathered in spite of a terrible storm.

The name of the last place reminds me that a gentleman in my own neighbourhood, to whom I happened to speak of Ouseley's papers, told me that his mother, " a dear old saint of eighty," living near Broseley, had told him that she found peace with God on the occasion of the visit of Ouseley, the Irish missionary, to that town. As to Wolverhampton, he says that "blessed preacher, Mr Millward," and his dear wife, lamented that not so much as an Amen could be drawn out of their dead souls; but a tolerable congregation came to hear the Irishman, which was visited by the power from on high. Mr Millward invited those who were under deep impressions to meet him the next day. "We had a fine company of awakened souls."

It is often remarked that spiritual children bear some sort of family likeness to the father in the gospel, and one of the sons of Gideon Ouseley manifested through a lifetime of considerable length, and great individuality, not a little of his spirit. The following is from Coley's " Life of the Rev. Thomas Collins : "—

" In the year 1818, Gideon Ouseley, the famous Irish missionary, preached at Redditch. His word was clothed with much Divine power. The heavenly flame melted many. Thomas, just entering on his ninth year, was there. Under that mighty ministry his heart, prepared by grace prevenient, broke utterly. The public service closed, but he would not leave. Touched by such inconsolable sorrow, Ouseley himself led him into the house of the Rev. John W. Cloake, with whom, and with the father, the holy man continued in prayer until the tears of the weeping child were wiped away ; and he indubitably received the spirit of adoption. The glad memory of that hour never failed. Warm gratitude to the instrument of God never grew cold. The portrait of the venerable evangelist formed always one of the few adornments of his private room. Life through, that parlour was esteemed sacred. One of his last visits in Redditch was paid in order that once again he might offer praise upon the very spot where that joy unspeakable thrilled him first."

At this time Ralph, then Colonel Ouseley, was serving Portugal in Brazil, and the following few sentences from a letter dated Pernambuco, 29th July 1817, show that he had the old British spirit :—

" The brig *Calliope*, from Messina, R. Goodwin, master, run aground yesterday evening near the bar, and was lost. Fortunately, however, the crew and greater part of the cargo were saved by the indefatigable exertions of the colonel, who is governor, and who instantly put the troops under arms, and repaired, in person to the spot, where he assisted from five o'clock in the evening till twelve at night, often up to his chin in water, and in danger of being dashed to pieces.

"When pressed to quit his most fatiguing and perilous situation, he said, 'No; for Britons never failed their friends in a breach; and there is some difference between wading in blood and in salt water.' 'Can I forget,' said he, 'Salamanca, Roderigo, Badajoz, Vittoria, St Sebastian? No; I shall never leave an Englishman in his distress.' This reply redoubled every exertion, and had the happiest effect."

After Mr Ouseley's return from England, we find letters from the South to his beloved colleague, the Rev. John Armstrong, in which facts and feelings crowd so fast, that he can hardly find time for letters, or in the letters find expression for what he has to say. Writing on 22d February 1819, he states that he had not been able to see his dear wife since last November but once. He was hurried night and day, for in the last ten days no less than four hundred persons had joined the Society in the counties of Wicklow and Carlow, while in the few weeks preceding that time, hundreds more had done so in different places which he names. He gratefully mentions the usefulness of different preachers, especially of Mr Andrew Taylor, and " a blessed, fine young man, Fossey Tackaberry," then a local preacher. He said that the Society at Arklow, which was only 40 at the last Conference, had increased to 200; that in Bandon they had added about 200; that in Cork he had been greatly encouraged; and nearly all the principal circuits in the South are mentioned as being in the enjoyment of a remarkable visitation and blessing from on high.

Mr Reilly, writing after this visit, says, " I cannot express my astonishment at the work in Arklow and Wicklow since you and Brother Noble were there. The most extraordinary conversions I have ever seen or heard of have taken place in this country."

One of Mr Ouseley's letters to William Hamilton tells how George James, a boxer at Wicklow, came to the meeting on the evening of Christmas day, being under engagement to serve as " second" to another boxer, John Connor, in a match taken for the following, or St Stephen's day ; and how " the Lord mercifully struck him." That night, George, with his wife and several others, joined the Society. On reaching home, he set off to Connor, and said, " I must not go with you to that bad work. No, no, I must not go. I have put it out of my power for ever ; and have joined the Methodist Society."

Connor found another second, and fought out his match desperately. " But last Monday night this same Connor came up with tears streaming down his face, and requested me to enter his name as a member of the Society." He adds, that " on Saturday morning last one hundred joined," and concludes by demanding from Hamilton " a long letter—small writing and closely written."

Mr Reilly adds, that a second visit was followed by similar results ; and Noble becoming exhausted, Ouseley says, " Brother Reilly has been on a short tour with me in Brother Noble's place." Reilly, on the other hand, says, that the short tour was one through all the counties of the south of Ireland, and lasted six weeks. In the course of it, he admired Mr Ouseley more than ever.

Mr Thomas Barber, speaking of Newtownbarry, describes his labours there. "He preached on Monday morning, and after preaching held a prayer-meeting, as he had done the evening before, when others professed to have found peace with God. His mode of preaching that morning was very peculiar, and did great execution among the people. His subject was the opposition between the flesh and spirit, as mentioned in Galatians v. 19. 'Every person under the dominion of the flesh,' said Mr Ouseley, 'is possessed by a monster with seventeen mouths, every mouth seeking food suited to its nature.' He here named the mouths. The people appeared horror-struck, and many of them roared aloud for mercy. The result of this meeting was sixty members added to the Society." The returns of the Conference for that year showed an increase in the Societies in Ireland of three thousand five hundred members.

It is about this time that Mr Reilly fixes the conversion of Philip Rorke, a man about fifty years of age, who could not read, though belonging to several confraternities in the Romish Church. He had heard some Methodists near Borrissokane read the Bible, and wondered, and was to some extent enlightened. He heard Ouseley, and was impressed. He repeated many rosaries, but was still troubled in spirit, and went on vainly seeking rest. He applied to priest after priest. One said to him, "Go to Loch Dergh;" another, "Go to Lady's Island;" another, "Receive the Lord's body."

" Does your reverence think you can make the Lord's body for me ? "

" I have that power, Philip. Can you doubt it ? "

" Then, your reverence, I have two little hens, but no cow. Now, if you can turn them into two milch cows for the children, to give us milk, I shall believe you have the power you say." ·

" Get a'gone ! get a'gone ! "

And so ended Philip's connection with the priest. Ouseley got him spectacles and a spelling-book, and Philip lived a witnessing disciple, in his artless way, praying and talking with his neighbours, so that they " would rather have him than the priest."

In 1822, during one of Mr Ouseley's visits to Sligo, as he was preaching to a crowd in the street, Priest O'Connor dashed up on horseback, and using his whip, scattered the people. That evening, in the old chapel by the river-side, Ouseley took down the names of forty persons who joined the Society. Among these was William Graham Campbell, then a lad, who sometime afterwards found peace with God under the ministry of the late Rev. John Holmes. Mr Holmes once told me that a person in Dublin asked him if he called Mr Ouseley eloquent,—a very natural question on the part of any one who took elegant language, graceful delivery, or polished composition, as essential to eloquence. Mr Holmes replied, " Eloquence is often defined as the art of persuasion ; and, judging by that rule, will you tell me of another man so eloquent as Mr Ouseley ? " He then went on to say that, once, at a large meeting, somewhere in the county of Fermanagh, where several preachers were delivering able sermons, Mr Ouseley unexpectedly appeared. When called upon to address the people, he began in his own fashion, by saying, "If you knew where there was a crock of gold hidden, that might be got by digging and searching, you would spare no labour to find it;" and he could tell them where there was a crock of gold. And Mr Holmes said it was not long before he had the whole of the people in tears, "and he did more good with his crock of gold than all of us had done with our fine sermons."

In 1824, he heard that the noble race of his beloved Charles Graham was drawing to a close. To the last he had laboured according to his strength, and not fainted. As late as 1817, the Lord had given him, as a spiritual son, that same John Feeley who witnessed the scene at Binghamstown in Erris, when Ouseley contended with Father Jordan. According to his own statement, Feeley had been such an earnest Romanist that, whenever he passed a Protestant place of worship, he put up a prayer for the destruction of the heresy; but he afterwards became one of the ablest and best of Ouseley's helpers, sweetly speaking the Irish tongue, and adorning the gospel in his walk. His training for the priesthood had left a stamp upon his *physique* which never forsook him; and, but for the more open countenance, to his dying day, he would have been taken for a priest. How he did revere the memory of Charles Graham!

Ouseley was naturally much moved by the tidings that the comrade of the earliest years of his career was about to pass over to the triumphant host. He dreamt that there was to be an ordination, and

Graham was the man to be ordained, and that he was called upon to state his character. "I spoke aloud, and said, 'Brother Graham's character is that he always did promptly, and with all his might, everything he conceived to be right to promote the glory of God and the good of the cause he was engaged in. This ye all know.'" Having related this in his letter, he proceeds, "Yes, Charles, we have seen happy and prosperous days together; and many a time were we refreshed together of God, so that we were filled with joy unspeakable and full of glory, which, when I now think upon, my eyes begin to overflow." He then rejoices in the hope of their meeting "in our Father's house above, never, never to be severed again," in which hope he is joined by "my Harriet, who loves you much."

The Rev. John Nash says, "I shall never forget my first meeting with him, on my first circuit, Newtownbarry, in 1824. I had just arrived at the house of an humble farmer at Old Ross, when Mr Ouseley rode into the yard. Having put up his horse (as was our usage), rubbed him down, and given him some hay, he entered the house. How lovingly did he salute each member of the family, even to the youngest child; go into the kitchen to speak to the servant-girl; inquire for the absent; and then proceed to his life-work! Sitting down, he inquired of each individually concerning his or her spiritual state, not passing by myself; and then gave us some happy incidents of his own experience. He preached that evening to the roomful of neighbours, and he laboured to win those few as if they were a thousand—

> ' With cries, entreaties, tears to save,
>   To snatch them from the gaping grave.'

Rising from the concluding prayer of the first service, with seeming inadvertence he stepped to the door, and placed his back against it; and commenced to sing a verse of a hymn. He related his own conversion, and its effects; and then called on each to state what they believed their position to be in regard to God and eternity. Were they yet in their sins? Careless? Unawakened? and so on; and lovingly and *entreatingly*, 'with tears,' pressed on them to ' close in' at once with the offers of salvation made to them.

" One evening, in Dundalk, he preached with remarkable power and effect. The next morning, while we waited in the street for the coach by which he was to leave, a military officer came up to us, and, shaking hands most cordially with him, expressed his admiration of the sermon and its effect on the previous evening. The venerable man took him instantly by the arm, and, walking him backward and forward, applied the truths to his heart and conscience. The officer had strolled into the chapel in plain clothes.

" When on the Castlebar circuit, I had a visit from him there and in Westport. In the latter place he preached to a very respectable congregation, and engaged to preach the next morning at eleven o'clock. We walked to the Mall, where the chapel stood, a little before the hour. Turning the corner, he raised his hat, and commenced to sing a hymn, in the Irish language, to a very plaintive air. Soon, several people ran together to see what was the matter; and in a short time about twenty of the lowest class gathered, and followed us. When he stopped outside the gate, a motley group faced him. Most were disposed to interrupt; but his manner, and the affecting expressions in the Irish tongue, held them in suspense. He sang another verse, which evidently touched them; and then some loving Irish thoroughly arrested them. At several expressions women curtsied, and men raised their hats, and very soon deep feeling was manifested. Amongst the group was one man who particularly engaged my attention. Tall, gaunt, and haggard; in rags, and without a coat; with a most forbidding countenance, ready, you would say, for any act of atrocity; for some time I feared he was bent on mischief. Gradually, his countenance began to change, and he seemed to quail under the earnest appeals. At last his lip quivered, he raised his tattered hat from his head, and, with eager eyes riveted on the blessed man, he drank in every word. I never witnessed anything like it. The picture rises in my memory to this day. At the outskirt stood a poor beggar-woman. She held her little wallet before her. The tears ran down her pallid face, her eyes fixed on the preacher while he spoke of the love of Jesus *for them.* Just at this moment an oysterman turned into the Mall, singing out his wares: I feared his noise would break up our interesting work, but, seeing the group, he quietly walked up to us, led by curiosity. For some minutes he stopped, heard words in his own tongue, and saw their effect on his fellows. Apparently as his instinct dictated, he pursued his accustomed course, leading his horse to the upper end of the Mall, still keeping his face turned toward us; then returned, having utterly forgotten to cry or sell. He stood, and looked, and listened; and deep were his emotions. Eleven o'clock had then nearly come; but Mr Ouseley, seeing the poor fellow, addressed him specially. What a sight it was to see the tears run down his rugged face, and the tattered skirt of his old coat raised to wipe them off! The preacher invited them into the chapel " to hear more." *Not one followed;* but, as he retired, earnest blessings were given him by all that group, the women curtseying, and the men lifting their hats, and amongst them all, the most earnest were the oysterman, the beggar-woman, and the tall, fierce-looking, ragged man.

We find, about this time, in the *Methodist Magazine,* an extract from the Rev. George Morley, describing Mr Ouseley preaching in the street of Trim to sixty or eighty people in the market. Reading the Douay version of the Bible, he made Mr Wilson read the authorised one, and comparing the two, commented upon them to the people. One of his allegations was, that every point of the Protestant faith could be proved from the Roman version of the Scriptures. Mr William Banks mentions the same proceeding in the streets of Athy, with this difference, that Mr Ouseley there read the Irish Testament, while he made Mr Edward Banks and another read the authorised and Douay versions alternately, and he commented upon them.

The following statement of one of his street difficulties, which appeared in the *Sunday at Home,* from the pen of a clergyman of the Church of England, has

P

left no trace in his own papers; but that is his way.
Only few of them would have been heard of, but for
others :—

"In the town of Roscommon, where I lived in
1812, I first saw Gideon Ouseley. It was on a
Saturday, the market-day, when numbers of the
peasantry round flocked to the town. About noon a
stranger rode on horseback into the market-place,—a
man not beyond middle age apparently, but of grave
and venerable aspect. He was dressed in black, with
long black gaiters, and a velvet cap on his head.
Looking about him, as if considering where to go,
he turned his horse toward a dead wall, which
belonged to a tobacco factory, the gable-end of which
abutted on the street side, with a trap-door through
which goods were hoisted. Having backed his horse
against the wall, he took from his saddle-bags a Bible
and a hymn-book. His appearance and proceedings
had attracted the notice of many people, who already
formed a semicircle in front of him. In youthful
curiosity, I was standing close to his horse's head.
Opening the hymn-book, he read a hymn, and, giving
out two lines, each verse was sung to a plaintive,
familiar air, in English and Irish alternately,
thus :—

> ' Behold the Saviour of mankind
> Nailed to the shameful tree !
> How vast the love that Him inclined
> To bleed and die for thee ! '

The unwonted sounds soon attracted a crowd, and
the latter verses, in the Irish at least, were sung
with loud, sweet melody. After the hymn, he
offered an earnest prayer, and then, taking his Bible,

he read some verses, and began to address the multitude. He had not proceeded far when the trap-door overhead was opened, and some men looked out. Suddenly a large pail of tobacco-water was discharged by these evil-doers upon the preacher, and the door was closed. What ensued I could not see, having been blinded for a time by some of the acrid fluid getting into my eyes; but I heard a great tumult. Some of the crowd climbed the wall, determined to punish the perpetrators of this outrage. The meeting was dispersed in the confusion, and, on my recovering, I had the pleasure of taking Mr Ouseley home, and my father insisted on his remaining the next day. A fortnight after he returned, on a Saturday also, with a companion; and the two on horseback addressed a large and deeply interested audience, without molestation, and with much acceptance. What results of his labour appeared in Roscommon I am unable to say, having shortly after to leave for Trinity College, Dublin; but the work of Gideon Ouseley for forty years in every part of Ireland was much celebrated, and is worthy of being now brought to public remembrance."

Another clergyman of the Church of England, the Rev. Dr Spencer of London, states that he cannot forget his first sight of Ouseley. On a Sunday in the winter of 1829, coming from church in Irvinestown, in the county Fermanagh, in company with "the young Irvines my schoolfellows," they were arrested on their way to the castle by the appearance of a man with a velvet cap, on a chair, in the act of giving out the text, "Without faith it is impossible to please God." "Utterly impossible," said the old man, and proceeded to preach. Dr Spencer subsequently often had "the great privilege of meeting him with and without his brother Sir Ralph Ouseley." He often also met "that truly good man Mr Noble, and noted down their wise saws."

One of the few cases in which the authorities sided with those who offered him violence, occurred in Dublin in 1815. He had been preaching in Oxmantown Green, and Mr Bonsall coming up found a riot beginning. One of Rooney the brewer's draymen flung a stone, which struck a peace-officer, and Bonsall succeeded in arresting him. He, however, and two others who had been seized, were discharged by Mr Walker, the recorder, without trial; for he said that the preacher was the rioter, and that he would gladly have punished him; he also reproved Dixon, the peace-officer, for not having arrested him. The counsel for the prisoner was the gentleman who became the successor of Mr Walker in the recordership, afterwards Sir Jonas Green.

In one of Mr Ouseley's hasty letters about this time, we find a notice of Summerfield, who became really celebrated in America as a preacher : "I never heard such a young man for his time; no, nor for any time. Crowds ran after him everywhere. He is humble and holy. I pray God to keep him so."

One of the few exceptions to the rule, that no trace of street assaults exists in his own papers, occurs in June 1819. When writing to Mr Bonsall, he tells how, when preaching in a fair at Monaghan, the rabble had attacked him, he tried all his arts of conciliation, but in vain. When he was beginning to move off, "the stroke of a cudgel fell on my mare,

and she flew off, you may be sure, as did Noble also.
Showers of stones came flying after us, but through
mercy we escaped uninjured. Our hats, which flew
off in the struggle, they beat heartily. Noble did not
get his, but mine was brought to me with some holes
in it." In the very next breath he says, "Almost
every day since I wrote last I have had the unspeakable happiness of witnessing the awakening of precious
souls."

It is in the year 1820 that we first find him making any mention of medical treatment. Writing to
his dearest love, as he generally called Mrs Ouseley,
then in Dublin, he confesses that he had been in
affliction ; but then the friends take such pleasure in
attending upon him ! However, it comes out that
he has had, for two days past, "twelve skilful
lancers " at him, but they were not foes, only friends,
and took away nothing good, nothing but what was
corrupt; and they relieved him. Still he acknowledges that his head felt like a cracked egg-shell.

It was about this time, and not very far from
Monaghan, that he became known to the Rev. Charles
O'Neill Pratt, then a boy, the late Vicar of St
Paul's, Burslem, who was never tired of talking about
him, and left behind him the following memorandum
prepared for this biography :—

"My father, the Rev. William Henry Pratt,
was Vicar of Donagh, in the diocese of Clogher,
county of Monaghan. He had known Gideon Ouseley
for many years, and was much attached to him. My
father, who had distinguished himself as a scholar
in the University of Dublin, and was a man of
brilliant wit, could thoroughly appreciate the scholar-

ship of Gideon Ouseley, and his rich store of sanctified humour. But he valued him most for his fearless advocacy of the gospel, in the midst of daily dangers, which might be almost spoken of as daily deaths.

"My father's vicarage was always open to Gideon Ouseley when he was travelling in the north of Ireland. No guest was ever more welcome at the house of any man, than was this good man at the vicarage.

"My first impression of Gideon Ouseley gave me the notion of a man of great determination of character and physical power, with a hearty, genial disposition, which made every one about him feel at ease. He always wore thick cord breeches, with top-boots—*mahoganies;* and his dress was that of a man who spent a great portion of his time on horse-back, and was constantly exposed to all sorts of weather. The first time I saw him—about the year 1820—he rode up to our house, and, as there did not happen to be any man about the place, he took his stout pony cob to the stable door, unstrapped his little travelling valise from behind his saddle, took off the saddle and bridle, gave the pony a drink, put a head-stall on him, and took him into the stable. I am not sure that he did not first partially groom him. Then, when he and my father got together, what an endless flow of conversation would go on !

"I remember his one blind eye ; but the blemish was soon forgotten in the clearness of the other, which beamed with intelligence, and even drollery. As a child, however, I could at the same time estimate his deep and earnest piety. I have seen him at our parish church of Glasslough, about three miles from the vicarage, receive the Lord's Supper from my father's hands; and, with very few exceptions, all the other communicants were Wesleyans. My father's clerk, Billy Walker, was a local preacher and a class-leader, and so was good old Robert Cherry, band-master of the Monaghan Militia, the staff of which was quartered in Glasslough. (Colonel Charles Power Leslie, M.P. for Monaghan, and first cousin to the Duke of Wellington, commanded the regiment. His son, Colonel Leslie, M.P. for Monaghan, commands it now, 1870.) There were also several pious men among the staff-sergeants, who were class-leaders or members in the Methodist Society. These men never absented themselves from the Lord's table. On the particular Sunday I allude to, Mr Ouseley preached in the morning, in the little Methodist chapel, before church service; and after service he got on the steps of the market-cross in the village, and, having put on his black velvet cap, preached to a congregation including my father and all the families of the church congregation, the Presbyterians, who had just come from meeting, and a goodly number of Romanists, who had come from mass. For the benefit of the latter, he now and then spoke in Irish.

" I recollect him visiting our house on one occasion when a young lady, Miss M'Dermott, was supposed to be dying of consumption. I remember how earnestly he prayed by her bedside, and how he kissed her at parting, as he did also my stepmother, my aunt, and sisters. Indeed, it was his custom, and the kiss of peace generally went round whenever he came or went.

" I can remember my father expressing his regret

at the decision of the Methodist body to celebrate the Lord's Supper in their own places of worship; and I have an idea that, subsequently, we did not see so much of Mr Ouseley; but of this I am sure, that there never was any estrangement between him and my father. I believe that, for many years afterwards, they corresponded and met as warm friends.

"I can remember that, fifty years ago, about the only decided Christians in my father's parish were the Methodists. He used to take us all often to see an old couple in the village of Glasslough—Mr and Mrs Barber, then nearly eighty years of age—persons who had often spoken to, and heard John Wesley. I began my ministry in October 1836, in my father's parish; and there were no people whom I then found so earnest as the Methodists; and, even then, with a few exceptions, they stuck to the Irish Church.

"The last time I saw Mr Ouseley must have been in 1820 or '21, after which I went to school. The occasion of his visit was a melancholy one. My father had lost his eldest son, a fine young man, who died in New Orleans of yellow fever. I was too young to understand it all, but I recollect Mr Ouseley's comforting my father and the family with great affection."

The stories associated with the name of Mr Ouseley have often a touch of the grotesque, sometimes due to his own humour, sometimes to his regardlessness of conventional manners, and sometimes to the rudeness of those with whom he had to do, or the strange circles in the midst of which he acted. The following tale, though strange, is not more so than many which were frequently repeated in the neighbourhoods where he

had been known. Mr Graham Campbell, who
had it from an eyewitness, thinks that the occurrence took place in 1820, it was in the county of
Limerick :—

" Mr Ouseley took his stand in the street, near a
butcher's stall, to preach ; but immediately the stones
began to fly, and some of them struck Mr Ouseley,
and cut him desperately. He went into Mr Ruttle's,
a Palatine, where he lodged ; and, after washing off
the blood, he went a second time to the same spot,
and began to preach, when the stones began to fly
again. But the ringleader saying, ' Let us not
kill him,' immediately seized a pig, and, having
gagged its mouth, he held it by the tail, while the
screams of the animal were so loud as completely to
drown Mr Ouseley's voice. At length the pig became
exhausted, and then Mr Ouseley began again, and,
suddenly stopping, called the butcher to him, and
said to him, ' My good man, the Lord will extort a
cry from you as loud as the cry of that pig.' The
man soon fell, and raised one of the most unearthly
screams ever heard from human voice, and continued
it for a considerable time. All thought he was
possessed with an evil spirit, and strove to raise him,
but could not. The priest was then sent for, who
brought a whip, and laid it on him with all his might,
but all to no purpose. He still roared aloud, until
exhausted. He was at last dragged into his own
house. None [afterwards] would venture to go near
him, or to purchase at his stall. So he had to leave,
and go to reside in Limerick, and finally to the county
Carlow, where some of his children are well-to-do
in temporal matters, but under a name somewhat

changed, and all thorough Protestants. The old man
never returned to the Church of Rome."

About this time we find a letter from Portarlington,
and it may have been on the same visit that the
Rev. J. Hughes took into his memory the impression
which he has reproduced in the following picture—
a picture which seems to me to present Gideon
Ouseley in private, exactly as I have often heard
him spoken of by those in whose house he had
stayed.

The Rev. John Hughes writes:—"My first remembrance of him goes back to my very early youth. On
a raw November evening, he preached at the corner
of the street in which we resided in Portarlington.
After preaching, he came into our house for some
refreshment, and to wait until his time came again
to preach in the chapel. When he took a seat in
the little back apartment, it was dusk. A turf fire
played fitfully, and there was no other light. I
crouched in an obscure corner, and Ouseley thought
himself alone. He took off his cloak and hat, ejacu-
lated 'My blessed Master!' and wiped the perspiration from his head and face. He then poked the fire,
and spread himself out before it. After musing a
minute, he wept. Tear after tear rolled down his
rugged cheeks. He repeated, in a low but distinct
voice, the first two verses of the 210th hymn :—

> 'Thee will I love, my Strength, my Tower ;
>   Thee will I love, my Joy, my Crown ;
> Thee will I love with all my power,
>   In all Thy works, and Thee alone;
> Thee will I love till the pure fire
> Fills my whole soul with chaste desire.

'Ah, why did I so late Thee know !'

(Here he smote his forehead with his big hand.)

> 'Thee, lovelier than the sons of men !
> Ah, why did I no sooner go
>   To Thee, the only ease in pain !
> Ashamed I sigh, and inly mourn
> That I so late to Thee did turn !'

" Thus far, memory serves me clearly. I have a hazier, yet still a tolerably satisfactory remembrance that he repeated the third stanza; and then, in his strong, hoarse voice he sang the fourth :—

> 'I thank Thee, uncreated Sun,
>   That Thy bright beams on me have shined ;
> I thank Thee who hast overthrown
>   My foes, and healed my wounded mind ;
>   I thank Thee' (*louder*) 'whose enlivening voice
>   Bids my freed heart in Thee rejoice.'

" He preached that night to a crowded house from Galatians v. 19–21, dwelling forcibly on ' the seventeen works of the flesh.' There was a sprinkling of Romanists in the congregation ; and there were two there—Tom Dunne and Biddy Whitefield—who had been Romanists, but who were then, and who continued, until peaceful death, to be exemplary Methodists.

" My last remembrance of Ouseley dates from 1838. I had come to Mountrath on a bitterly cold winter morning, just in time to commence the usual Sabbath service. The congregation was small, and the chill depressing. Just as I had given out a verse, before announcing my text, Ouseley came in. I suppose he had lodged with a friend outside the town on the Saturday night. He waited until the verse was sung, and then came up the aisle, saying, ' Come down, John.' I gladly vacated my stand, and Ouseley preached that morning and met the class. He spent the Sabbath with us at Mr John Lyster's, and seemed cheerful, but was evidently feeble.

" The late Mr Henry Bournes, of Crossmolina, told me that Mr Ouseley came to his house on a very wet day, late in the autumn. Being engaged to dine with a gentleman of the neighbourhood, he merely threw off his outer wrappings, saw his horse groomed and fed, and walked out in all the rain to dinner. He returned to Mr Bournes's in time to preach. He retired to his room early, having ridden forty Irish miles—upwards of fifty English—that day. He would not allow his clothes to be removed from his bedroom to be dried. Next morning Mr Bournes heard him singing a hymn. He knew that Ouseley usually began the day with sacred song, but thought it strange he should sing but two lines at a time, with pauses between the couplets. He got out of bed, looked into the street, and saw Ouseley standing on a block, addressing a company of labourers, who were waiting to be hired for the potato digging.

" Pat M'Donagh, a half-converted Romanist of this vicinity (Monastereven, Queen's county), could have supplied many an anecdote of Ouseley. He was a man of shrewd wit, far-reaching thought, and, alas! the immoral life of despair. He was but a labourer. His children were bitter Papists. He yielded to home persecution, went to mass, drank. Yet his aspiration ever was, like that of the friar over Bedell's grave,—' Let my soul be with Ouseley's, wherever it be!' "

Mr Ouseley speaks of Mr Feely as the right kind of Irish preacher, and says, that he preaches from thirteen to fifteen times a week. On the other hand, Feeley, speaking of him, exclaimed, " Oh, how did he labour in prayer, both before and after these services ! . . . Often have I seen him weep, and agonise, and wrestle with God."

In September 1824, the *Sligo Journal* tells how a fellow rushed furiously up certain steps, where Mr Ouseley was standing to preach, in Monaghan, and struck him so violently on the breast, that respiration for a time was suspended. He attempted to repeat the blow, but was seized by the people. When able to speak, Ouseley's first word was, " Do him no harm ; he did it because he was drunk." In December of the same year, the *Kerry Evening Post* indignantly describes how the magistrates of Kilrush were, as it says, driven out of court by the violence and menaces of a Roman Catholic clergyman, when they would themselves have wished to protect Ouseley who had been assaulted in the streets. He had now gained a point at which the Protestant press, as a rule, warmly defended him. But the case related by the *Kerry Journal* is one which illustrates the condition of public justice at that time, when the priest chose to interfere. The magistrates were browbeaten by the priest at two sittings, and prevented from acting according to their view of the case.

When the controversy respecting Roman Catholic emancipation approached its crisis, he frequently took part in it by letters in the newspapers, or by pamphlets ; and to the surprise and perplexity of all his friends, though a strong opponent of

emancipation, propounded a scheme for taking priests
into the pay of the Government.   One of the many
correspondents who sought information and advice
from him on public affairs was the Honourable
Henry Maxwell, the member for the county of Cavan,
in one of whose letters we find the following words,
touching the proposal in question :—" I cannot agree
with you.   I consider it a *malum in se*, and a most
inexpedient measure." · In the same letter, Mr
Maxwell speaks of the evidence of Dr Doyle before
the Parliamentary Committee, which has now become
more celebrated than ever since the publications of
Mr Gladstone on the Vatican Decrees.   One observation of Mr Maxwell's illustrates the need of having
men who practically know Romanists to judge of the
effect and value of what they say, a function in which
ordinary Englishmen are, all over Europe, noted for
being rather more than defective.   Mr Maxwell
regrets his own absence when the evidence was given,
for after the statements of Dr Doyle, disclaiming views
usually ascribed to Roman Catholics, as to the power
of absolving subjects from allegiance, and other con-
comitants of Papal Infallibility, he felt that some such
question as the following ought to have been put: Such
being your sentiments with respect to these errors, is
it your practice, and that of the Roman Catholic
priests in general, to undeceive the minds of their
flocks in respect of them ?

In 1826, Mr Ouseley writes from Cavan with great
delight, stating that he had seen the church crowded,
and sixty-three Romanists recanting the errors of
Popery, making 257 in all ; that he also had heard Mr
Pope, then a famous controversial orator, address a

large audience for two hours. The Reformation movement, as it was called, then proceeding in the neighbourhood of Cavan, owed much to the influence of Lord and Lady Farnham, whose guest Ouseley occasionally was, and with whom he corresponded, holding them in hearty respect.

Public discussions between Protestant and Romish champions were, at this time, very popular. One which was to take place in Derry appears to have had particular interest for Mr Ouseley. He feared beforehand that the Catholics would flinch, and this proved to be the case. When he visited Derry immediately afterwards, he states that the fact of the priests having done so, " opened their people's eyes, so that they now came in crowds to hear." Shortly after this, he was in Dundalk, and in a ball-room preached to a great crowd, among whom was the truly noble and good Lord Roden, with his family, " and an immense mass of the lower orders, although the priests had been threatening them." Mr Marmion, a political speaker, created a disturbance at the close, but Mr Ouseley was escorted home by a magistrate and the police. We are not told at what particular period of Mr Ouseley's life it was that, in this neighbourhood, an event occurred, which procured him the honour of a notice in the biography of a celebrated highwayman. All that is stated is, that this worthy, being on the watch one night, heard the tramp of a horse, and was on the alert; but, recognising in the figure the well-known Methodist preacher, he knew that there was no *loot*, and let him pass unheeded.

From this time forward we find invitations pouring in upon him, in most of the places where he goes, to the houses of persons of consideration both among the clergy and laity; and he occasionally is able to accept of them. He seems to have antici-pated Pius IX., for in 1827 we find him announcing and preaching a sermon on the Infallible Protestant Faith. About the same time, he mentions with grati-tude the exertions of Dr Henry Cooke, the memorable champion of Orthodoxy in Ulster; for he regarded the purgation of the Presbyterian Church as certain to be productive of much good.

He does not seem to have preserved letters, those that exist being mostly such as he received late in life, and such as might have remained in the hands of Mrs Ouseley, or Mr Bonsall, without any intention on his part to preserve them. There is one affectionate letter from Dr Bunting, in 1828, invit-ing him to Manchester to take part in the anniversary of the Missionary Society, and saying that Mr Watson and himself thought the good cause would be greatly served by such a speech at each meeting as they had heard him deliver at the Conference in Belfast. Then comes the only case in which he mentions having shared with others the responsibility of any debate. This was in Omagh in 1828, at a Reformation meet-ing, when three priests set themselves forward as champions of Rome. On the Protestant side were " the Rev. Messrs Jones and Athill, Captain Gordon, and myself." Mr Reilly gives a good reason why he was not found among those holding formal discus-sions. The priests refused to meet him. His " Old Christianity " had taken more people from them than any book of controversy published within the memory of man, and his oral feats were to them a familiar cause of anxiety.

The visit paid to Manchester was a source of great enjoyment to him. He felt the cordiality of his reception. Visiting York, Leeds, and Bradford, he found traces of his former labours. Very many persons called him father, and earnest applications were made for visits here and there. The secretary of the Missionary Society in Hull, Mr North, writing to invite him, says, " You have many friends and spiritual children in Hull, who would rejoice to see you once more." One of his brief remarks is, " The Protestants of this side of the water are filled with apathy about Popery, as if the case were hopeless, or not worthy of notice."

Mr Hay narrates, as he received the account from Mr Waterson, an attempt at the wholesale destruction of Mr Ouseley and his congregation, in Bloomsbury Chapel, Tradeston, Glasgow. Mr Ouseley, he says, had preached in the street, in the neighbourhood of the chapel, and at the close announced that he would preach in the chapel at night. The Sunday school had been held as usual in the schoolroom under the chapel, and had been dismissed by Mr Waterson, the school superintendent, who saw everything in its proper place before he left, and who noticed that the fire in the stove, near the centre of the room, had nearly burned out. In the evening, the chapel was crowded long before the time of service ; and Duffus, the chapel-keeper, about half-past five, went down to the schoolroom for some forms. The only way to the schoolroom was by a stone stair, by the side of the chapel nearest the river. When Duffus reached

Q

the first window of the room, he was surprised by a glare of red light, and on hastening into the room he found the stove filled with blazing coal, and almost the whole of the four sides in a red heat. The table was close up to the burning stove on one side, and on its opposite side was a long form, placed on end, and reaching up to the ceiling, and as close to the stove as it could be. Duffus quietly removed the table and form to a safe distance, raked out the burning coals, and secured the room against further intrusion. That night a man was found in the gallery with a horse-pistol in his possession.

The Rev. John Liddy states that he remembers hearing Mr Ouseley speak of having seen Dr Chalmers on this visit, and that when he observed that one great evil in Christian Churches in our day was a lack of discipline, the Doctor replied, " You are right, Brother Ouseley." To us the " Brother " does not sound Chalmerian. But the Doctor's great heart was as warm as his own, and he may have slipped into the way of speech which he knew and felt was like the man.

In 1829, he mentions, with pleasure, labours in the neighbourhood of Ballina, and says that in Westport he was entreated to return; also that the Bishop of Killala had personally been very kind, and given him two guineas to assist in building a chapel. " It is pleasing to see such crowds everywhere, and the blessed effects produced; only in Dublin am I lumber." The plain language of this last sentence gives one a key to otherwise obscure hints scattered here and there among his letters, which thus interpreted, show that he was very conscious that the Dublin people did not relish his rough-and-ready preaching; and he evidently sometimes thinks that Dublin preachers also did not give him a welcome. We do not know the particulars of the case, and cannot judge how far he or they were to blame. On the one hand, it is very probable that many of them may have been incapable of overlooking the drawbacks of his manner, for the sake of the religious benefits of his labours. On the other hand, it is quite possible that he was not fully aware how unlikely he was, in permanence, to keep up city congregations, being as unsuited to that work as the men whom he found doing it were to accomplish, by occasional visits, those great results which made his own path through the country like a fertilised furrow.

Writing from Tuam in 1830, he says that for several years not a drop of his blood had been spilled; but that the evening before, being assailed by a shower of stones, turf, dirt, and eggs, many of them had hit him; and one turf striking his mouth, " made me bleed a little." However, he did not desist from preaching, and closed his outdoor service with solemn prayer. The fact is, two teeth were knocked out. But as soon as it was possible he proceeded, pausing now and then to relieve himself of blood. Dean Seymour, of Tuam, in a communication to the Rev. Oliver M'Cutcheon, mentions that, when he first commenced his labours in the cathedral town, the people often quoted the words of Gideon Ouseley, who, being there when the Roman Catholic cathedral was being erected, told the men that they were not building it solid enough; and when they asked why, said that they would have Protestant clergymen preaching in it one day. And Dean Seymour says that when the people saw some movements in his own missionary experience, they often said the prophecy of Gideon Ouseley would one day be fulfilled.

On one of his tours through Galway, in company with Mr Feeley, crossing the country after heavy rain, they had to wade a stream; "down went my mare suddenly, and while she plunged, off I tumbled, and was thrown on my back in the water." Mr Feeley coming up to help, "down he and his little Rosinante went." However, they both gathered themselves up, "nothing hurt that signified."

Part of a letter is found without the date or the name of the person to whom it was addressed ; but we can scarcely doubt that it was to the Rev. John James at the Mission House in London. It contains messages to Brother and Sister Edwards, Dr Townley, Mr Morley, and to kind Mr and Mrs Hunter, a well-known surgeon in Islington. It speaks of an inflammation of the liver, of sixteen teacups of blood being taken from the arm, of thirteen leeches, and a blister. "Here I lie in peace, upon a bed of doubtless salutary affliction, under the care of a kind wife, and a merciful Father who neither slumbers nor sleeps." A letter follows from the Rev. John James, affectionately conveying, on the part of the Missionary Committee, an expression of sympathy with Mr Ouseley in his afflictions. Not long after this serious note of failing health, comes the statement that, when leaping his mare across a fence somewhere in Roscommon, she stumbled, and something in his heel gave way with a loud crack. It appeared that the Achilles tendon was broken; and though he hardly ever mentions the accident or its effects afterwards, he never ceased to suffer from them. In 1831, speaking of a visit to Mohill, in the county of Leitrim, he says that he was cordially received at the house of Mr Norris, a magistrate; but, as no place to preach in was opened, he was on the point of setting off. " 'However,' said I, ' the sky cannot be taken away,'" and under that kindly roof he sought and found a large congregation. After this he procured a large schoolroom, and preached, as usual, night and morning, seven sermons in all. Shortly afterwards, returning to Mohill, we find his congregation in the street "as attentive as if the priest was the preacher," and indoors such a crowd that he came out as wet as if he had been in the river. But next morning he was just as fresh as ever, and exclaims, " Delightful toil ! " He now dined with the rector, and breakfasted with the curate, and had to decline the invitation of Colonel Walsh—a variation upon some of his experiences.

In June of 1831, while passing along the street of Armagh, a man came up to him, and taking him by the hand, said, " It was in the county of Mayo I heard you, sir, and now I and my family are Protestants, thank God." As another reminiscence of Mayo, and also as a specimen of the letters he often received, but of which he preserved scarcely any, we may give the following, signed by some one of the name of M'Greal. If we touched one word of its English it would be less like its author, and less like what Mr Ouseley heard and read every day. The letter is without date :—

" A LETTER TO MR GIDEON OUSELEY, Preacher of the Gospel.

" SIR,—It is my intention to state to you, in as accurate a manner as I possibly can at present, the true cause of my conversion from Popery. In the year of our Lord 1812 or 1813, I was in the fifteenth year of my age. It happened on a day, I believe, in the month of November, as I returned from school, I saw a large crowd standing on the street of W——. I went to see what was the cause of it. When I drew nigh I beheld two gentlemen preaching the 'glad tidings' to the people. I immediately inquired as diligently as possible what was their motive in preaching to the people; but I could not learn. I paid the greatest attention to what I heard, and in a few moments I heard you, sir (for you were one of the gentlemen), express these words :—   .

"'There is no other name given among men whereby we can be saved,' &c. 'Is this possible,' said I, 'that what he says is true? If it be true, I am wrong; but if I am, the world is so as well as I.' It was not long after until I saw the priests lashing the people away; and I ran away also, and gave myself a great round on my way home, in order that I might avoid seeing the priests. I sat myself down to think on what I heard. 'But,' said I, 'the priests know better than any person. And why should I imagine that these gentlemen should be as knowledgeable as the holy servants of God? But, then,' said I again; 'how well they did not hold their tongues when the priests came present! That is one great instance to think they had truth on their side. Well,' said I, 'I shall return to them again.' I came back the same way, and found the priests and the most part of the people gone. I found myself very happy. I thought and listened with attention to every word that was said. At length I heard you say, sir, you would preach that evening in the preaching-house. I then made the best of my way home. I was asked what delayed me, but gave some frivolous excuse, which satisfied my parents for that present.

"Coming on the hour you appointed to preach, I told my parents I would be very willing to go see a young man, my relative, who was going to college. At length, to please me, they allowed me to go. But my object was to go to the preaching-house. I got a large, loose coat, and wrapped myself in it, in order that no person should know me; and on going into the preaching-house I hid myself in the darkest portion of it. When you began to preach, you set forth sin in all its colours, and showed its enormity in the sight of God; but what struck me more than all [else] I heard was, you raised up your hand,

and pointed to me, and said, ' Blessed be the Lord, you are here to-night!' I thought you stared me in the face, while you brought to my recollection every sinful deed I ever did. I got ashamed, and would give anything in my possession to be outside doors. I also thought some persons must have told you all about me, whilst I was getting into the remotest corner. I thought every eye ought to be fixed upon me, through the means of your pointing to me and telling me all I ever done. When preaching was over, and that you pronounced the blessing, I thought you prayed for none else than me. I returned home, and I was asked some questions about my friend; but I answered nothing lest I should be guilty of a lie—what I never before thought to be sinful, but that night I heard him [the liar] ranked with the adulterer, fornicator, and murderer.

"At that time I was deprived of every means that would cause me to get forward in the knowledge of the Saviour. First, I being too young to make steadfast resolution; and secondly, having no opportunity, being always at school. But when I arrived at the nineteenth year of my age, I was taken from school; and, being one day alone, there came in a young man, a neighbour's son, who had a few leaves of a Douay Testament. I took the book into my hands, and opened it, and read that text in the First Timothy, 'There is one God, and one mediator between God and men, the man Christ Jesus.' I got astonished. But, in a word, it brought everything I heard in the street and in the preaching-house to my remembrance. I made a firm resolution then, and said I would and should see more about it. I set to work, and spent very near two years in reading and comparing books, and seeking after the works written by the ablest advocates on both sides.

"At length that work of yours fell into my hands, entitled ' The Defence of Old Christianity.' In this volume ended all my pursuits in the discovery of truth and error. After a study of near two years, I embraced the Reformed Church, and then encountered persecution on every side. Argumentarians, both lay and divine, thought to confound me. My father brought three priests together on me; but, to their shame, I possessed the Word of Truth, which they could not withstand. A friar assailed me at another time in his presence. I asked him at length, ' Is the Babylon of the Revelation Rome?' He answered,

'Yes, but it is Rome heathen.' 'If so,' said I, 'the inhabitants thereof ever since must have been devils, and every unclean bird.' He was struck dumb, but stood up and blessed and crossed himself, and then swore on his breviary no man out of his Church could be saved. I said, 'Thank you, sir, but I am not convinced.'

"In a few months after there came a young man whose name is Peter F——. This young man's parents took every pains to prepare him for the office of a priest, and intended to have him sent to Maynooth College. He asked me several questions concerning my conversion, and said he was very sorry for it, such proceedings to be taking place in me. But I soon let him understand the Church of Rome, which he was intended to be a pastor of, could in no wise bear examination by that unerring standard, which is the Word of God. I immediately produced the Holy Scriptures of the Old and New Testament, and pointed out her principal errors. I then told him I could not trust the salvation of my soul with any Church which taught such doctrines, contrary to the Word of God. I also produced your 'Defence,' and left him to peruse it, which he did, and kept it for three weeks, during which time he compared both versions of the Scriptures, and saw plainly the errors of Popery. He embraced the Established Church, and I trust is no disgrace to her members.

"Opportunity would not allow me to state every occurrence that afterwards happened, especially through the channel of degradation.

"I remain, sir, with the greatest respect, your most obedient and humble servant in the Lord Jesus."

In 1831, Mr Ouseley mentions a young man who heard regularly during a visit to Mohill, and whom the priests offered to send free of expense to their English College, and have him ordained; but refusing to go either there or to Maynooth, he went to Trinity College, Dublin, and out of seventy-three candidates for entrance, took the first place. He also mentions a priest who, after hearing him in Ballyjamesduff, came to call upon him. They had much free and friendly conversation, and the priest cordially invited him to his house; " but I had to go forward."

The next day we find him at Ballinamore, preaching, in all, four times. He states that, in the market of Killashandra, in a great crowd there was nothing but peace and goodwill, satisfaction beaming on their faces, and no distinction being perceptible between Romanist and Protestant. While at prayer every head was uncovered. He confesses that he lay down pretty tired, but meaning to be off early again for Ballinamore, and to preach by the way; but acknowledges that the excessive rain had prevented him.

In 1832, when his threescore years and ten had come, we find strong expressions of gratitude for the recovery of his brother Ralph, who was then, evidently, with Mrs Ouseley, coupled by earnest solicitude for the welfare of his soul. He says that in Brookborough, from which place he writes, a great work of God was going on; and that last Sunday upwards of thirty souls found peace in Enniskillen, and more than twenty in Irvinestown. That day he had preached twice in both of these places, twice or three times on Monday and Tuesday—an odd uncertainty of memory, especially after so short an interval, for he was writing on the Thursday. On the Tuesday evening he had an immense crowd in Maguire's Bridge; on the Wednesday morning, in the market there, a peaceable crowd. At night, a great company in a country place, and also the following morning. "My health stands it amazingly." He rejoices to see the throngs that come "to hear me once more;" and cries out, "For thirty years past no such work has been seen in this country.

"'O Jesus, ride on till all are subdued!'"

In another of his hasty notes to that dearest love whose presence seems to have always followed him, rejoicing that Ralph has had time granted for the great preparation, he exclaims, "What a wonderful mercy that, in the day when we thankfully submit to Christ to be His disciples, the book of our former follies is closed, never to be opened against us while we continue to learn of Him!" The next letter shows him to be in Queen's County, at Abbeyleix. He sends loving words of grace to Ralph, and then, "Accept all my affections yourself, my own dear wife; and may the Lord, who has again restored you to me, bless and keep you day by day to the end! Good-night—past twelve! Yours again,   G. O."

A fortnight later he is at Baltinglass, where he hears of "wars and rumours of wars" at Dunlaven, in Wicklow. The police and a troop of horse had been employed from three in the morning, and apparently all day, "in pulling down what the people called pinnacles; that is, mounds on high ground for signals. The people sounded horns, rapidly assembled, and built them up again." About three miles from the town the crowds faced the police, to whose aid twenty yeomen hastened, and an express came into the town for the dragoons. Before the latter reached the ground, the leader of the insurgents had been seized, and afterwards thirteen more were caught. Notices were put up in Dunlaven that, unless the prisoners were released, the people would rise and murder all before them. The cause of the disturbance is stated in a word. " The cattle were seized by the police and army for tithes, and, in spite of the people, will be sold. I saw a letter to-day with the magistrate, who read it for me, saying that a great seizure of this nature had been made [evidently in another locality] ; and a host of soldiers and police, upwards of seven hundred, were present, with two pieces of cannon, and many thousands of the peasantry ; but the cattle were sold, and the people durst not stir."

Ouseley looked no farther than the obvious truth that the law was to be obeyed, and if resisted, must be enforced ; and thus for him the whole of the wrong lay on the side of those who resisted the law : but to a distant spectator, it was a case in which both the peasantry and the police were to be pitied ; and, perhaps, still more the clergy for whose support the temporal arm was stretched out.

As illustrating Mr Ouseley's notion about giving State payment to the priests, Mr Campbell tells that in 1833, when the former visited him at Boyle, they went together to Rockingham Castle, where Lord and Lady Lorton were delighted to see Mr Ouseley. His lordship said, " I have read your letters in the ' Sligo Journal,' and I must say that I do not agree with you in recommending the Government to pay the priests."

" But, my lord, if you throw a bone to a dog he will not bite you."

" Yes, Mr Ouseley ; but it would be a violation of

principle, such as is condemned in Scripture, namely, doing evil that good may come."

" Not at all, not at all ! "

But his lordship shook his head. However indisposed to adopt Mr Ouseley's political notions, Lord Lorton showed his kindly feeling a few days afterwards, by sending him a ten-pound note, begging him to spend it in circulating his tracts. On the same occasion, the two missionaries went to the house of Archdeacon Oldfield, "one of the best of men," in whose parochial schoolroom Mr Ouseley preached. The archdeacon always welcomed Methodist preachers, and ascribed his own conversion, under God, to the instrumentality of an old Methodist woman in Lurgan. He did not believe that it would be better for the Church if Methodism were extinguished; although such a theory, till tested by practice, seems not only plausible, but self-evident. But in practice, it has always proved that where "the Church" existed alone, it languished : in England, letting the people slide back towards irreligion; in Ireland, letting them lapse into Romanism; and in the colonies, letting them take very much the form that circumstances prescribed. Side by side with Methodism, and other forms of Christianity, Anglicanism exerts a spiritual and moral power much greater than it ever did alone; and probably the same remark would apply, if not with equal, yet with considerable force, either to Methodism or any other of the several systems which are but variations of the Catholic whole. Unity placed in the construction of the fold, is a poor substitute for that unity which lies in the person of the Shepherd and the nature of the sheep.

Our next trace of the septuagenarian evangelist is in a letter to the Rev. Theophilus Lessey, which is begun at half-past eleven at night. " After all the blessed business of the day," he cannot write very long, especially as he has to preach at half-past six in the morning. He had apparently parted from Mr Lessey at Cork. Then he went to Killarney, and preached in the evening in the street, some hearing attentively, some yelling loudly. He then preached indoors, and the next morning " both out and in." He sent a short letter in Latin to the Roman Catholic bishop, enclosing a copy of his reply to a challenge of Father Tom Maguire, with another of his pamphlets on the case of the Hon. and Rev. Mr Spencer, then a recent convert to Romanism. He had also sent a tract on Transubstantiation to the curate.

After this he spent three days in Tralee, preaching both in the street and in the chapel every day. " I sent Priest M'Henry a piece for his edification." On his journey, on a Saturday, a priest sat next to him, probably on one of Bianconi's cars. "Although I upset every position of his, he only cleaved all the more to me, so that we were like brothers. He bought my book, 'The Plot Opened,' a three-shilling book." He states that his heart is set on having Scripture readers employed, and hopes that Mr Lessey will lend a helping hand to "good and kind Mr Bunting " in procuring sanction and aid.

The Rev. Dr Robinson Scott says, "I was first introduced to Mr Ouseley in the house of Mr John Love, Banbridge, which was his home during his visits to that town. He greeted me with a fatherly affection, and spoke to me words of wisdom, which, although not now remembered, I then deeply felt.

" On that and subsequent occasions, I was much struck with his zeal, aptitude, and power in parlour preaching. His loving and tenderly sympathetic spirit seemed to gain the confidence of every one ; and the veneration with which he was regarded added greatly to the force of his words. He did not so much talk about religion in general, as about the religious experience of the individual. ' Is your soul happy in Jesus ? Are you sure you love Him ?' or words to that effect, I have often heard him address to persons when introduced to them for the first time ; and, when his words seemed to take effect, he was not the man to leave the work half done. With a masterly skill, and yet a loving hand, he would probe every sore to the bottom, but would so pour in the healing balm that the patient himself longed to know the worst of his case, that he might have a perfect cure. In these personal appeals, he never overlooked the *servants* of the household where he was a guest. His special efforts for their salvation were often the subject of remark, and not a few of them was he permitted to number among his children in Christ.

" My recollection of one of the sermons I heard him preach is still quite vivid, and from what I can learn, I believe it was a tolerably fair specimen of his preaching on ordinary occasions. He was not inattentive to the precise meaning of his text, but he made no attempt at elaborate exposition. In the early part of the discourse, he dwelt upon the love of Christ to sinners, upon how able and willing He is to save *now*, and upon the fact that He is now as truly going about to seek that He may save, as when He dwelt among us in human flesh in Palestine. He then showed that sinners need this salvation now as much as then—nay, more; that their condemnation is now greater, because of the clearer light of the blessed Spirit whom they have so much grieved. When he had thoroughly arrested the attention of the congregation by this course of general remark, he entered on what seemed to me his special forte in preaching— namely, that of describing particular characters, and adopting the truth to them. In the chapel to which I refer, the men and women sat apart. Looking first to the men's side of the house, and as if fixing his eyes on particular persons, he began to describe imaginary characters, under familiar names, as James, John, Thomas, &c. *James* was a decent worldling, who for decency's sake would go to church or preaching, and would like to have just so much religion as would not require him to come out from the world. *John* had got a deeper insight into the nature of religion and conversion, but had got so terribly entangled by certain besetting sins, which the preacher particular- ised, that, while he was a man of many resolutions, he was 'unstable as water.' *Thomas* was the son of pious parents, having had great advantages, but by wicked companions was laughed out of religious no- tions, and, in order to silence the voice of conscience, was trying to be a real sceptic. For each of these, and for others not now named, he had a word in season. Then, turning to the women's side, he had familiar names and descriptions of character peculiar to the sex, not less graphic.

" To say that this depicting of character was so
done as not to give offence, is to say little. It was
done with all the feeling of the most tender of
loving fathers towards beloved, though erring children, and sometimes, as it seemed, in a half-apologetic
strain, because of the sinfulness common to our fallen
nature, and the devices of Satan, who seeks to perfect
the ruin in which he has involved our race.   His
' hits ' at particular characters did seem for a time
to amuse some of that class who hear for others rather
than for themselves; and now and again there was
a smile, and a nod towards a neighbour, as if to say,
' That's you.'   This state of feeling, however, was
transient. Conscience soon began to speak. Every-
one seemed to be individualised. Involuntarily, there
was a restless anxiety exhibited to evade the eye of
the preacher, lest the John, or the James, or the
Thomas, on one side, or the Jane, or the Emily, on
the other, might seem to hit, and mark the person
for undesirable notice. As he reasoned, conscience
did seem indeed to give its verdict that the preacher
was speaking ' the words of truth and soberness ; '
and, whether the hearer desired a more convenient
season or not, the preacher did not fail to put the true
issue—' Now, or never ! '

" One incident touching myself I must not omit
to notice. During my first year in the ministry
(1835–36), I paid a short visit to my home in Banbridge. I preached on the Sunday, and it was
announced that I would preach again on the Tuesday evening, before leaving for my Circuit early next
morning. Meanwhile, Mr Ouseley came to town ; and,
as a matter of course, I invited him to occupy the

pulpit in my stead. By an arrangement, however, between him and the friends, it was settled that I was to preach first, and he to follow. In singing, prayer, and preaching, I occupied only forty minutes. He then immediately announced his text, 1 Tim. iv. 16: 'Take heed unto thyself, and unto the doctrine; continue in them : for in doing this thou shalt both save thyself, and them that hear thee.' I sat behind him in the pulpit; and he, instead of addressing the people, as was expected, placed me in the position of Timothy, and assumed to himself that of Paul, occasionally turning round to enforce particular counsels upon his ' beloved Timothy.' He dwelt upon the care I should take of my soul and of my body, and upon the watchfulness I should exercise over my behaviour both among our Societies and before the world. He urged diligence in study, and in the acquisition of useful knowledge ; and, above all things, that I should be instant in season and out of season in preaching the Word, both publicly and from house to house, enforcing all by the consideration that only by such a course could I 'save myself and others.' Of the address generally I can now recall only the outline ; but two of the similes he employed, and the use he made of them, I have never forgotten. ' Preachers,' said he, ' are fishers ; they catch men. Some fishers like to have full nets, but do not like the toiling to fill them. If their nets never contained fish but of their own catching, they would be empty indeed. Be not ye like unto them.' Again : ' Preachers are hunters. Hunters do not wait until the game comes to them ; they go in quest of it.' His description of the fowler, with his dog

R

and gun, and mud-boots, toiling through morass and over mountain after his game, was so graphic that I should fail to do it justice ; but, just when he had sketched the picture to the life, turning round and addressing me where I sat, he inquired in his deepest and most thrilling tones, ' For what does *he* toil ? ' Then, replying to his own inquiry, in a softer voice, and with gestures somewhat theatrical, he added, ' That he may bag a few little birds, and bear them home as the trophies of his gallant exploits ! You,' continuing to address me, ' must encounter greater difficulties, must endure greater toils. You hunt for souls. You need a steady hand, a practised eye, and a brave heart. Quit you like a man. Be a Timothy.'

" As to the feeling in the congregation, a mother in Israel said to me immediately after, that at first it was one of sympathy with me that the eyes of the congregation should be directed to me so particularly ; but that, as Mr Ouseley proceeded, this feeling became lost in that of an awful sense of the responsibility of preachers of the gospel ; and that, on several occasions during the discourse, she could scarcely see an eye that was not filled with tears. This exactly tallied with my own feelings. For a few minutes I sincerely wished I could make my escape unseen ; but soon my thoughts ran in a different channel, and for such an address, I could not but thank God from my heart. Before it was brought to a close, my heart was full. The privilege of the occasion, I felt, did indeed involve additional responsibility ; but my feelings were so carried captive that I could have fallen on the neck of my venerable preceptor, and embraced him.

" Among all the eminent men raised up by God in Irish Methodism, I doubt if any other was ever so successful in winning souls for Christ as Mr Ouseley. Testimonies to this effect I often heard during the early years of my ministry in Ireland; and during my several visits to the United States and Canada, one time including Nova Scotia and New Brunswick, these testimonies were greatly confirmed.   Frequently I there met with his spiritual children. They were generally persons advanced in life, and deeply experienced in the things of God.   They loved to dwell upon his name, and upon the incidents connected with their conversion through his ministry. The case of Mr Patrick Connolly, of New York, a convert from Roman Catholicism, I gave in the " Irish Evangelist" a short time after my return from America in 1858.

" I have often reflected upon his almost unrivalled power in reaching the consciences and hearts of his hearers, and have contrasted it with that of some who are considered oratorical preachers.   The latter have appeared to me like a man with a large sledge-hammer, dealing tremendous blows at random against a huge rock, only to receive a rebound from the unconscious block without any material result; while the former seemed like a man with a much smaller implement, looking out carefully for a particular vein in the rock, and, by one skilfully-directed stroke, splitting it with the greatest ease, and illustrating God's own saying, ' Is not my Word a hammer that breaketh the rock in pieces ?'

" His appeals were generally accompanied by remarkable unction.   His tears often flowed copiously;

and while his voice, at the time I heard him, as described above, was husky, it often became tremulous with emotion, and was then exceedingly tender and insinuating. His style was perfectly colloquial, as well as sententious and direct; and when he would sometimes address his audience as ' children,' it seemed as natural and fitting in him to do so, as for ordinary men, even of equal age, to address them as ' brethren.' "

The Rev. J. W. Mackay writes as follows :—

" When I was a little boy, my father lived in that barony of the County Monaghan that adjoins both Cavan and Louth. The great bulk of the population was Roman Catholic and Irish-speaking. Mr Ouseley occasionally came there. A poor drunken creature, who was well known as ' Paddy the Friar,' attempted to interrupt him on one occasion. He stopped and said, ' that if there were questions to ask or objections to propose, he would hear and reply to them at the end of the service, but would not permit himself to be turned aside from his discourse.' Paddy disappeared, however, before Mr Ouseley's sermon was concluded.

" I was at that time impressed by Mr Ouseley's manner as *seeming to have one business in hand*, and to take hold of every opportunity for engaging in it —addressing personally every member of the family whom he could influence by some kind, pointed inquiry, exhortation, or advice. I cannot forget how, one day, just before he bade my mother good-bye, he spoke to me about being born again, referring to our Lord's conversation with Nicodemus, explaining 'that which is born of the flesh is flesh, and that which is born of the Spirit is spirit,' by reference to Paul's treatment of the flesh and the spirit in the fifth chapter of the Epistle to the Galatians; then kindly urging me to pray for this Spirit, he put his hand upon my head, saying some encouraging words to my mother as to my future. Some years afterwards, at a love-feast in Shinrone, which he conducted in company with the Rev. Samuel Downing, he was the first Methodist preacher at whose call I engaged in public prayer.

" I was in Parsonstown when he spent a week in that town in 1834 or 1835. The then rector of the parish, Mr M'Causland, took considerable interest in his visit, and had several ministers to meet him at the glebe. He preached every evening in the Methodist chapel to large congregations. There was at the time an evangelical movement in the church, in which Mr Trench, then perpetual curate of Cloughjordan, was chief leader. Mr Darby also, and Mr Edward Synge, were actively engaged in calling the attention of some of the upper and middle classes to spiritual concerns; but their efforts were very much marred by the kind of Calvinism that mixed itself up with all their teachings. One evening, when some seven such clergymen were present, Mr Ouseley, in his sermon, supposed the Lord to address some young Calvinist just entering the ministry, in the language of the great commission, ' Go ye into all the world, and preach the gospel to every creature,' and then himself accosting the young clergyman who had been so personally addressed, he inquired, ' What would you say, child? what would you say? Would you hesitatingly say, " Yes, Lord, but I don't believe that doctrine"?' I think it was in the same sermon he quoted the first and great commandment as presenting both duty and privilege; and the brief comment impressed my memory

—' "Thou shalt love with all thy heart," affectionately; "with all thy mind," intelligently; "with all
thy soul," passionately; "and with all thy strength,"
the energy of all thy powers.'

"A young man who was then altogether thoughtless
and unconcerned about his soul, went with some like-
minded companion to hear Mr Ouseley. Before entering the chapel they had been indulging in some
frivolous mirth, and he had got into such an im-
moderate fit of laughter, that decency would not permit him to enter for some minutes. He was that
evening deeply convinced of sin, joined the Society
immediately afterwards, endured some opposition from
his relatives, but held fast faith and a good conscience,
and is to-day, I believe, a consistent and influential
member of the Methodist Church in the Roscrea and
Parsonstown Circuit.

"As well as I can remember, Mr Ouseley did not
much resort to preaching in the street during that
visit. He did not seem to think it expedient, or to
hope for much good result from it at the time. But
one day he was persuaded by Mr Synge to take his
stand near the monument in the Duke's Square; and
I was greatly struck by the manner in which he
addressed a large number of people that gathered
round him, many of them Roman Catholics. The
subject was the importance of searching the Scriptures for themselves, and his aim was to show that, in
allowing the priests to keep the Scriptures from them,
and in taking what they said for scripture, they were
acting contrary to their own common sense, and to their
common practice in everyday life. He said something to this effect: ' Suppose, children, you all had
one father, and that he died, leaving a will. This will

comes into the hands of an attorney, and you come to him to know all about it. He tells you that it is in his possession as sole executor of the will; he is to have the entire management of the property, and you are to take all your direction from him as your guardian: he'll take care of you during your minority, and put you in possession of what you are entitled to when you come of age. You go out and meet a neighbour, telling him where you were, and what the attorney had said; and he looks at you and says, " There's not a word of truth in it, for I saw the will, and your father has made a clear provision for you during your minority, and you are to be put in free and full possession of the property when you come of age." What would you do, children? What would you do? Wouldn't you go and insist upon seeing the will? You would, children, you would. You wouldn't be duped by any roguish attorney. Now, your Heavenly Father has left a will, and the priest there claims the sole right to be the administrator of the will, and he tells you to do so and so, to be governed by his direction, and on these conditions he will take care of your souls, and see it all right with you here and hereafter. But here's a man ' (putting his hand on the head of one standing near) ' who has a copy of the will, and he knows there's not a word of truth in all this.' And then he appealed to them to act like themselves, and to assert their right to read the Scriptures—God's Testament to man.

" During this address the people heard with great attention, though a few moved away when one or two priests came in sight, who, however, passed down the street without further notice."

CHAPTER XV.

A LETTER signed John Flanagan, Wesleyan minister, and dated St Thomas's, Upper Canada, March 20th, 1834, tells Mr Ouseley that the writer, before leaving Ireland, had never been near a Protestant place of worship, or heard of a Methodist preacher but one, and that was Gideon Ouseley. He describes the familiar scene of a man on horseback, with two others at his side, in the town of Cootehill, near the White Cross, by the house of George Dunbar the watchmaker. "I thought you the worst man in existence. I had heard so much about you, of your burning so many Catholics, that I really wished that God would kill you." Mr Flanagan was then only fourteen years of age, and remembered nothing more than the fact of the man preaching; but that he did remember, as if it had happened yesterday. In Canada, the Word had come home to his heart, applied by the Spirit of God; and no sooner was he convinced of sin than "I thought of you." No sooner had he found the Lord than he "wanted to see Father Ouseley. I thought of you, I dreamt of you, I longed to see you, I wanted to tell you what the Lord had done for me." Feeling that this was not possible, he writes, "But, thank God, I am happy; happy,

happy in the Lord. May God support you in your declining years, and may He give me now in my youth something of the spirit of Ouseley !"

With the sanction, and by the aid of the Missionary Committee, he succeeded in establishing a Scripture Readers' Society, employing ten men ; some of the leading Irish preachers, however, never co-operated in the plan, which is said to have eventually failed for want of agents. But the fact is, that opposition often dries up the sympathies from which agencies would spring ; and it is strange, how ready some men are, in all Christian Churches, to take the responsibility of checking the usefulness of others, and how much alarmed they are at assuming the responsibility of letting good be done in a way that they are not accustomed to. He gave £50 a year himself towards the cost of the readers, and we often find sums going from him to this, that, and the other object. The Rev. John Saul stated that he had sometimes given him as much as £20 at a time.

It would seem that Dr Hoole had been a principal helper at the Mission House, in carrying out his design for the employment of Scripture readers. Cordial letters passed between them at different times, in one of which Dr Hoole pays a tribute to a speech of Mr Reilly at Great Queen Street Chapel, in 1835, congratulating his early associate, Gideon Ouseley, who always loved the man that had so often stood by his side, who, with his light hair and flowing speech, kindling into high excitement, displayed in his happiest moments some of the striking qualities of real Irish eloquence.

A long letter from a man in the Island of Achill,

which lies off the coasts of Mayo, beyond the bogs and beyond the mountains, shows how various Christian agencies co-operate with one another, even when the shortsightedness of the agents may make them mutually distrustful. This man had first been led to read the Scriptures through the Rev. Mr Willing, a well-known clergyman in Cavan, connected with the Irish Scripture Readers' Society. He had become a Protestant through reading Mr Ouseley's "Old Christianity," and, though the letter does not expressly say so, evidently had become a Methodist. Having sent for a Protestant clergyman to baptize his child, he lost all his earthly friends. After several years, he had been employed by the committee of the Achill Mission, originated and up to that time conducted under the zealous superintendence of the Rev. Edward Nangle, to whom and to his colleague Mr Duncan, a very able man, the writer bears an unaffected testimony. But he is grieved with the doctrines of Reprobation which he hears preached, and would gladly dwell and labour where grace free for all sinners, and grace saving from all sin, was fully proclaimed. He alludes also to good Mr Stoney, the rector of the adjacent parish of Newport, coupling him with the other two clergymen named; and as to them all the only fault he seems to have found is, that they are "up-the-hill" Calvinists, which probably means very high.

The Rev. Jeremiah Wilson writes, "In 1835 I travelled with Mr Ouseley in his gig from Elphin to Strokestown." Having related how Mr Ouseley twice pulled up on the road—once to speak to a butcher who was buying a pig, and once to say a few words to about a dozen men whom he met—Mr Wilson proceeds: "Having put up his horse in Strokestown, he came out to the street, and seeing a few of the constabulary, he said to them, ' You're king's men. Now, what a fine thing it would be if you were men of the King of kings!' 'Yes,' said they, 'but we can't be.' ' Pooh !' said he, ' what is there to hinder you? There are just two points, faith and love. Follow these, and there's no fear of you.' ' O sir, we can't,' was their reply. ' The evil nature that is in us hinders us.' ' Pooh ! I tell you you're all wrong. You know, children, it's just the way I would be in if I had the ague. If all the men in the world would shout, "Ouseley, don't shake," Ouseley would shake on; but if I had the cure for it, and was cured of the ague, then, if all the men in the world would shout, " Ouseley, shake as you did when you had the ague," Ouseley could not shake that way. Oh, no, children, when I had got the cure for it, the shaking would go away. That's the way you'll be when the evil nature is taken out of you, and the good nature is given you ; then you'll be able to follow faith and love. But don't believe in any man, or any set of men. If you do, you'll be ruined. You policemen are doing your duty in the streets of Strokestown, and the people say, " Oh, the police are all wrong." But you look at the book of orders, and you see you have been doing what's right, and you laugh at the poor ignorant people. But suppose the officer bids you do what's wrong ; you go to the book of orders, and you see that what he bids you do is contrary to it, and you know you are not safe in doing it. That's the way, children. The God of heaven has given us a Book of Orders; and if what man bids us do doesn't agree with that Book, we're not safe in doing it. But they'll stamp their foot at you! Well, what about that? Sure, they're dying men, like ourselves, and they'll soon be dead, and rotting in their graves, and, it may be, you and I standing over them; and,' giving a snap of his finger, he raised his voice, and cried, 'What about them, then?'

"Passing across the street to his lodging for the night, an old man, a pensioner, ran after him, saying, 'O Mr Ouseley, how is your brother? I was under him in the army, and a dear, good man he was. When did you hear from him?' He replied, 'I heard from him two weeks ago.' 'And how is he?' 'Oh,' said Ouseley, 'he is very well, dear; but how is your soul?' 'O sir,' said the man, 'I'm not of your way of thinking.' 'Well, and what way of thinking are you, dear? Don't you wish to go to heaven?' 'Oh, I do,' said the man. 'Then,' said Mr Ouseley, 'sure, I wish to go there too. Now, dear, you see we are of one way of thinking.' And, still holding him by the hand, he talked to him of the love of Christ, until the tears streamed down the old soldier's face."

"Yesterday," says Ouseley, "once more I was four times employed." By that, he means in preaching; the places being Warren Point, Rostrevor, and Newry. This was in 1835, when for a time he made Armagh his centre, and thence made this excursion to the neighbourhood of the Mourne Mountains. This year he was again coupled with one of his own sons in the gospel, George Burrows—a Christian, if ever one breathed in human body—mild and happy and holy; anything but a singular or remarkable

man, except for the one thing that an excellent
spirit was in him; and the more you knew him, the
more you felt how the grace of God could make a
man good;—a man who, after all, was just like
other men, only that he was so unlike all that was
evil.

Speaking of a visit to Galway, to assist in raising
funds for a chapel there, Mr Ouseley says that he
met with no annoyance, "only that one man came
up to me on the street, and gravely accosted me,
saying, ' Sir, one of your eyes is not good, and the
devil soon pull out the other!' 'Thank you,' said
I." At this, he was confounded, and became civil.
He states that when in that city twenty-four years
ago, his two favourite posts for street-preaching
were near the barracks, and before the window of
an apothecary—a kind of window at which a mob
would be slow to throw stones.

We next find him at Trim, Athboy, and Arva, in
which last place "the kind church clergyman"
stood by while he preached in the market, and then
took him to his home. Hence he went to the
house of Mr James Armstrong, of Coraneary, where
he was seized with violent illness. Reluctant to
alarm Mrs Ouseley, he did not consent to her being
called for until matters had proceeded very far.
She found him "lying like a corpse," with his eyes
closed and sunk into the sockets. It was not long
before he rallied a little. "Our dear friends,"
wrote Mrs Ouseley to Mr Bonsall, "are all affection
and attention. What a providential mercy that he
came to this house!"

His brother writes to Mrs Ouseley: "I am most

truly grieved to hear of my dearest Gideon's situation. But that can't mend the matter; and should it please God to take him, you shall not be left either poor or destitute while I have the means; for you are, and ever were, my sister most beloved, and in me you shall find a friend and a brother. Let John Bonsall advance you what you want on the present occasion, and draw on me at sight for the amount." In a subsequent letter he resents the thanks which this one had, doubtless, called out from two hearts as grateful as those of Gideon and Harriet. "Oh, with all your wisdom you still don't know me, though Gideon thinks he knows all things."

He then touches a point in which, as in many other things, Methodist preachers and soldiers have some relation to one another: "I hope, my dear sister, that the Society to which you belong, and for which Gideon has laboured incessantly, is not like the Government of most countries, in their feelings towards soldiers in particular, and those who have risked most on their defence. They not unfrequently forget services before the wounds received in the performance of those services are healed. How is poor Gideon provided for? What have they done for him, who dedicated his whole life to a cause in which they pretend they are so interested???"

When able to move towards Dublin, his first letter is written from Ballyduff, apparently from the house of a clergyman, Mr Eades. "I left the dear Coraneary family yesterday, and John, the doctor's son, came with me to this place. He will

accompany me to Dublin." The progress of his
recovery was but slow. Reaching home in November,
he was not able to preach until the end of the year.
Then he did so once, on New-Year's Day, at Lucan,
a few miles out of Dublin, but not again till Good Friday, when he preached in Whitefriars Street Chapel,
in Dublin. Writing to his brother, he declares, with
his usual disregard of ailment, that he is perfectly
restored ; " and my Harriet is tolerably well, though
complaining of much bodily weakness. This is not
strange, for I am in my seventy-sixth year, and she
is not far behind." Then comes a burst of praise
and thanksgiving to His Father and Redeemer in
heaven.

During the interruption to his ordinary toil, occasioned by this illness, he wrote letters, which were
inserted in the " Dublin Evening Packet," and also a
pamphlet. He has, moreover, brief as his notes are,
a serious loss to record, that of his horse, " that had
carried him the previous seven years many thousands
of miles." He had been kicked by some other horse,
and never recovered. After a trial trip of a week or
so, in the Queen's County, he ventured on a journey
to Enniskillen in May; but the loss of his horse drove
him to the coach, which he never seems to have taken
kindly to. It brought him to his destination on the
Saturday evening, and on the Sunday he preached,
went to church, preached in the afternoon in the
street, and again at night in the chapel. He had
already passed his seventy-fifth year, but, in the sixteen days now spent in that part of the country, he
preached six-and-thirty times, of which eight were in
markets and streets ; and his own account is that he

was "nothing the worse, nor even fatigued." Besides Irvinestown, he visited Pettigo in Tyrone, and Ballyshannon in Donegal. In the latter place, he states that another Methodist preacher, belonging to the Primitive Society, had been violently assailed while attempting to preach in the street; but he was heard by an immense crowd " as quietly as if they had all been our own people."

In returning through Enniskillen, he stayed with " kind Brother Halliday and his family." He was ill, took remedies, did not sleep, and in the morning feared that he must disappoint the people, who, according to announcement, expected him to preach three times. " However, I rose from my bed, bowed myself in humble prayer to my Lord, and laid the matter before Him. He heard me—adored be His name; I was well at once, breakfasted, preached at eleven, went to church, as has been my manner from the beginning, and in doing so I found the Lord blessed me; —spoke to many in the street, and in the evening preached without either illness or weakness to a crowded chapel." He again preached to them next morning, and the same evening at Lisbellaw, " where I saw a heavenly work thirty-seven years ago among the brothers and sisters, and other relations, of our late blessed Brother Copeland." He probably here refers to the Rev. W. Copeland, another of his spiritual sons in the ministry, who ran but a brief, though useful course, before he was taken home. Several who bore the name of Copeland were frequently mentioned amongst the most respected friends of Methodism in Fermanagh.

A friend communicates the following, through the

Rev. Wm. Burnside, who " was well acquainted with some of the persons mentioned : "—

" Seventy years ago, on Mr Ouseley and Mr Graham's first visit to the north of Ireland, manifest tokens of the Divine presence invariably accompanied their ministrations ; and, as in the late revival [that of 1859], it was no unusual thing, while they were holding their meetings, to see the people weep, fall down, apparently without sense or motion, for a considerable time, then suddenly rise up praising God for having pardoned all their sins, and given them an assurance of His love. A striking instance of this I heard related by an eyewitness.

" On the missionaries' visit to Clones about this time, they stopped at the house of a Mrs R——y, a widow lady, who carried on a most extensive drapery business. In that establishment there resided then a young man, son to a gentleman, a Mr L——, who lived near the village of Redhill. This young man's mother (who was a most excellent woman, according to her light) heard from her servants of the missionaries' preaching in the street of Clones. They told her they were broken priests, and possessed by the devil—that they rode on horseback, and preached with black caps on them. Her curiosity became aroused, and she became anxious to see and hear them for herself. At this juncture she had a letter from her son, saying that Mr Ouseley and Mr Graham were to be in R—— fair on a certain day, and that it was his earnest wish they should be invited to stop at his father's. The mother accordingly requested her husband. He reluctantly consented, but desired her to get his eldest son to wait upon them with the invitation. The son declined, as Methodism was little known and little thought of then in that neighbourhood. However, Mrs L—— prevailed on her husband to carry the invitation himself. Accordingly, after the missionaries had preached to the vast number of people who attended the fair, Mr L—— made his way through the crowd to where the preachers stood, introduced himself to them, spoke of the communication from his son in Clones, and said, ' I have come, according to his wish, to ask you to dine with me to-day, and to make my house your home while you are here.' They thanked him, and Mr Ouseley said, ' Mr L——, have you a place for us to preach in ? for we make it a rule never to accept an invitation where liberty is not

S

given us to preach.' Mr L—— was very much puzzled how to act. He was unwilling to bring upon himself the illwill of his Roman Catholic neighbours and others by such a proceeding; but he was also unwilling to give an impression to the missionaries that he was not sincere and hearty in his invitation, for he was a most hospitable man. Very soon he said, 'Well, I have a very large parlour, and I suppose you must have it.' Mr Ouseley at once turned to the large crowd, mostly Roman Catholics, and announced a great revival meeting that night at Mr L——'s. The vast crowd gazed at Mr L—— in astonishment, and he was glad to get out of the village. At the time appointed, a multitude of people who had attended the fair, and from the country all round, came flocking up Mr L——'s avenue, filling the house and the entrance-hall. All were filled with wonder, as this was the missionaries' first visit to that quarter. When the missionaries began to preach, the people began to weep and pray, and numbers fell stricken to the ground, and amongst them Mr L——'s eldest son. This being a new thing in the country, and young Mr L—— lying in a swoon, with no appearance of recovery, the mother became alarmed, and inquired of Mr Ouseley the meaning of it. He told her plainly he had never seen anything like it; but he hoped the enemy had not got power to drive them out of the neighbourhood (as would have been the case had the young man not recovered). The eldest daughter, seeing her brother in this state, said, 'It is full time for us all to begin to think of ourselves when *he* has done so.' Up to that time she had been influenced only by curiosity, and when, at prayer, those around her were falling down and weeping, she had just turned round to look on. Just then, however, an old Wesleyan classleader, whom she had not before known, touched her on the shoulder, and desired her to *look into her own heart*—an expression she never afterwards forgot. Not long after this, young Mr L—— recovered from his stricken state, and, rising up, praised God and exhorted the people. The sister afterwards, through Mr Ouseley's instrumentality, became truly pious, and lived and died a devoted Christian.

"Mrs L——, conversing with Mr Ouseley on religious subjects, related the following dream : For some time previously, she had felt more than usual anxiety respecting the state of her soul. One night, while in this state, she dreamed that she stood at her own hall door, that the night was lovely, the stars bright and shining. The sight was so beautiful that she continued looking upward. Just then the clouds parted, and she saw a person of most benign countenance appear, moving towards the earth. She immediately thought, 'This is my Saviour!' As she continued gazing, the person came nearer and nearer. 'Now,' thought she, 'this is my opportunity! When my Lord and Saviour visits my house, surely He will not reject my prayer.' She bowed herself before Him, and said, 'My Saviour, as You have come under my roof, surely You will bless me, and bless my family.' She thought the Saviour smiled upon her graciously, and that a sweet peace visited her heart, and she then felt that she loved her Saviour above all things, and could trust in Him. The sense of peace was with her when she awoke, and *that* she never lost. Mr Ouseley said to her, 'You have it, you have it. Never give up your confidence.' Shortly after this, fever visited the family. She took it, and died. Mr Ouseley attended her during her illness. Immediately before her death, she requested to be raised up in her bed, and began to sing

'The voice of free grace cries, Escape to the mountain,' &c.,

and sang it to the end. She then lay calmly down, and, without groan or sigh, her happy spirit passed away to a better world.

"Mr Ouseley never ceased to be the firm and attached friend of this family. To the eldest daughter he was particularly attached, as was also Mrs Ouseley, who was a frequent visitor at the house. He used to say to Miss L——, 'I shall get away to a better world before you. But, remember, I will be looking out for you, and, if I find you not coming, I will then say, "Poor B——y, you have missed your way."' This, however, she never did. The Rev. Henry Deery came from Dubin to Monaghan to preach her funeral sermon. He said at the close, 'I have known Mrs R—— for upwards of forty years, and have been coming into and going out of her house during all that time, and can say with truth I never saw a change in her countenance—always the same ; a truly devoted Christian.' A gentleman, not connected with Methodism, who went to hear the sermon, remarking on it to one of her friends, said, 'That man has told the truth. There never was her equal in Monaghan.'

"She was heard to relate the following in connection with the introduction of Methodism into her father's family. Her grand-mother—a very old woman at the time, and requiring to use a staff for support—got frightened at *the stricken cases.* She must have thought that the missionaries had power to strike the people down; for she went artlessly to Mr Ouseley to request that, if she had to fall, it might be in the house. Mr Ouseley's reply was, ' O grandmother ! I am afraid you are too *stout* to fall.'

"Another very strange occurrence took place in that country about that time, which caused a great sensation. As Mr Ouse-ley was preaching at a cross-road, near a Roman Catholic chapel, the greater portion of the congregation having to pass that way homewards, they, hearing him speak in English, and then trans-late into Irish, stopped to listen. A man called ' the Chevalier,' on account of his self-consequence, who was in very comfortable circumstances, and had been very useful to Mr L—— in busi-ness matters, but had become enraged at the missionaries' hav-ing obtained a footing in Mr L——'s house,—this man, seeing the crowd gather round Mr Ouseley, strove to drive them away, but failed. He called Mr Ouseley a false prophet, and other opprobrious names. Mr Ouseley, as was his wont, paid no attention to this, but preached on. The man became very much excited, went home, took to his bed, and not long after died. On the following Sabbath, as Mr Ouseley was preaching, at the same hour, and on the same spot, a funeral was seen in the dis-tance approaching. Mr Ouseley, who had not heard of this man's illness or death, was deeply affected, and was seen to weep. After this, great fear fell on the country around, and they were careful not to interfere with the missionaries in that neighbour-hood afterwards."

Had some men been as often mobbed and stoned as Mr Ouseley, they would have made something of it. He, however, says, " Is it not a great mercy that I have escaped uninjured for so many years ? more than forty since I began to preach in the streets! Though I have been ill at intervals, I have not been so much as one year laid aside ; thanks to my Father and God, through Christ my Lord."

In the June of 1837 we find him at Carlow and Fermoy, on his way to the Conference at Cork, where Dr Bunting presided. In August of the same year, writing from Abbeyleix, he says that he had preached nineteen times in eight days; and, after praising God who enabled him to do so, seems to think that this ought to be taken by his friends as a proof that they might be quite at ease about his health. The idea that it might cause them anxiety does not appear to have crossed his mind. In the same vein, writing in September from Spring Park, near Borrissokane, he assures Mrs Ouseley that, after preaching four times, he was " not a whit the worse." At Roscrea his friends were terrified when he resolved " to take the street," because of the disturbed state of the country. " They came not near me, but I went and preached, and returned quite safe." He finds Borrissokane altered by the hand of death. " The dear old friends are gone—gone home before us. My heart melts within me while I write and recollect the times that are past. May God be with me now also ! " This last is evidently a prayer that the labours he is about to enter upon may be fruitful, as those had been which now lay so many years behind.

About this time some of his letters to his brother Ralph, then in Lisbon, begin to be preserved. He tells him with delight of the exposure of Dens' Theology, by M'Ghee and others, and says that it has brought the priests to their wits' end. Ralph, in his letters to him, betrays strong affection and admiration, without ever expressing anything of the sort. He begins one by thanking him " for your short letter and long sermon." In another, he says that as to the sermon, Gideon might as well omit it. He thinks if he tried, he could perhaps preach as good a one himself.   Then he is taken with solicitude for Gideon's spiritual welfare, and fears that the success of his books may lead to spiritual pride—a sin quite as bad as some of his own.   He boldly proclaims the breaking of the Achilles tendon to be a judgment on Gideon for running up and down the country on one wild-goose chase after another, instead of staying at home like a sensible man.   He tells him that he " might as well whistle jigs to a milestone, as preach to the Papists."   Some of his letters he addresses to him as " Captain" Ouseley, apparently to indicate his idea of his militant qualities.   Once, in writing to Mrs Ouseley, he confesses to reading some of Gideon's books, and wonders how he ever got all the information.   " He might have been the Pope's private secretary all his life." · In a letter from London, referring to Mr (afterwards Sir Philip) Crampton, with whom he had become acquainted through Gideon, he unwittingly says what would confirm the latter in his opinion that the service and friendship of the world were hollow : " This man's acquaintance would be more valuable than all the others I have, as a shining example which one might be glad to imitate, and as an upright, enlightened character, in whose acts and words one might place (what nowadays is not to be placed in any) unlimited confidence."   One point in Mr Crampton pleased him greatly : " While he stands firmly by the saint, he does not *hang up* the sinner, as some of your sect are accustomed to do."

If this expression is not directly connected with

that in the following extract of a note from Mr Crampton to Sir Ralph, it is at least illustrated by it: " I do not hesitate to say that in your becoming a knight, you will confer more honour on the order than the order can confer upon you. At the same time, I cannot admit that a knighthood of any order which terrestrial sovereigns can confer, will raise you to the rank of your brother *Saint Gideon*, as you justly term him."

Meantime such topics as the controversy about Dens opened up, gave him new subjects for frequent letters in different newspapers. Now a gig begins to be heard of, and not exclusively the old pulpit— the saddle. Writing from Tandragee, he speaks of preaching three times in the day, once in the fair of Portnorris, as he passed through, " standing in my gig." We find him preaching on a Tuesday night at Banbridge, and again on Wednesday morning, both in the street and the chapel, after which he drives to Tandragee, and there preaches first in the market, and afterwards in the chapel. He " was then pretty well tired, and slept well, thank God."

Then we trace him on tours from Belfast as a centre, first in Down, through Donaghadee, Newtownards and Downpatrick; and next in Antrim, through Carrickfergus, Larne, and Lisburne. In one of these he was the guest of good Lord Roden at Tollymore Park, one of the most beautifully situated mansions in these isles. A kindly letter from Lord Roden is among his papers.

At the close of 1835 we find him riding or driving twenty miles to Dromore, and holding a watch-night service, which lasted from ten o'clock to one in the morning of New-Year's Day. He preached altogether five times, and dined with Mr Boyd, the rector.

One letter is dated from Benburb Castle, and he tells Mrs Ouseley, " Were this couple my son and daughter, they could not show me more love. They are longing for you to come." Another of those illnesses, which now, in spite of his aversion to notice them, begin to reappear every now and then, had, immediately before this visit, laid him up for sixteen days. But he speaks with delight of his congregation; the large parochial schoolroom could not hold them, and would have been too small even had it been as large again. He and his host and hostess spent a day with Dr Griffin, the rector.

In 1836 he made a visit to England on business of his brother's. He preached in Liverpool soon after landing, in the morning, and again in another chapel at night. In London the kindness of Dr Hoole enabled him soon and easily to get through his business affairs. He preached in two London chapels, and makes lamentation over the stagnation of Methodist work in Wandsworth, where it had existed, without extending, ever since the days of John Wesley.

Traces of letters pressing him to visit different quarters remain. From Bramley the Rev. James Blackett reminded him that on his visit to Chester, twenty years before, the Lord graciously poured out His Spirit, and saved many precious souls, who are still walking in the way of righteousness. At Leeds he found that different friends had planned to waylay him as he arrived, and carry him to their home, claiming kindred as his children, or as having some of his children in the family. In a letter written thence he tells Mrs Ouseley how he had preached four times in Birmingham, on Sunday, "among friends indeed," one of the times being in the street. There also he met with many who hailed him as their father. He proceeds to tell her of what, we suspect, with all his love for her, was not a frequent experience with her, the purchase of a silk dress: "In Chesterfield I lodged with my old friend Mr Owen, and bought in his great shop twelve yards of beautiful silk and lining for you, chosen by the good sister and himself out of many pieces."

At Leeds they had "a blessed band-meeting on Saturday night;" and on Sunday morning, at six, he preached in St Peter's Chapel to the largest congregation he had ever addressed. "My God so strengthened me that I felt no difficulty, nor was I even tired." At Hull, also, many of his children gave him a warm welcome, and the general cordiality of preachers and people warmed his heart.

"I am quite glad that I have taken this course through this fine country," he says, writing to Mrs Ouseley from Liverpool; "there is nothing like poverty or misery, but prosperity and comfort everywhere. . . . The preachers are blessedly alive—kind-hearted and affectionate men." After visiting Preston, we find him on the other side of the Channel, about the middle of May (1836). The next letter to his beloved correspondent is from Enniskillen.

During the preceding week he had preached four times in Monaghan, two in Cootehill, two in Clones, two in Brookborough, three in Maguire's Bridge, and three in Newtownbutler. Paroxysms of illness now frequently attacked him, but the old fisher would not be driven from the boat, and when not prostrate, would fling out the net once more. He preached twice in Enniskillen on the day of his arrival. " I was nothing the worse," he assures Mrs Ouseley, " when all was over. The Lord removed the violent pain the night before. I slept well last night, and preached this morning again, and am to do so this evening also; which will be the twentieth time since yesterday week, notwithstanding the affliction I have passed through. And I am now stout and well. To God be all the glory ! "

The following extract from a letter to Dr Hoole, as missionary secretary, throws light both on his spirit and his plans : —

" I shall close by stating what has often struck me would do vast good indeed to this country— namely, If a few, even two, of our brethren were selected by our Conference, and sent through all parts, either together or separately—men of some education, good talents, and possessing fearlessness to preach in the streets, &c. ; that could speak in Irish, and have by all means an accurate knowledge of the religion of Rome—some of the professed tenets of which are exquisite, pure, and apostolic, and essentially sound Protestantism; but its practical doctrines, framed by men of great parts, and by Councils, in order to uphold the glory of the Papacy, and support of its numerous clergy, are the very reverse, and are with all diligence passed on the credulous for *divine mysteries of faith, without which none can be saved,* and which to even doubt in any one point is heresy, and leads to certain damnation, for that to doubt in one is to doubt in all. While these latter are diligently inculcated from infancy to hoary hairs, the former, though constantly extolled and professed, are with equal diligence neutralised and set aside, as the unceasing opposition to the Scriptures of truth clearly shows. Thus are the poor, unsuspecting people taught darkness for light, and are deceived and ruined, and the followers of the gospel proscribed as detestable heretics that should be extirpated. Thus is our country filled with anarchy and untold mischiefs. Of this state of things not a few of our rulers seem not to be aware. Oh, tell it not in Gath !

"Now, the Christian missionary, knowing these things, must see it his wisdom to bring forth these *pure tenets,* as found in their catechisms, standard writings, in the three ancient creeds, and in the gospel, and to insist that no Protestants, however learned, no angel from heaven, could possibly in truth object to them, and of course that all doctrines contrary to them must be false and damnable. To all this will the people freely agree. Then should he mildly adduce the contrary tenets, and, *without ridicule or sarcasm,* contrast them with the pure. The people will instantly perceive how these matters are; for many of them are candid and intelligent, and, so far from being enraged with the preachers, will return home *satisfied that these*

pretended mysteries of faith are ruinous deceptions,
will insist on having the Book of God in their
houses that they may search every point to the
bottom, will cease from their prejudices against
Protestants, and hesitate no longer to send their
children to their schools. These would be fine and
salutary effects truly. This blessed plan have I
adopted, and for many years past have been endeavouring to follow, both in my preaching and
writings, and not wholly in vain. Thank God, I
have been given to see various pleasing fruits of it,
and I trust the seed sown shall yet spring up abundantly under God, if duly watered especially.—I
am, yours in Christ,   GIDEON OUSELEY."

"To the Rev. ELIJAH HOOLE,
Secretary, Wesleyan Methodist Mission House,
   77 Hatton Garden, London."

Athlone is the next point where we get another
glimpse of him. There he is once in the street, and
twice in the chapel, on the Sunday, casting the net;
and on the morning and evening of Monday casting
it again. Lord and Lady Castlemaine stood by him
on the street till he had concluded. Galway is the
next point. " I preached much, as I came along, from
house to house." Here he was helping to raise funds
for building a chapel; and gratefully mentions the
hospitality of Mr O'Hara.

In October of the same year, writing to his friends,
he declares he is safe and well, "except a wound on
my right leg from the kick of a horse in the dark, as
I was passing through Maryborough on foot, about
three weeks ago. Though it was painful, it did not

hinder me in the work of the Lord. I preached in and out of doors fifteen times a week. This caused my wounded leg to swell by day; at night it got down again, and now I intend to rest a while until it becomes healed, or nearly so." Then he tells how one hundred had given in their names to meet in class. "From Sunday morning, August the 27th, to Thursday morning, September the 21st, I was enabled by my Lord to preach fifty-four times in and out of doors—not far off my seventy-seventh year!" In Mountmelick, where he appears to have preached seven times during a short visit, he says, "I have not had so blessed a season for a long time. Between thirty and forty persons came forward, and with tears gave me their names to meet in class." In November 1837 he tells how a pressing invitation of the Tullamore preachers, Messrs Crook and Cather, had brought him again to Mountmelick. He rejoiced in the prosperity of the work, but lets it out that his leg is rather worse since he left home. Still he means to go on for another week, and hopes to do so "without much injury." He tells Mr Bousall how Mrs Ouseley had been near to death, but "the Lord heard prayer and relieved her, and me, poor me! thanks to Him!"

It is plainly a note of failing strength when, on returning from his work in the Tullamore Circuit, although he tells how Brother Crook had taken him almost everywhere in his gig, he could only say that he had got back in tolerable health.

It was during this series of services that, among other precious lambs, he gathered my friend John Hay into the fold.

In the spring of 1838 we find him anticipating with great interest an impending discussion between Mr Tresham Gregg and Father Tom Maguire. " I had a conversation with Mr Gregg this day and yesterday, on the approaching discussion. He is a very pious, ardent, good creature, and full of hope of flooring his adversary, and doing wonders. I pray it may be so. I should not take the plan he means to take." This is dated May 23, 1838. In another letter he speaks of Father Tom as a trickster, but hopes that he will meet with more than his match.

A new preaching - place now begins to make its appearance, namely, the canal boat, which at that time formed a quaint but convenient conveyance on more than one important line from Dublin to the provinces. In going down to Galway, he mentions that, for nearly seven hours, he had been preaching or reasoning ; and in coming back by the same line, he had done so for nearly six hours. During this visit to the capital of his native county, he heard in the church, from Mr Medlicote, of Loughrea, " one of the best sermons I ever heard delivered by any minister." He also mentions that at Athlone, a Presbyterian minister, who attended a missionary meeting, did speak like a true Christian. He writes with as much zest as if he were twenty-five, about a controversy in the local Galway papers in which he bore the principal part. It is now, I think, for the first time, that he mentions dining at the house of Judge Crampton, who, with his admirable wife, was held in high esteem by Christians of every denomination, and was a constant friend of Methodist preachers, and particularly of Mr Ouseley.

We might take an expression in one of the letters written in the close of 1838, as describing all the time between then and the last-named date—"I came with a pleasant course to Kilrush, and had no little preaching as I came along." As to his mode of returning on the tour from Kilrush, it is plain that the horse is now out of the question, and that he is forced to choose between coach and boat; and he expresses a decided preference for the latter—a sign of increasing inability to bear fatigue.

In a letter addressed to Marshal de Campo, Major-General Sir Ralph Ouseley, 64 Rua da Amparo, Lisbon, and dated Abbeyleix, February 21, 1839, we have the following:—

"I came to Dublin nearly two months ago, and intended to write thence to you without delay. But on the very evening I came, I was, for the first time in my life, attacked by robbers between five and six o'clock, in Whitefriar Street, to take my watch and run off. I seized one of them, and cried out, '*Robbers!*' No policemen or others were near to help. Another of them joined him, and I was, with one of them, tumbled on my back in the street. He got up quickly, and fled, leaving his hat behind. Another, when I got up, made at the chain of my watch again, which broke, leaving the watch. A third took up a small bag I had in my hand, which contained some linen, papers, &c., and made off, but to no serious damage to me. In the scuffle I received a hurt in my right side—I suppose a kick from one of them; but am now quite recovered, thank God." . . .

Immediately after this attack, we find him visiting Mr Campbell,. at Selbridge, who says he laboured away as if nothing had happened, while his own note is, that he preached in the chapel and in the street. He evidently thought of settling in Lucan, and told Mrs Ouseley how they could find rooms in the same house with amiable Mrs Campbell, while, on the other hand, he told Mr Campbell that, if the Conference should appoint them both for general mission-work the next year, they would spend two months at a time from home, and one at home. " But what would our wives do? " inquired the other. " Oh, they could live together, and would do very well." Alluding to the blow given him on the side by the robbers, his words were, "The hurt in my side is no more."

" Closing my seventy-seventh year," he says, writing to his dear old colleague Reilly, about a week before the last birthday he was to number among mortals. He praises his blessed Master, as was his wont—

> ' Through waves, and clouds, and storms,
>   He gently cleared my way.'

Praises be to Him that sitteth upon the throne, and maketh all things new, Amen and Amen! Oh, eternity, blissful eternity—

> ' Sin, earth, and hell, I now defy,
>   I lean upon my Saviour's breast.'

God be thanked, Amen! The end shall soon come. Joyful news!" This was not written under any presentiment of closely-approaching death. On the contrary, in the same letter he speaks with his usual dogged opposition to infirmity, saying that he feels no such diminution of strength as would "prevent him from labouring as usual." Nevertheless, he takes leave of his colleague with the words—

> " 'There, there, at His feet, we shall suddenly meet,
> And be parted in spirit no more.' "

His letters now show increasing anxiety to make Mrs Ouseley feel that he is "finely." He often alludes to good Mrs Moore, at whose boarding-house in Dublin he was accustomed to stay, and to the great kindness that she always showed him; but he manifests a sense of the coldness of the Dublin people and preachers.

We soon find that he had to consult Sir Philip Crampton, the eminent surgeon, a brother of the judge, who treated Ouseley as a personal friend, as may be inferred from the extract before quoted of a note which he wrote to Sir Ralph in reference to the knighthood of the latter.

Sir Philip let Mr Ouseley know that a surgical operation would become necessary, but allayed all apprehensions of danger. "I must put myself quietly under his care, for about three weeks after I return from the country." He then plans to meet Mrs Ouseley far away in Tarbert, to return with her, and stay at Mrs Moore's so long as he is in the surgeon's hands, and then to settle at Lucan. He speaks with interest of the meetings for the celebration of the centenary of Methodism, then about to be held in Dublin. Having got as far as Abbeyleix on his way

T

to Tarbert, he writes to Mrs Ouseley, and repels some suggestions on her part that he had not been as well as he had led her to think.

From Rushin, he writes the following to the Rev. J. Nash, then in Dublin, attending the centenary meetings :—

"Yesterday I began my seventy-eighth year in this world, and a day of happiness to me, and, I trust, to others too, it has been. To God be glory and praise for ever! I preached in Mountrath at ten o'clock, and met the class ; after that I went to church and heard a good sermon ; I then went out, and preached in the open air to many, without interruption from any but one man, who again and again vociferated, 'I'll prove there is no hell—so I will.' Having ended my short sermon, I returned to Rushin, and after dinner preached at five to a nice congregation in the parlour; and after tea we started again for Mountrath, and I preached there at seven o'clock. The blessing of the Lord was with us through all, praise to Him for ever! Thus, having preached four times, and met the class, and gone twice into the town, &c., on the first day of my seventy-eighth year, I was not even fatigued! Thank God, thank God, O my soul, Amen and amen! Why, I feel as able to labour in my Lord's work as I did twenty years ago, now that I am closing my fortieth year in His ministry.—You may read this paragraph to Dr Bunting, and present him my love.

"I am to preach at our friend Conway's this evening, and after some days my beloved and I are to proceed to Dublin. I am to attend there for some time on Surgeon-General Crampton, for a complaint which he doubts not he can shortly remove.

"God bless you and yours, my dear brother, prays yours affectionately in the Lord,

"GIDEON OUSELEY."

He returned to Dublin in the middle of April, preaching at Maryborough on his way five times on the Sunday and Monday. The two days following he spent in Mountmelick, and there once more the Lord rejoiced His aged servant by the sight he loved above all things, that of souls pressing to the feet of the Saviour and into His fold. Having called upon those who were resolved to flee from the wrath to come, to give in their names and join the Society, several came forward. "On writing each name," says Mr Hay, "he solemnly repeated it, and said, ' I write your name before God, and the Lord Jesus Christ, who shall judge the dead at His appearing, and His kingdom.' Then followed in each case a brief, but earnest supplication, that God might write the name in the Lamb's book of life. A friend who was present with me at the time writes, ' The good done on that night, only the Great Day will tell. I know some who gave in their names on that night who are holding on their way, and some are fallen asleep in Jesus.' "

He writes to Mrs Ouseley, "On Tuesday night a dense crowd attended in Mountmelick, and on Wednesday night (April 10, 1839) the like, and in the morning a few. . . . I suppose about twenty have given in their names to begin in the heavenly service. Our meeting lasted from seven to after ten o'clock. . . .

May the Lord continue to bless this fresh revival also! Glad, indeed, were that kind people to see me among them once more." And he never had to tell of preaching again. The "few" that heard him at Mountmelick on Thursday morning, heard his last sermon. Those, "about twenty," whose names he wrote that Wednesday night, were the last he gathered into the Methodist Societies. The friends who said "Farewell" at the canal boat on the Thursday, were the last who received the prophet in the name of a prophet—the last of a long succession, many of whom felt that in leaving them he had left behind him a prophet's reward.

Once more on the canal boat he glided along the level country towards the capital, doubtless bearing much testimony for his blessed Master as he went. He had left Mrs Ouseley at Abbeyleix, from which place she could easily come to Dublin; but the Surgeon-General thought that there was no occasion for her presence; and at another consultation, six days later, he still "thinks that all will be well."

It would seem that the last table at which Ouseley ever sat as a guest was that of Judge Crampton, where he dined twice in the week before he was finally confined to bed. He speaks of having been pleased and edified with the Judge, Mrs Crampton, and their friends; and does not fail to tell that they affectionately inquired for Mrs Ouseley. On the 19th of April, he informs her that the Missionary Deputation from England will be in Dublin the next day, and, thinking it probable that he will not be able to be with them at the meeting, he imagines they will consider it strange. "But my health requires me to keep still for some time." So far as we know, what follows is the last sentence he ever put upon paper : concluding this letter to the wife who had shared his lot for six-and-fifty years, he says :—" My work was the Lord's, who never left nor forsook me, but blessedly sustained me in my labours and dangers. Glory, glory, glory be to Him, Amen." The day after this was written, alarming symptoms set in, and it soon became evident that the labourer's toil was closing. Mrs Ouseley was presently at his side. She had watched by his sick-bed at Dunmore, young as she was, looking back upon a cloudy past, and forward on a future dark and uncertain for both worlds,—with Young's terrible pictures for all of religious consolation. She now again took her place by his bedside; but oh, with what a difference! Nearly fifty years of shining day separated their memories from the dark times of chaos. The future opened to the eye of both, filled with light and gold. Even yet, Ouseley did not think that he was going to part from Harriet; but Harriet saw the angels waiting for her Ouseley, and with them a numerous company of his own spiritual children.

To the Rev. John Fraser Matthews he said, "that, if he had any wish to recover, it was to do something more to hasten the downfall of the dire apostasy that overspread the land." When Mr William Banks, a friend and the son of a friend, was praying by his side, he found the old man's hand laid upon his shoulder, and heard him say, "Stop, dear; pray that I may recover and live to see the end of that foul apostasy."

His sufferings became intense, and he would cry,
" My Father, my Father, support Thy suffering child.
Thy will be done, my Father God." He frequently
repeated the hymn :—

> "And let this feeble body fail,"

but most of all the last stanza—

> "Oh, what are all my sufferings here,
>   If, Lord, Thou count me meet,
> With that enraptured host to appear,
>   And worship at Thy feet !
> Give joy or grief, give ease or pain,
>   Take life or friends away :
> I come, to find them all again
>   In that eternal day."

On the day before his death, namely, the 13th of
May, he took leave of his relations, and prayed
especially for them, for all his friends, for the
Church of God at large, and for the whole world.
He dictated messages to some religious friends
through Mr Bonsall, and especially his grateful
remembrance to a lady from whom he had received
much kindness, coupled with the testimony, God is
Love,—a testimony that, in life and strength, he had
made to resound in the ears of many a thousand.
He asked for the prayers of all, that he might be
endued with a thankful spirit, and in the midst of
his crushing tortures might be " saved from stupidity
and neglect." Late that day the Rev. Dr Appelbe
saw him. " He called to me, and said, ' Come near,
my son.' I placed my ear near his lips, and he said,
' Hear what the great Master said, Learn of me,—not

of councils of popes and cardinals, but of ME.' Then his mind began to wander."

As Mr Bonsall sat beside him that evening, he began uttering sentences in Irish, and, when requested to do so, translated them into English. They were the repetition of the reasonings that had passed through his mind when under conviction of sin,—the beginning of his spiritual and the close of his mortal life thus coming into remarkable connection. "Is there an eternity—a hereafter beyond the grave? My mind replied, There is. The next question was, What will you do? when instantly, and altogether, my sins sprang up to my mind's view like a hostile army. I then reasoned with myself, If all these come against me in the day of judgment, I shall be ruined most certainly."

Being asked by his nephew, "What do you now think of the gospel, which you have preached all your life?" He replied, "Oh, it is light, and life, and peace."

Instead of the words of Young, which had rolled in upon his ear in his illness at Dunmore, he now had the blessed words of the Bible constantly read to him; and every now and then they called out from himself expressions of confidence and joy. About three hours before his death, he told them to read the 14th chapter of St John's Gospel. He spoke upon discipleship, upon being one with Christ, and upon the teaching of that chapter as to the Holy Spirit, dwelling on which he said, "I have no fear of death. The Spirit of God sustains me. God's Spirit is my support." Apparently this was the last word that he ever uttered; and a little after the noonday, he entered into the everlasting light. A few days afterwards, the old Methodist chapel, in Whitefriars' Street, beheld an unusual solemnity, and presently, men with full breasts stood round an open grave in Mount Jerome, and there returned to mother earth all that was now earthly of one of the best sons of Erin that the green sod ever covered.

CHAPTER XVI

Mrs Ouseley had travelled hand in hand with Gideon for six-and-fifty years. Now, she remained behind alone. He had often left her to go on his Master's errands, after the lost sheep. We have no hint from any one that she was ever known to repine either at his long absences, or his snatch visits. The latter must have been sometimes very trying. One story is told of his coming home after weeks of absence, and, no sooner had he attended to the horse, than he came into the house and said, " Harriet, fasten on this button for me, till I go off to such a place, where I am expected to preach." Now he had left her to go home, and abide in his Father's house. It was not far away, the way was not unknown, and it would not be long.

Still, it proved to be fourteen years. She made her home with Mr Bonsall, who writes, " And what shall be said of her during those fourteen years? To describe her spirit, conversation, and manner of life, for one day, is to describe it for the entire period. It was throughout uniformly Christ-like." He says

again, " Not how to be great, but how to be holy
and happy, was the example presented by Mrs
Ouseley."

A great deal with her Bible, and often in prayer,
saying little and loving much, she made all in the
house feel how beautiful is the life of God in the soul
of man. Mr Hay, in whose class she met for some
couple of years, says, " She was so sweet, and calm, and
saintly ; but she had little to say." The first care
of her widowhood would appear to have been that of
assuring Sir Ralph that she was exceedingly well off;
and yet we cannot make out that she had anything
to speak of, beyond her pittance of annuity as a
Methodist minister's widow. Thus happy herself,
and, like the happy, willing to serve others, but unwilling to be a charge to any, she glided in health,
peace, and fulness of hope, through the ten long
evening years lying between eighty and ninety.
" On the 12th of February 1853," says Mr Bonsall,
" when settled in her bed, and after prayer, she expressed her thankfulness to God that she felt so well,
and, in her usual loving manner, poured forth blessing upon my good wife and myself, for our affectionate attention to her, and her gratitude to God
for His favour during a long life."

Long before the day broke, Mr and Mrs Bonsall
were called to her bedside. They were able to make
out a few words of prayer. They thought of what
they had heard her sweetly say, that " soon she would
arrive at that blissful state, where, in the presence
and enjoyment of God, she should be restored to a
deathless union with many who had gone before
into the heavenly mansion." And then, after a few

minutes, serenely, as her spirit had shed the light of
Christ around, did it pass into His hands.

Though Sir Ralph was ten years junior to Gideon,
he survived him less than three. As Mr Bonsall
stood by the bedside of the one uncle in Dublin, so
was he found by that of the other in Lisbon. The
soldier had often faced danger, but this was death.
Mr Nelson repeats what I have heard from other
quarters, that, in battle, he would say, " I shall not
be killed ; Gideon is praying for me ;" and many a
prayer of which he knew not waited for its answer
by that death-bed. Before Mr Bonsall arrived, the
Jesuits had already made their way into the sick
man's room. "Friar Joyce," says the nephew, speaking of the first day that he was with his uncle, appealed to him to facilitate the reconciling of the old
man with the Church. Baptizing him now could do
no harm, and it would remove doubt. When he
found this sternly rejected, he began to speak of
the blessing procured by his Church through unifor-
mity ; but he received an answer which silenced that
gun. The old general, who had shed his blood for
Portugal, and who was the only Protestant, except
Sir James Yeo, who had been made a Knight Com-
mander of the highest military order of the kingdom
(Avis), and who was a proportionately desirable prize,
then so expressed his " detestation of Popery" as to
compel a retreat. The next day, when Mr Bonsall
re-entered the room after a walk round the city, he
found another with his uncle, whom he calls the
Jesuit Davies.

Sir Ralph hailed " John," saying that it was well
he had come just then ; and addressing the priest,

said, " My nephew so completely floored father Joyce, that unless you can manage him, you may despair of managing me." Mr Bonsall simply told the friar, that he declined to convert the sick-chamber of his relative into a theatre for disputation.

When alone, the nephew and uncle had much conversation together, and the former tried to fix his mind upon his own case as a sinner, and to direct his thoughts to repentance and faith in the Lord Jesus Christ, and to the effects of faith. And so day passed after day. The old soldier would say, " Oh, if I was with Harriet and Mary (Mrs Bonsall), seated by the fire, I would cast myself into their lap, and feel comfortable and happy." After a time, he began to offer up "ten thousand thanks to God," for the mercies He had shown to him. Coupled with this would still arise the wish to be in Dublin with " Old Harriet and Mary." In his walks, Mr Bonsall surveyed the establishment of the Inquisition, and his reflections were directly personal. He thought, if it was now in force, what would become of me ? Mr Prior, the Protestant clergyman residing in Lisbon, was now sent for by Mr Bonsall, with his uncle's concurrence. The old man solemnly acknowledged his sins against God, and said that he could now trust Him with soul and body. " I should not," he said, " have had this interview with you, had not my mind been made up to forsake sin, and to cast myself upon God for mercy. Yet, what confidence can I have in myself; for, if God were to restore me to any degree of health, I fear I should violate my present purpose to serve Him."

When he came to speak of his body, knowing that Mr Bonsall intended to remove it to Dublin, he said,

" No matter where my body lies, it shall be gathered at the resurrection." When Mr Prior spoke of the Lord's Supper, he said, " Yes, I wish it; but it will, I fear, be a burden to my mind, lest I again turn to sin."

A few days later, when all was nearly over, Mr Prior told Mr Bonsall that, had he not arrived, the priests " would have managed for a triumph, and had intended to make a great display." That day, the Jesuit Davies called, and though Mr Bonsall sent him a message, saying that he could not see his uncle, he kept the servants so long in talk, that Mr Bonsall went out and reproved him " for not taking his answer, and for keeping the attendants of a dying man away from him." Though plainly told that Sir Ralph did not desire to see him, but the contrary, he persisted, " Does he say so?" " He has said so, nay more, he does not admire you, and says you are a very self-sufficient man." He then wanted to enter upon a controversy. When this was declined, he still pressed to see Sir Ralph, till he forced Mr Bonsall to say, " I tell you he desires it not; and, if your Holy Inquisition were in force, I should not be deterred by it from resisting such unmannerly intrusion." The Jesuit then actually said he had been informed, by two or three, that Sir Ralph had expressed a wish to see him. " You could not have been so informed by any person," replied Mr Bonsall, " and to so monstrous a statement, I can only reply by saying that it is a lie." The cool answer to this was, " Charity prompted me to come." " Nay," replied the indignant nephew, " not charity, but to make a pretext for a party triumph; for you know that he detests your doctrines. But, no matter for that, if you could only make a colourable pretext for reporting that a Protestant had become, not a convert to truth, but a proselyte to your system. But, sir, you must excuse me, I cannot, will not, suffer a further trespass upon my time. Good evening!"

Thus, the influence of Gideon presided in the dying chamber of Ralph, within telling him to—Behold the Saviour of mankind, and without guarding him from the irruption of the Jesuits. We must firmly hope that the spirits of the two brothers met at the feet of Him before whom they who repent early, and they who repent late, equally know that they have nought wherein to glory, although they will also know that only the former had the best of both worlds.

Mr Bonsall brought away the remains of his uncle, thankful that the teeth of the Inquisition were drawn. He laid him in the same grave with Gideon, and erected one monument over the two brothers. Over Ralph, he wrote—

> " The strong man of war and turmoil
> Lay down like a meek and humble child,
> Forgetful of
> The glories and vanities of the world,
> Seeking salvation eternal
> Through Christ crucified."

CHAPTER XVII.

CONCLUSION.

WE have made no attempt to give any general estimate of the character or labours of Mr Ouseley. It
never entered into our plan to do so. Rightly or
wrongly, our conception of our proper task was fixed
by the first survey of his papers ; and, instead of
being shaken, was only confirmed by every subsequent
one. We thought the best thing we could do was to
aim at letting Gideon Ouseley on paper appear as
like as it was possible to Gideon Ouseley in the
saddle, in the pulpit, and in the home, and having
done this, to leave every reader to take his own impression, just as every witness of the man in action
had to take his.

However incompletely what we proposed to do has
been done, we do not doubt that the appearance of
this record of true evangelistic work, at a moment
when the Lord is quickening the spirit of evangelism
afresh in many branches of the Church, will, in some
small degree, contribute to encourage and stimulate
labourers. John Wesley used thankfully to record
that the revival of religion, which the Lord had
begun in his earlier days, had lasted more than forty
years, which Luther had said was the longest term
that any revival had been sustained. But it has
lasted till this day. It is now spreading wider and

striking deeper than ever. Men of more nations and tongues now feel and diffuse its influence than in any previous stage. It never was confined to one channel, whether of sect or nation. It at present runs in many channels, broad and deep. Now within the banks, and now overflowing from some one till it reaches the others, and all seem united into one flood. In this work the members of one denomination are made the instruments of blessing to those of another, and the citizens of one nation to those with whose fathers their fathers were at war. Thus life is being made the power to spread peace both among churches and nations.

The connection of holiness with evangelistic power is illustrated at every step in the course of Ouseley and his fellow-helpers, especially that of Charles Graham, the well-beloved. They were mighty with men, because of their power with God. That unction from the Holy One which taught Ouseley how to win souls is the one all-sufficing cause, and the only cause, of his extraordinary usefulness which can be assigned. Through it every natural qualification, and every acquired one, was endued with spiritual, in addition to human, power. The elements of human power were many and evident; but not these, but the Holy Spirit using them, led lost men to their Saviour. The one cry that seems to rise from every period of the labouring life of Ouseley is,— Evangelise! evangelise! evangelise! and that ye may do so with success, "Tarry ye in the city of Jerusalem until ye be endued with power from on high."

PRINTED BY BALLANTYNE, HANSON, AND CO.
EDINBURGH AND LONDON

Works by the same Author.

THE TONGUE OF FIRE;
Or, The True Power of Christianity.

Twenty-second Edition, Crown 8vo, price 3s. 6d. bound, or 1s. 6d. limp cloth.
Cheap Edition, Royal 32mo, price 1s.

THE SUCCESSFUL MERCHANT.
Sketches of the Life of Mr Samuel Budgett.

Thirty-seventh Edition, Seventy-fifth Thousand.
Crown 8vo, 5s. ; Small Crown 8vo, 2s. 6d. ; limp cloth, 1s. 6d.

THE DUTY OF GIVING AWAY A STATED PROPORTION OF OUR INCOME.

Price Sixpence.

ALL ARE LIVING.

Sermon on the Death of Mrs Beecham.
Fourth Edition, price Eightpence.

REPORT OF DISCUSSION ON THE QUESTION WHETHER ST PETER EVER CAME TO ROME,
Held on the 9th and 10th February 1872,

In the ACADEMIA TIBERINA, ROME, between ROMAN CATHOLIC PRIESTS and PROTESTANT MINISTERS. Translated from the authenticated Official Report. Eleventh Thousand. Price Sixpence ; Cloth, One Shilling.

THE MODERN JOVE:
A Review of the Collected Speeches of Pio Nono.

Second Edition, Crown 8vo, cloth, 2s. 6d.

"A searching review of the contents of the first volume of the 'Discorsi.'"— Right Hon. W. E. Gladstone, M.P. (*Rome, and the Newest Fashions in Religion.*)

This work was translated into Italian by Signor Sciarelli, and published in Rome. *Il Diritto*, a leading journal, says, "Mr Arthur shows, by the expressions of Pius IX. himself, that the mythological name of the modern Jove is that which best fits the proud, self-styled prisoner at the Vatican."

LONDON: HAMILTON, ADAMS, & CO.
WESLEYAN CONFERENCE OFFICE,
AND ALL BOOKSELLERS.

PUBLICATIONS

OF THE

WESLEYAN CONFERENCE OFFICE,

2 CASTLE STREET, CITY ROAD, AND
66 PATERNOSTER ROW, LONDON, E.C.

NEW BOOKS AND NEW EDITIONS.

A Compendium of Theology; Biblical, Dogmatic, Historical. By the Rev. W. B. POPE. Demy 8vo, 800 pages. Price 15s.

The Mother of Jesus not the Papal Mary. By the Rev. E. J. ROBINSON. Crown 8vo. Price 6s.

The Living Wesley, as he was in his Youth and in his Prime. By the Rev. J. H. RIGG, D.D. Crown 8vo. Price 3s.

Sermons for Children. By the Rev. MARK GUY PEARSE, Author of "Daniel Quorm, and his Religious Notions." Crown 8vo. Numerous Illustrations. Cloth Extra. Gilt edges. Price 2s. 6d.

Daniel Quorm and his Religious Notions. By the Rev. MARK GUY PEARSE. Crown 8vo. Numerous Illustrations. Cloth Extra. Gilt edges. Price 2s. 6d.

Henry Wharton: the Story of his Life and Missionary Labours in the West Indies, the Gold Coast, and Ashanti. By the Rev. W. MOISTER. Crown 8vo. With Portrait and Illustrations. Price 3s. 6d.

Long Life and Peace: Memorials of Mrs ELIZABETH SHAW, of St Austell. By the Rev. ROBERT C. BARRATT. Foolscap 8vo. With Portrait. Price 3s.

" *Out of Darkness into Light;*" or, *The Hidden Life*
made Manifest through Facts of Observation and Experience : Facts
Elucidated by the Word of God. By ASA MAHAN, D.D., Author of
"The Baptism of the Holy Spirit," "Christian Perfection," &c.
Crown 8vo. Price 5s.

Missionary Anecdotes, Sketches, Facts, and Incidents,
Relating to the State of the Heathen and the Effects of the Gospel in
various parts of the World. By the Rev. WILLIAM MOISTER. Crown
8vo. Price 4s.

The History of Methodism in Macclesfield, Cheshire.
By the Rev. BENJAMIN SMITH. Crown 8vo. Price 6s.

Gems Reset; or, The Wesleyan Catechisms Illustrated
by Imagery and Narrative. By the Rev. BENJAMIN SMITH. Crown
8vo.

The Prophet of Sorrow; or, The Life and Times of
Jeremiah. By the Rev. THORNLEY SMITH. With a Frontispiece
from the Fresco of Jeremiah by MICHAEL ANGELO. Crown 8vo.
Price 4s. 6d.

Lectures on the Foundation of John Fernley, Esq.
Volume I. Demy 8vo. Price 12s.

CONTENTS.

I.—The Holy Spirit : His Work and Mission. By G. OSBORN, D.D.

II.—The Person of Christ : Dogmatic, Scriptural, Historical. By the
Rev. W. B. POPE. (New and Enlarged Edition.)

III.—Jesus Christ the Propitiation for our Sins. By the Rev. JOHN
LOMAS.

IV.—The Holy Catholic Church, the Communion of Saints. By the
Rev. B. GREGORY.

Ecclesiastical Principles and Polity of the Wesleyan
Methodists. The whole compiled by WILLIAM PEIRCE, and revised
by FREDERICK J. JOBSON, D.D. Third edition. Royal 8vo, cloth,
15s.; half morocco, cloth sides, 20s.

This work contains a correct Transcript of all the published Laws and
Regulations of the Wesleyan Methodist Connexion, from its first organisa-
tion to the present time, and affords full and authentic information on the
History, Discipline, and Economy of Methodism.

COMMENTARIES, DICTIONARIES, &c.,
ILLUSTRATIVE OF THE HOLY SCRIPTURES.

Aids to Daily Meditation: being Practical Reflections and Observations on a Passage of Scripture for each Day in the Year. Crown 8vo, cloth, red edges. Price 3s. 6d.

The Holy Bible: with Notes, Critical, Explanatory, and Practical. By the Rev. JOSEPH BENSON. With Maps and a Portrait of the Author. Six Volumes, Imperial 8vo, cloth, red edges. Price £3, 3s.

A Biblical and Theological Dictionary: Illustrative of the Old and New Testament. By the Rev. JOHN FARRAR. With a Map of Palestine and numerous Engravings. Crown 8vo. Price 3s. 6d.

An Ecclesiastical Dictionary: Explanatory of the History, Antiquities, Heresies, Sects, and Religious Denominations of the Christian Church. By the Rev. JOHN FARRAR. Crown 8vo. Price 5s.

The Proper Names of the Bible; their Orthography, Pronunciation, and Signification. With a brief Account of the Principal Persons, and a Description of the Principal Places. By the Rev. JOHN FARRAR. 18mo. Price 1s. 6d.

A Commentary on the Old and New Testament; Containing copious Notes, Theological, Historical, and Critical; with Improvements and Reflections. By the Rev. JOSEPH SUTCLIFFE, M.A. Imperial 8vo, cloth, marbled edges. Price 12s. 6d.

A Biblical and Theological Dictionary: Explanatory of the History, Manners, and Customs of the Jews, and Neighbouring Nations. With an Account of the most remarkable Places mentioned in Sacred Scripture; An Exposition of the principal Doctrines of Christianity; and Notices of Jewish and Christian Sects and Heresies. By the Rev. RICHARD WATSON. Royal 8vo, cloth, red edges. Price 12s. 6d.

An Exposition of the Gospels of St Matthew and St Mark, and of some other detached parts of Scripture. By the Rev. RICHARD WATSON. Demy 8vo. Price 6s. 12mo. Price 3s. 6d.

The New Testament, with Explanatory Notes. By the Rev. JOHN WESLEY. With the Author's last Corrections.
Pocket Edition. 18mo. Price 2s.
Large-Type Edition. 8vo. Price 4s.
Library Edition, fine paper. Demy 8vo. Price 6s.

An Exposition of St Paul's Epistle to the Romans. By the Rev. HENRY W. WILLIAMS. Crown 8vo. Price 6s.

An Exposition of the Epistle to the Hebrews. By the Rev. HENRY W. WILLIAMS. Crown 8vo. Price 6s.

www.ingramcontent.com/pod-product-compliance
Lightning Source LLC
Chambersburg PA
CBHW020952030726
47496CB00005B/1474